ALL
MY
SECRETS

Also by Sophie McKenzie

Teen Novels

Girl, Missing
Sister, Missing
Missing Me

Blood Ties
Blood Ransom
Split Second
Every Second Counts

THE MEDUSA PROJECT
The Set-Up
The Hostage
The Rescue
Hunted
Double-Cross
Hit Squad

LUKE AND EVE SERIES
Six Steps to a Girl
Three's a Crowd
The One and Only

FLYNN SERIES
Falling Fast
Burning Bright
Casting Shadows
Defy the Stars

Crime Fiction

Close My Eyes
Trust in Me

ALL MY SECRETS

Sophie McKenzie

SIMON & SCHUSTER

First published in Great Britain in 2015 by Simon and Schuster UK Ltd
A CBS COMPANY

Copyright © 2015 Rosefire Ltd

1 3 5 7 9 10 8 6 4 2

Simon & Schuster UK Ltd
1st Floor, 222 Gray's Inn Road
London WC1X 8HB

Simon & Schuster Australia, Sydney
Simon & Schuster India, New Delhi

A CIP catalogue record for this book is available from the British Library.

PB ISBN: 978-1-47112-221-7
eBook ISBN: 978-1-47112-222-4

Typeset by Hewer Text UK Ltd, Edinburgh
Printed and bound by CPI Group (UK) Ltd, Croydon, CR0 4YY

www.simonandschuster.co.uk
www.simonandschuster.com.au

For Louisa Goodman

Irina Galloway

One

If I hadn't answered the doorbell that afternoon, would I ever have known the truth? Or would Dad have found a way to carry on hiding it from me? After all, if Mr Treeves had turned up just a few days earlier, I'd still have been at school enduring a long, long week of GCSE exams. But that's what my life turned on: a riddle wrapped in a coincidence, bound tightly by a lie.

And covered up with a massive secret . . .

So, the exams are all done and it's the middle of the afternoon, but I'm still in PJ bottoms and one of Mum's old sweatshirts, lolling on the sofa and thinking about making some hot chocolate. The window is open and a warm breeze is drifting through when the doorbell rings. Actually, it chimes, an annoying sound that Mum for some reason thinks is classy because it was featured on some stupid home makeover programme. She's always redecorating the living room. And their bedroom. And the twins' room. Dad puts up with it all in his solid, steady way. But he'll get totally on my case if I don't answer the door just because I feel lazy.

Even so, I wait a sec to see if he'll come. Some hope. He's in his office, at the top of the house, and he knows full well that I'm down here. The chimes sound again.

3

'Evie!' Dad yells from upstairs.

I sigh and haul myself up from the sofa. Dad and I are the only ones at home right now as Mum's gone to pick up Jade and Jess from school. As I plod to the front door, I catch sight of myself in the hall mirror. I've been growing my hair for nearly a year and it's now past my shoulders. It's dark and shiny. Which is good. But the ends are *really* split, as Mum never tires of pointing out. 'Like rats' tails,' she always says. Still, I prefer it long and uncut and it's my hair.

I don't even think about being in my PJs until I'm actually opening the door. Then I feel a bit self-conscious because a man is standing outside in a suit. He's short – no taller than I am – and dapper with slicked back hair and a tightly knotted blue tie.

He stares at me for a second. 'Evelina Brown?' he asks. He has a soft Scottish accent.

I nod, a self-conscious knot twisting in my stomach. The man is looking at me in this weird way, like he *knows* me. Which I'm certain he doesn't.

'I'm Mr Treeves, solicitor with Stirling, McIntyre and Cox. Er . . . may I come in and talk to you for a minute?' he asks.

Now he's seriously freaking me out.

'Talk to *me*?' I ask.

The man nods. 'I have important news . . . I've been looking for you for a while . . . that is, my firm has.' He clears his throat. 'Of course, perhaps if you want a . . . an adult present?'

Jeez, am I in some kind of trouble? I rack my brains, trying to think if there's anything I could possibly have done that would mean a lawyer calling round. Nope.

4

'Dad!' I call. 'Come here!'

There's an awkward moment while Mr Treeves and I wait on either side of the front door, then Dad pads downstairs, barefoot in his jeans, rubbing his forehead like he always does when he's distracted.

'Do you need me to sign for some—?' He stops as he catches sight of Mr Treeves. He smiles. 'You're not delivering a parcel, are you? How can I help?'

Mr Treeves visibly relaxes. Dad tends to make people feel comfortable like that. All my friends love him. What they don't see is how strict he can be about going out and staying in touch and coming home at what he calls 'a decent hour'.

'I need to speak to your daughter, Mr . . . Mr Brown, is it?'

'Yes, er, OK. What's this about?' Dad asks, looking bemused.

Mr Treeves wrinkles his nose. 'It's a legal matter.' He hesitates, clearly not wanting to say more until he's properly inside.

'Very well.' Dad glances at me, eyebrows raised. I shrug. I have no more idea what's going on than he does. 'Let's go into the living room.'

A few seconds later, we're all sitting down: Dad and me on the sofa, Mr Treeves perched anxiously on the edge of an armchair.

'Please don't be concerned; this is good news,' Mr Treeves says, fishing some papers out of his briefcase. He looks up at me. 'You've been left some money in a trust fund, Evelina.'

'It's Evie,' I say automatically. 'What's a trust fund?'

'A way of investing money.' Mr Treeves hesitates. 'In this case, a considerable amount. You inherit it when you're sixteen at the end of August. As I say, we've been trying to track you down for a while now.'

I can't take it in. I've been left *money*? Who on earth from? I look at Dad He's frowning.

'I . . . we . . . didn't know anything about this,' he says.

'I realise that.' Mr Treeves gulps. 'Well, that's why I've come in person, to explain it . . . to you both.'

'Explain what?' I ask. 'Who's left me this . . . this trust fund? And what's "a considerable amount"?'

'Ten million pounds.'

I gasp. Is he serious? I look at Dad again. His jaw is hanging open. He's clearly as stunned as I am.

'Ten million pounds?' I echo.

At that moment the front door opens and the hall fills with Jade and Jess's shrieks.

'She *promised* she would let me have a go, Mum!' Jade is whining.

'But it's *mine*!' Jess, as usual, sounds utterly outraged.

'Girls, *please*.' Mum sounds weary.

A second later, my eight-year-old twin sisters, Jade and Jess, have barrelled their way into the living room. They're brought up short as they spot Mr Treeves, then dart away, out of sight. Mum puts her head around the door as they push past her.

'Oh, hello.' She glances at Dad, clearly expecting him to

perform an introduction. But Dad is still sitting stock-still, mouth gaping.

'I'm sorry, I've brought some rather surprising news for Evelina,' Mr Treeves says, standing up.

'Evie?' Mum turns to me, her eyes all curiosity.

It's the last moment that I trust her. Or Dad.

I stand up beside Mr Treeves. 'Somebody's left me ten million pounds in a . . . a trust fund or something.' I turn to Mr Treeves, ignoring the widening of Mum's eyes. 'Who is it?'

Mr Treeves clears his throat.

'You've been left the money by an Irina Galloway.'

Across the room, Mum slaps her hand over her mouth. Dad lets out a low moan.

I turn to Mr Treeves. 'Who on earth is Irina Galloway?'

'No!' Dad jumps up. 'Stop!'

'Please.' Mum's normally rosy cheeks are as pale as paper. 'Please don't say any more.'

Mr Treeves fidgets from foot to foot. He looks desperately uncomfortable.

'What's going on?' I demand. 'Who is Irina Galloway? How do you know her? Why has she left me all this money?'

'She has to know.' Mr Treeves is talking to Mum and Dad now. 'If you don't tell her, I'm afraid I must.'

'No.' Mum is clinging to the door. Tears well in her eyes.

'Tell me what?' Fear and dread rise inside me.

Dad shakes his head. 'We can't,' he mutters, 'Not like this. We can't.'

I turn to Mr Treeves. '*Tell* me,' I insist.

7

Mr Treeves draws himself up. 'I realise now, having talked to you. Evie, that this will come as a shock,' he says, a little shake in his voice. 'But Irina Galloway is . . . was . . . your mother.'

Two

There's a terrible silence. Mr Treeves shuffles from side to side, but I'm frozen to the spot. I sense Mum looking at me from the doorway. Dad sinks back down onto the sofa, his head in his hands.

'How?' The word squeezes out of me. I turn to my parents. Dad is staring down at the ground, but Mum meets my gaze.

Except, if Mr Treeves is right, she isn't my mother at all.

There is terror in her eyes.

'I don't understand,' I stammer.

Mr Treeves steps forward. He hands me a piece of paper.

'This is your birth certificate,' he says.

I look down, my eyes skittering over the words. Under 'father' it gives Dad's details, but there, under 'mother', is the name 'Irina Galloway'.

'This is just a piece of paper,' I say. I look at my parents. 'Mum? Dad?'

Dad stands up slowly. He seems to have aged about twenty years since he first sat down. I've never seen him so close to tears.

'It's true, Evie,' he says, his voice cracking. 'Irina Galloway was your birth mother.'

9

My jaw drops. I feel like I've been thrown out of a plane and I'm spinning, plummeting through the air.

Everything known and fixed is gone.

I sit down hard on the sofa. Mum rushes over and puts her arm around my shoulders. I shake it off, a thread of anger weaving through my shock.

'I don't understand,' I say again.

Mum and Dad stay silent. A beat passes. Then Mr Treeves holds out a folder.

'This contains details of the trust fund,' he says. 'As I said, we've been trying to track you down for a while. The fund has been well invested for fifteen years and, well, I've told you about the money. It will be released to you on your sixteenth birthday at the end of August.'

'Sixteen?' Dad frowns.

'Yes, that's younger than in England, I know,' Mr Treeves says. 'That's because the trust and the will were drawn up under Scottish law.'

I stare at him. 'My mother was Scottish?'

He nods. 'I think the best thing right now is for me to leave you with your, er, family. My card is in the folder. I don't have any direct knowledge of Irina Galloway myself, but you can call for more information about the trust fund whenever you wish.'

He hurries out, clearly desperate to get away from the tense atmosphere in the room. I can't blame him. Suddenly it's just me and Mum and Dad.

Outside in the hall, Jade and Jess are squealing with excitement over something.

Mum squeezes my arm. 'Oh, Evie, I'm so sorry it's come out like this.'

I turn to her. 'Tell me . . . everything.'

Mum glances at Dad. He nods. I'm vaguely aware that his hands are shaking. I feel numb.

'The first thing to say is that Mum is your mother first, last . . . in *every way*.'

I hold up the birth certificate. 'Not first,' I say.

'OK.' Dad rubs his forehead. 'Irina and I had a relationship before I met Mum.'

'You were born,' Mum says, 'but . . . but Irina . . . she wasn't well . . .'

Dad coughs. 'Janet,' he says, a warning note in his voice. Mum stops talking.

'The point is that Irina died in a hit-and-run accident shortly before your first birthday,' Dad goes on. 'I was on my own with you for a bit, then Mum came along and . . .'

'. . . and I loved you *as if* you were my own right from the start.'

I nod, letting what Dad said sink in. 'So my real mum died when I was a baby?'

Beside me, Mum winces.

'Mum is your real mum,' Dad insists. 'Irina only knew you for the first few months of—'

Anger seers through me again. 'Don't tell me what's real and not real,' I snap. 'Why didn't you tell me?'

Dad and Mum exchange helpless glances.

'We thought it was for the best,' Mum says shakily. 'A few

11

months passed and we moved here where we didn't know anyone, and of course everyone assumed you were mine and . . .'

'There was never a good time to tell you,' Dad urges. 'We didn't want to upset you.'

'Well, you've upset me now.' I stand up. 'You should have found the time. You've been lying to me all my life and—'

But I can't finish the sentence. A huge sob rises inside me like a claw clutching at my insides. Out in the hall, Jade and Jess's excited squeals have turned into some kind of argument. Normally, Mum would be straight there, sorting them out, but now I'm not sure she even hears them. She's weeping, hunched over on the sofa.

'What about Jade and Jess?' I ask, teeth clenched. 'Are they even my sisters?'

'Of course they are,' Dad says.

'Yes.' Mum nods eagerly. 'They're mine and Dad's.'

It suddenly sinks in. 'Yours and Dad's,' I echo. 'But I'm not yours.'

'Of course you are, Evie. This doesn't change anything,' Dad argues.

I glance down at the folder in my hand. What did Mr Treeves say? That I would inherit ten-million-pounds on my sixteenth birthday.

'No Dad,' I say. 'This changes everything.'

The next twenty-four hours are the worst of my life. Mum doesn't stop crying and Dad is torn between comforting her and dealing with me. He refuses to answer any of my questions about Irina: from how he met her and what their relationship was like, to what she looked like and where the original money invested in the trust fund came from. He says that none of this matters, that Irina was never a proper mother to me, not like Mum has been, that she's just a set of genes and, now, this legacy of millions of pounds.

He's not even happy for me about the money. He's been on to a lawyer about setting up a new trust fund that he and Mum will control until I'm twenty-five.

No way am I agreeing to that.

As time passes, his refusal to talk about anything other than the fact that it's crazy for me to have access to too much money too young makes the whole thing a zillion times worse. My early shock gives way to pure, coruscating rage that he and Mum clearly want to carry on as if the entire revelation hasn't happened. Mum sobs the whole time the twins are at school, insisting how much she loves me and how little my having a different birth mother matters, while, at the same time, begging me not to tell my sisters.

'So you want me to lie to them too?' I can't believe it. 'If it doesn't matter, why can't I tell everyone?'

But the truth is I don't want to talk to people either. How can I tell anyone that my parents have been lying to me all my life? In the first heat of my fury, I go to call my best friends, Mina and Carrie. I want to tell them I've been deceived and betrayed – and that I'm about to be very rich. Vague ideas about how we could spend some of my inheritance flit through my head: we could go on a fancy holiday and buy millions of clothes, maybe even follow a band on tour around the world . . . But as soon as we're talking I realise I'm too embarrassed to explain either the money or the lies. At least not until I've found out more.

But neither Mum nor Dad are prepared to talk to me about Irina Galloway so I lock my bedroom door and search for information on the internet. I'm imagining it won't be easy to find anything, but to my surprise there are loads of hits. I examine them more closely. The Irina I've discovered was a dancer from Edinburgh and the youngest person ever in the UK to become a prima ballerina.

Could this be my mother?

I find a picture. This Irina doesn't look anything like me; she's got fine fair hair and blue eyes, while my colouring is dark, same as Dad and the twins. Also she's clearly tiny with delicate features and a heart-shaped face. I can see that maybe I looked a bit like her when I was little, but I've grown nearly ten centimetres in the last two years and am definitely on the tall side, again like Dad.

I hurry downstairs to show him.

'Is this her?' I demand.

'Yes,' Dad says. 'Please stop looking. You can't rely on anything you find on the internet.'

'Then *you* tell me about her,' I insist. 'How did you meet? What was she like? Why didn't you tell me about her before?'

Dad frowns. 'There really isn't anything to tell. It was a

14

brief relationship. I don't know anything about her really, other than that she was a successful dancer who, er, died young in a traffic accident.'

For goodness' sake.

I scurry back up to my room and start investigating more deeply. I find a Wikipedia entry which explains that Irina changed her name from Irene when she was eighteen and several videos on YouTube of her dancing. She looks amazing, so graceful and beautiful as she moves, entrancing. I've never been interested in ballet. I grit my teeth, wondering if Mum and Dad deliberately avoided cultivating that side of my abilities. Mum doesn't have an artistic bone in her body. She's all about practical things like baking and gardening and putting up tents on our definitely unglamorous camping holidays.

It's not fair, what they've done to me.

'Evie?' Mum knocks gently on the door.

'Go away,' I say.

I can hear her crying and for a second I feel guilty. Then something inside me twists and breaks. I shouldn't have to feel guilty. My parents have brought this situation on themselves and my life with them will never be the same again. In that moment, I make a conscious decision to stop calling them Mum and Dad. From now on they'll be Janet and Andrew.

And, when I get my money at the end of August, never mind holidays and clothes . . . I'm going to buy my own place. Cheered up by these thoughts, I go back to my web search. After a few more minutes, I find a fan site for Irina, complete with background biography, performance dates and memorabilia sales details.

Excitement grows inside me. I read the biography eagerly. It hadn't occurred to me before, but maybe I've got lots of brothers and sisters, a whole alternative family.

It's soon clear that I don't. Irina was the daughter of elderly parents, both of whom are dead. The biog covers the details I'm already aware of: how Irina left home to study ballet abroad at the age of twelve, her early successes, her decision to change her first name from Irene, her unplanned pregnancy and the year-long hiatus this brought to her career right up to her triumphant comeback, followed swiftly by her sudden and tragic death at the age of twenty-one in a hit-and-run accident in Nottingham.

I'm mentioned at the end of the biog as the baby girl Irina leaves behind, but my name isn't given. Does the writer not know it? I peer at the note at the bottom: the biog was written by a Gavin Galloway, Irina's brother. I turn back to the fan site and do a search. It turns out that this man, Gavin, is not just Irina's younger brother but also the manager of her fan club, responsible for the sale of the memorabilia. The site is clearly regularly updated and there's an email and a postal address in Edinburgh.

I quickly start an email: *Hi, Gavin*

I stop. What on earth do I say next? It doesn't sound as if he has any idea about where – or who – I am. How do I break the news that I'm out here, eager to meet him, to find out more about Irina and her life?

16

Mum – Janet – is knocking on the door again, calling my name. She's still crying.

My fingers hesitate, then I delete the draft. What I want to say can't be put in an email. Tomorrow I'm going to take a coach to Edinburgh and go and find my uncle. Even if he's not at the address on the website any more, whoever lives there will surely know how to reach him.

Andrew and Janet might not be prepared to tell me about Irina, but surely my Uncle Gavin will.

Three

I switch my phone back on as I leave the station in Edinburgh. There are four missed calls from Andrew and five from Janet, plus a stack of texts urging me to ring them and asking if I'm all right.

I send a quick message – no 'x's – saying that I'm fine. I already left a note on the kitchen table explaining that I'd 'borrowed' some money from Andrew's wallet 'which I'll easily be able to pay back at the end of August' and was going off to find out more about Irina 'as you won't tell me anything'.

Under any other circumstances I would feel sorry for them, but how can I right now? They've kept the truth from me for years. If I'm making efforts to find out about my own history now, they've only got themselves to blame.

I do a quick check on my maps app. The address from the website – a flat in Rose Street – isn't far away. I find the road, then switch off my mobile again. It's cooler here in Edinburgh than it was at home. I tug my jacket around me, wishing I'd worn proper shoes instead of sandals. As I reach Rose Street, it begins to rain. I scuttle past the rows of sand-coloured buildings, looking for the address given on the website. It's teeming down by the time I find the old wooden front door and ring on the bell.

No one answers.

I stand, feeling the rain trickling down the back of my neck, and press the doorbell again.

Still no reply.

For the first time since I left home, I'm forced to face the fact that I may have come on a complete wild goose chase. I huddle closer to the door, trying – and failing – to keep the rain off me. Surely *someone* must be in.

I'm about to turn away when the buzzer sounds and a sleepy voice mutters, 'Second floor, leave it by the door.' Is that Gavin? My heart is in my mouth as I head inside and scurry up the stairs. It's chilly on the stone floor, though the walls with their off-white paint and chrome-framed mirrors have a designer feel. I glance at my reflection. I look a mess, my hair lank against my face and my mascara smudged. I wipe under my eyes, my pulse racing.

There's only one door on each floor and I'm on the second-floor landing in seconds. I don't let myself stop to think. I hurry over to the door and give it a sharp rap. Then another.

After a few seconds. it creaks open.

'I said leave it by the—' The man who's speaking stops as he sees me. He's about Andrew's age – but much shorter – and pale-faced, similar in colouring to Irina, at least from the pictures I've seen of her. His hair is ruffled as if he's only just woken up – though it's almost 2 pm – and he's dressed in ripped jeans and a bright orange T-shirt with a diamond stud in each ear. 'Hello?' His accent is softly Scottish.

'Hi.' My throat feels tight. I've been planning this moment

19

for two days, but now I'm here everything I'd intended to say flies out of my head.

'Hello?' he says again.

I shake my head. 'I'm Evie . . . Evelina,' I blurt out. 'I'm Irina's daughter.'

What little colour there is drains from the man's face. His mouth gapes.

'Are . . . are you Gavin?'

He nods, still clearly speechless. Then he shakes himself. 'Where . . .? How . . .?' He stands back. 'Come in, darling. Please, come in.'

I go inside the flat, my heart still beating fast.

It's very smart, with polished wood floors and – though I'm no judge – what looks like proper art on the walls and expensive designer furniture in both the hall and the living room where Gavin leads me.

We sit down. Gavin stares at me in the same way that Mr Treeves did, like he's searching for something in my face.

'Are you really . . .?' he asks.

I hold out the birth certificate Mr Treeves gave me.

Gavin reads it and nods. 'Wow,' he says. 'Darling, I had no idea where you were, that you were even alive.'

'But you knew I existed?' My question comes out more accusatory than I mean it too.

Gavin looks up quickly. 'I was abroad when you were born and my sister died. My . . . our . . . parents told me about you, but, well, by that point they weren't in touch with you or your father so . . .'

Now I'm staring at him. 'Do you know my dad?' I ask.

'No, though I've seen pictures.' Gavin walks over to a cupboard and takes out a photo album. 'My parents left loads of these when they passed. I'm sure there's a picture of your dad with Irina in here. Have a look, darling.'

I take the album, feeling dazed. Gavin is still staring at me.

'Wow,' he says. 'Sorry, but this is totally freaking me out.'

'Yeah.' I look up at him. 'Me too. It's weird that we're related, isn't it?'

'Sure is.' Gavin hesitates. 'So . . . so I don't get it. I mean, I vaguely knew you existed, but when I came back from travelling your dad had already told my parents – your grandparents – they weren't welcome in your life. So they – all of us – we backed off.'

It's like a punch. 'My dad told them to stay away from me? *Why?*'

Gavin shrugs. 'Guess he didn't want the reminders of Irina.' He narrows his eyes. 'How much has he told you about her?'

'Nothing.' The word explodes out of me. 'He won't talk to me about her at all.'

'So how do you know about me? In fact, how come you're here?'

I take a deep breath and launch into an explanation of everything that happened following Mr Treeves' knock on the door. Gavin listens intently, wide-eyed when I tell him about the ten-million-pounds and appalled that I've been given so little information.

'I can't believe Andrew is keeping everything from you,

21

darling,' he says. 'I *totally* understand why you felt you had to come here.'

'Thank you.' Tears prick at my eyes. 'I just really want to find out more about Irina. I saw your fan site for her. It's obvious you and she were really close.'

'Not so close that she told me she had ten mill to leave anyone,' Gavin says with a grin. 'I knew she was a successful ballerina, but not *that* successful. That's some inheritance.'

'I don't think it was anywhere near that much money to begin with. Mr Treeves said it was a good investment.'

'I'll say it was.' Gavin raises his eyebrows. 'Look, darling, I'm happy to tell you everything I can about your mother. I've tried to keep her memory alive and I've still got a few of her bits and pieces I expect you'd like to take a look at.'

'Oh yes, please,' I breathe.

'Well, why don't you stay here tonight? I have to go out for a bit, but I've got a spare room and I am your uncle after all and . . . well, I've got sixteen years of uncle stuff to make up for.'

I hesitate. In so far as I'd thought about it at all, I'd assumed that I'd have to find a room in a hostel for the night. All I knew was that I couldn't go home without finding out more about Irina. But here was Gavin offering me a bed for the night *and* information. It was more than I could have hoped for.

'Yes,' I say. 'Yes, definitely.'

I switch on my phone, send Andrew and Janet another text, reassuring them that I'm fine, then turn it off again. Gavin goes out, leaving me leafing through another photo

22

album. He returns within the hour, carrying a couple of pizzas. He puts on a DVD of Irina dancing *Giselle* and I watch, transfixed, as my mother skips and pirouettes across the stage on screen.

'Oh, she was beautiful,' I gasp.

After the DVD finishes and our pizzas are eaten, Gavin fetches a small, faded canvas bag. 'Here.' He offers it to me. 'I think you should have these.'

Excited, I open the bag and take out two pink ballet shoes. The leather is creased and worn and exquisitely soft.

'They were Irina's,' Gavin says. 'Her favourite pair. I was going to sell them with some of the other memorabilia, but I've never quite been able to bring myself to.' His voice grows shaky. I'm suddenly aware that it isn't just me who has lost someone here. Gavin is all alone, without his parents or his sister.

'Thank you,' I say.

Gavin nods. 'No problemo, darling.' He shows me to my bedroom, a white-painted room with green furniture which he says once belonged to Irina. It's old and quirky and I love it instantly. I get into bed, feeling ridiculously at home. It makes sense, I guess. After all, Gavin and I are family and this room is full of furniture my own mother chose and loved. I just hadn't expected to feel like I belonged so quickly.

It crosses my mind that maybe I should send Andrew and Janet another text to let them know where I am and that I'm still OK, but, as soon as the thought arrives, it passes. I lie down, clutching Irina's ballet shoes. There's something

23

comforting about the soft leather. Before I know it, I'm asleep.

I sleep deeply, waking full of excitement for the day ahead. Gavin has promised to take me to the theatre where Irina danced her debut as a prima ballerina. Before that, we walk to a café where he says she used to go for coffee with her dancer friends. I order mine black with two sugars, like he says she drank it. Gavin has found some more photos overnight – mostly of Irina at my age, already dancing with a professional troupe. While Gavin answers some texts on his phone, I stare and stare at her, searching for some connection, but there's nothing in her heart-shaped face or fine blonde hair or dark blue eyes that resembles me. Plus, she's much smaller and slighter than I am.

It hurts that I don't look more like her and I push away the croissant that Gavin has bought me. I feel his gaze on my face.

'What's up, darling?' he asks.

'I just don't look anything like her.' The truth is out before I mean to say it.

'Puh-*leese*,' Gavin says. 'Your colouring might be darker, but you have the same cheekbones and the same smile.'

'Really?' I glance up at him, hopeful.

'And *that* look is one I saw her give our dad a million times, whenever she wanted anything.' He pauses. 'She had him wound round her little finger.'

I sit back and smile.

'Talking of dads, maybe you should send yours a text if you

24

haven't already? Let him know exactly where you are, that you're safe with me.'

I do as he suggests, then switch off my phone as we leave the café. The morning traffic is busy down on the main road. Gavin points to a church just visible on the other side.

'That way,' he says.

I glance up and down the street. Nothing's coming right now. As I step onto the road, I see movement out of the corner of my eye. A car. Coming towards us. In the split second that follows it seems to speed up until it's right here, black metal looming into view, and I just have time to step back before it zooms past, so close I could touch it.

I fall back, hard, onto the pavement. In an instant, Gavin is beside me as the car speeds off into the distance.

'Darling, are you OK?' He sounds breathless, terrified.

I nod, gasping, as a single thought fills my head: that car was driving fast towards me on purpose; it *meant* to run me over.

Four

Seconds later, I tell myself not to be so stupid. The driver of that car couldn't possibly have meant to run me down. It was just going too fast. And anyway I was at fault for stepping out without taking another look.

I push myself up off the pavement. Gavin is chasing after the car, almost out of sight. I can hear his yells, his Scottish accent stronger as he shouts out:

'You idiot! Hurtling along like that! You could have killed her!'

A few seconds later, he's back.

'Are you all right, darling?' he asks, dusting me down and patting at my arms as if to make sure they're not broken. 'Evie? Are you all right?'

'I'm fine,' I insist. 'Not even bruised.'

'Thank goodness for that.' Gavin hugs me, his voice full of emotion. 'I've only just found you. I don't want to lose you again.'

His words fill me with a warm glow. It strikes me that though Gavin has asked about my life, and he's certainly told me plenty about Irina's, I don't really know anything about him.

'What do you do for a living?' I ask.

Gavin shrugs, steering me carefully across the road. 'Bits and pieces of things.' He sighs. 'I'm a journalist of sorts, though not a terribly successful one. Irina's death hit me hard. Of course, it was even harder for our parents. And I think not being able to see you made it worse. They were both gone within two years of her passing. And I was on my own. I struggled to cope, to be honest with you. I mean, I had their money, but what good are material things if you don't have anyone to share them with?' He smiles. 'Remember that when you inherit your ten million.'

'Do you have a girlfriend?' I ask timidly. 'Or a boyfriend?'

'No one special,' Gavin admits. 'Not right now anyway.'

He sounds really lonely. I suddenly feel furious with Andrew and Janet for keeping me away from him all my life.

'I don't want to go away again,' I say. 'I mean, I'd like to keep in touch with you. And, once I've inherited my money, I think maybe I'll find a course I could do up here, maybe buy a flat?'

Gavin grins. 'Sounds fantastic, darling. Will your parents be OK with that?'

I pull a face. I can't imagine Andrew or Janet liking the idea of me moving away from home for the sixth form. But that's their problem. Not to mention their fault.

'They'll have to be,' I say. 'Er, I know it's a big deal and everything, but . . .'

'. . . could you stay with me while you sort out a course?' Gavin grins again. 'I think that would be brilliant.'

Feeling delighted, I let him show me around the sights of

Edinburgh. It's a sunny morning, though the air has a crisp edge to it. Gavin doesn't just take me to the theatre where Irina first danced, but a park where they played as kids and the hotel where their parents – my grandparents – met. I feel so sad that Andrew denied me the opportunity to ever know them. And even sadder when I consider that the two sets of grandparents I have known – his and Janet's – must have both been in on the whole secret from the start, lying to me like Andrew and Janet have done.

Apart from during a couple of phone calls, which Gavin wanders away from me to take, we spend the rest of the day out and about, heading back to his flat only after eating an early dinner in what Gavin tells me was the Italian restaurant his family used to go to on special occasions. I turn on my phone as we reach Rose Street to see if there are any messages from Andrew or Janet.

As the mobile powers on, I look up.

To my horror Andrew is here, pacing up and down in front of Gavin's apartment building.

'Oh no, it's my dad,' I gasp.

'Is that Andrew?' Gavin's eyes widen. 'He looks . . . different from in the photos. It must be the hair, or lack of it.'

As we draw closer, Andrew spots me. My guts twist and knot.

'Oh, Evie.' He rushes over, pulling me into a bear hug.

I let him hold me, arms stiff at my sides.

Andrew steps back, taking in Gavin, who instantly introduces himself.

'Oh,' Andrew says without smiling. 'I see.' He turns to me. 'Mum and I have been so worried. We—'

'D'you remember Irina talking about Uncle Gavin?' I interrupt.

'Er, yes.' My dad still doesn't smile. 'I guess I do.'

Irritated, I cross my arms. 'Uncle Gavin's been showing me round Edinburgh.'

'Well, I'm glad he's looked after you, but really, Evie, what do you think you're playing at, running off like that? Mum and I have been out of our minds with—'

'She's *not* my mum though, is she?' I say. 'And frankly you don't deserve to be my dad.'

Andrew looks stunned. Behind him Gavin shuffles awkwardly.

'Evie . . .' Andrew begins.

'No,' I snap. 'You both lied to me and then refused to tell me anything so, if I'm here, trying to find things out for myself, it's your own fault.'

Andrew stares at me. '*Please*, Evie, that one factor doesn't—'

'I'm not coming home,' I say. 'Gavin says it's OK for me to stay with him and—'

'This is none of your business.' Andrew turns on Gavin, who takes a step back, hands raised in a conciliatory gesture. 'You should have made Evie call us.'

'Don't blame him,' I say. And then, before I can even think, the next words shoot like bullets out of my mouth. 'I hate you, Dad. I'll never forgive you for lying to me and keeping me apart from my family.'

29

His lips tremble. I can feel my face flushing. Part of me feels bad for saying that. Yet a bigger part is relieved that I've finally, properly said how I feel. Andrew's eyes fill with misery. I'm suddenly aware of the bustle of the dusty street around us, all sorts of people going about their business, unaware of who we are and what we're saying and doing.

Gavin clears his throat. 'Look, I don't want to get caught in the middle of this,' he says. 'I'm thrilled that Evie's sought me out and I don't want to lose touch with her again. But Evie darling, this is your father. It's understandable he's been worried about you, that he wants you home.'

'Please, Evie.' Andrew looks up and there are tears in his eyes.

Perhaps I should feel sorry for him.

But in my heart there's only anger.

I go back home with Andrew. After all, what choice do I really have? I don't have any money of my own yet and, anyway, all my things are still there. But it's not the same and it never will be. Andrew and Janet try to talk to me; Andrew even offers a bit more information about Irina. I discover that they met when he was a student at Edinburgh University and – as I'd more or less gathered anyway – only went on a few dates.

'I was shocked when she said she was pregnant. To be honest, I didn't cope with it very well,' Andrew admits. 'Irina and I never lived together, not before or after she got pregnant, but once you were born I saw you every few days and you

30

stayed with me when she went back to dancing, and then, suddenly, the accident happened and she was dead and you needed someone to look after you.'

'What happened?' I ask.

Andrew looks uncomfortable. 'I told you,' he says. 'Hit-and-run, a lorry. The driver was never found.'

I shiver, remembering my own near miss with that car in Edinburgh, and ask what Irina was like as a person and why Andrew had such an issue with my grandparents. But at this Andrew clams up again and my fury surges back. In the end, I'm barely talking to either him or Janet. I don't want to see my friends and I can't be bothered to play with the twins. I spend all my time in my room, watching Irina's *Giselle* DVD over and over again, holding her ballet shoes for comfort as I fall asleep every night.

Gavin calls me every day to see how I am. We chat about Irina's childhood mostly. I love hearing his stories about her. And he repeats his offer to have me stay again, once my money comes through.

And so a week passes. I refuse to come down for the family meals that Janet insists on every evening. After all, I point out, we're not really family. I know that's cruel, but she was cruel first, letting me think she was my one and only mother all this time.

Janet pleads, then she shouts. So does Andrew. But I refuse to leave my room, going to the kitchen in my own time and living mostly off toast.

Another week passes and the end of June arrives. Still two whole months until I inherit my money. I take to planning what I'm going to spend it on: a flat in Edinburgh definitely, though if I'm honest the idea of living there alone is more than a little daunting. Perhaps I'll travel. I still haven't told any of my friends about either the money or Irina. The money is so big a thing it doesn't even feel real. And, anyway, it's just that Andrew and Janet lied to me all those years.

On the last day of June, Andrew knocks on my bedroom door to say that he's asked Gavin to visit. I'm shocked – I've gathered since leaving Edinburgh that neither Andrew nor Janet have a very high opinion of him.

'Bit of a waste of space, Irina thought,' Andrew says with an apologetic smile that makes me want to scream. 'And I'm pretty certain he's into some very dodgy dealings.'

'From what your dad told me . . . he looks and acts like a shark,' Janet adds.

I roll my eyes. What gives them the right to pass judgement? They don't even know Gavin.

My uncle turns up that evening. He looks different in our house than he did in Edinburgh – smarter and younger. He's wearing a designer suit and his hair is carefully gelled and slicked back. He might be around my dad's age, but he comes across as much more youthful.

I rush downstairs to greet him and he gives me a big hug.

'Are you all right, darling?' he breathes in my ear. 'Your dad's been terrifying me to death, saying that you're hardly speaking, refusing to come out of your room.'

I shrug, throwing Andrew an angry glance.

'Anyway, I'm here now, darling,' Gavin goes on. 'I'm *always* here for you.'

Beside us, Andrew stiffens. It's a tiny gesture, but I know he's irritated. Which he has absolutely no right to be.

'Your uncle has a suggestion for you,' Andrew says, tight-lipped.

Uncle Gavin smiles, revealing a set of very small, even, white teeth. I remember what Janet said earlier about him looking like a shark. Then I push the thought out of my head. Janet was just being mean.

'What suggestion?' I ask.

'It's a place for you to go, Evie darling,' Uncle Gavin says. 'A place to sort your head out after all the . . . the revelations.'

I frown. 'What do you mean? What sort of place?'

Andrew and Gavin exchange a glance. My throat suddenly feels dry. The last thing I expected was to see the two of them in cahoots over anything.

It doesn't just feel strange.

It feels wrong.

'Tell me,' I insist.

Andrew plucks his laptop out of his bag and places it on the kitchen table. 'Sit down, Evie,' he says with a sigh. 'We've got something to show you.'

What was coming now?

Andrew opens the computer. I glance at Gavin, but he is looking at the screen. I slide into a chair as Andrew turns the laptop to face me.

'What is this?' I lean forward, trying to make sense of the picture of an island sparkling in sunshine.

Andrew clears his throat. 'It's the brochure for the Lightsea Young Adult Development Programme.'

'The *what*?' I peer more closely. Underneath the main photo of the island is a row of smaller close-ups. One picture shows an ugly grey stone house, with the sea beyond. Another a cluster of trees. A third an expanse of uneven rocks leading down to the shore. I scroll down to the page of text below the pictures.

Lightsea House offers guidance and development opportunities for troubled teenagers. Our discreet team of highly trained staff know exactly how to get the best out of each adolescent in our care. We take a highly individual approach to every member of the group and keep staff-to-student ratios high: we take a maximum of six teens on every self-development course and emphasise the need for discipline and responsibility.

'What do you think?' Andrew asks.

I frown, my stomach twisting into an uneasy knot. 'Why are you showing me this?'

'Read to the end,' Uncle Gavin urges.

I turn back to the screen.

Personal possessions are limited and there is no internet access or signal network on the island. Attendees are only

allowed a small number of clothes and other items for
personal use. We encourage each teenager in our charge
to explore the issues that trouble them in a supportive
environment, enabling them to confront their past and
take responsibility for their future.

'This sounds like a boot camp,' I say.

Andrew glances at Uncle Gavin, who sits down beside me.

'We think it sounds like exactly what you need, darling,' he says.

'What?' I'm as shocked as I'm horrified.

'Seriously, Evie, I know you've been unhappy since . . . since you found out about your mum . . .'

'*Birth* mum,' Andrew interjects.

'I – we both – think you should give Lightsea a chance,' Gavin goes on. 'It might help you heal from all the trauma of your recent discoveries.'

I can't believe it. I'm not surprised by my dad's desire to punish me for following my heart. Uncle Gavin wanting to send me to some hellhole for teenagers is quite another matter.

'But . . . but . . .' I can't even find the words.

'I don't know how to explain what Lightsea offers in a way that will make it appealing to you,' Uncle Gavin says. 'But the man who runs the place – David Lomax – is the son of some old family friends.'

'*Our* family?' I ask. 'Yours and mine?'

'Yes,' Gavin says. 'David Lomax's parents knew mine and

Irina's – your grandparents. They knew us too, when we were children.'

'Oh.' I'm thrown. 'What about David Lomax?' I ask. 'Did you spend any time together when you were a kid? Did Irina?'

'I don't remember meeting him, but he's a few years older so he may well remember better.' Gavin smiles. 'It's not just that connection. He's the real deal, Evie. I've followed his career. He used to be a therapist, then he spent ten years on an ashram in India. Now he's running his own residential development courses. He's a good guy. And he specialises in helping . . . er, young people. You've had a lot to process recently and I really think this might help.'

'I don't know.' I'm torn. On the one hand, I'm intrigued by the sound of this man with his family connection to Irina. On the other, it's still basically just a jumped-up boot camp.

'Evie.' Andrew runs his hand over his head. 'I don't want to force you, but your mother and I are at our wits' end. We don't know how to help you and Gavin has come up with this idea and he's generously offering to split the costs . . .'

I stare at him, then at Uncle Gavin who looks away. 'Where is this Lightsea place?' I demand.

'It's off the west coast of Scotland. I spoke to David Lomax earlier. He's very happy for you to come for the August course.'

'The whole of August?' Is he serious?

'At the end of which time you'll come into your inheritance and you'll be free to make future decisions for yourself,' Gavin says with a smile. 'Lightsea isn't like any other institution for teens. It's supposed to be a great place.' He pauses. 'I think it's what Irina would have wanted for you.'

'Really?' I gaze up at him.

'Definitely, darling.'

I doubt very much if Lightsea will help me feel any better about Andrew and Janet lying to me all my life, but it's a connection to my real mother and, because of that, I want to find out more.

'OK.' I turn to Andrew. 'OK,' I say. 'I'll go.'

Lightsea

Five

It's a long journey to Lightsea from Hertfordshire and Andrew hates being late for anything so is furious when our car breaks down on the motorway. As a result, we miss the boat sent to pick everybody up from the mainland and take us to the island. David Lomax, the head of the Lightsea YA Development Programme, organises a local fisherman to bring us over. The man, whose name I don't catch, settles himself at the back of the little motorboat, his gnarled hand on the tiller. He looks like a walking cliché of a salty seadog with white hair and weather-beaten skin. Andrew tries to talk to him when we set off, but the guy just grunts so Andrew gives up and the two of us sit at the front in total silence, the spray misting in our faces.

My chest tightens as we draw closer to Lightsea Island. All the other teenagers will have met each other by now. I'll be the one coming in late . . . last . . . an outsider. This was *such* a bad idea. Why on earth did I ever agree to come here? I close my eyes, trying to focus on the fact that David Lomax must have met Irina when they were children, that he may have memories, stories to share with me. And Gavin thought I would like being here . . . that it might help me come to terms with

41

finding out about my real mother – and the fact that it was kept a secret from me.

'OK, Evie?' Andrew asks.

Ignoring him, I lean back against the rough wooden hull and take out my mobile. Now that we've left the mainland there's no signal at all.

No phone and no internet for a month. I can't imagine what that's going to be like. The prospect of no contact with friends or family bothers me far less. Right now, I've got nothing to say to anyone. Except Gavin of course.

We power along for another few minutes. I keep my eyes on the murky water ahead. At last, the island comes into view. The pictures in the Lightsea brochure must have been taken when the sun was shining and the sea sparkling. On this grey day, everything looks stark and barren – a load of old rocks.

'I guess the trees we saw in the pictures must be further along the coast,' Andrew muses.

I shrug. Who cares where the trees are? The whole place sucks.

It drizzles for a minute or two as we draw close to the island, making everything even duller and greyer than before. We're at the south-east tip of Lightsea, Andrew explains, where the island is at its narrowest. All I can see is an endless stone beach and the edge of a wooden jetty.

'There's a boathouse along the rocks, I think,' Andrew drones on.

'Wow,' I say. 'Fascinating.'

Andrew sighs. For a second, my throat pinches with guilt

at being mean, then I shake myself. Andrew has lied and lied to me all my life. Even now, he has only given me the minimum possible information about Irina. He doesn't understand me at all. Goodness knows what *she* ever saw in him.

The motorboat slows as we reach the empty jetty. The drizzle stops completely as the fisherman moors us to a wooden rail.

'I'll be leaving again in five minutes,' he mutters, his accent so thick I can barely make out what he's saying.

'Thank you,' Andrew says.

We walk onto the jetty, carrying my big rucksack between us. A woman appears out of the trees. She strides towards us, about Andrew and Janet's age, and slim and muscular with neatly bobbed hair. She's wearing dark green, soldier-style combat trousers. There's a big smile on her face, but she looks seriously tough.

'Ah, here's someone,' Andrew says approvingly, setting down my rucksack.

I say nothing, but my legs suddenly feel like jelly. The woman reaches us.

'Evie Brown?' she asks. The smile is still there, but her eyes pierce through me. At least she has an entirely understandable northern accent.

I nod. Not for the first time I imagine what it would be like to have my mother's name: Galloway. Brown is Andrew's name, of course, though he and Irina weren't married. It's solid and conventional, just like him.

'I'm very sorry we're late; the car broke down as I explained

43

when I called. I'm sorry if we've inconvenienced you,' Andrew says.

'It's fine. I'm Miss Bunnock.' The woman purses her lips, her eyes lingering on my hair. It's loose, right down my back. The Lightsea regulations – as Janet reminded me ten times before we left the house – insist that long hair must be tied back at all times. I bite my lip, expecting Miss Bunnock to make some comment, but instead she turns to Andrew.

'I would offer to show you around, Mr Brown, but your boat won't wait and I'm sure you're keen to get home.' It isn't a question. Andrew nods. He looks at me.

'You'll be OK here, Evie.'

That isn't a question either.

I press my lips tightly together. For some stupid reason, I feel like crying. For a second, I actually want to throw my arms around Andrew and beg him to take me home. But the bigger part of me is too proud to show him I care.

'Bye,' I mumble.

Andrew turns to Miss Bunnock. 'I know you said no communication, but . . .'

'You can call the office if you wish for an update,' Miss Bunnock says crisply. 'And obviously we'll contact you in case of an emergency, should there be such a thing.' She makes it sound as if she'd be astonished if an emergency dared to happen anywhere near her or Lightsea Island.

'Right.' Andrew hesitates.

'All those who're coming, be coming,' the fisherman calls out.

'Bye then, sweetheart.' Andrew leans forward and kisses my cheek. 'Be good. I love you.'

'Yeah,' I mumble, giving him the briefest of hugs back. But there are tears in my eyes as he turns and heads back to the boat.

'Come on then.' Miss Bunnock indicates the rucksack on the ground at my feet. 'Pick that up, we need to get you settled before the welcome talk. Dinner has been delayed to allow time. Everyone else is up at the house.'

I frown. It isn't quite 4.30 pm. What time is dinner usually served? I follow Miss Bunnock through the trees and along a gloomy path strewn with twigs and leaves. It's far colder here than it was at home. In fact, it doesn't feel like summer at all. I tug my jacket around me. The instructions said to bring three pairs of leggings and/or tracksuit bottoms, plus three T-shirts and three sweatshirts or jumpers. There was no mention of coats and I'm beginning to wish I'd brought something warmer than my cotton zip-up.

Miss Bunnock doesn't speak as we walk. After a couple of minutes, the trees thin out and we emerge onto a wide patch of heath with the sea in the distance on either side. It's completely deserted.

'How far is the house?' I ask. 'Aren't there any other buildings?'

'No.' Miss Bunnock clears her throat. "Apart from the boathouse, Lightsea House is the only building on the island.'

The ground is rough and uneven; not easy to cross in my favourite sandals: silver, with a wedge heel. My boots are tucked at the bottom of my rucksack, along with my favourite bits of make-up. The instructions said no cosmetics would be allowed, but I'm hoping no one will notice the mascara and BB cream I've shoved in the toes of my boots.

Miss Bunnock is striding hard across the scrubby grass. I have to walk fast to keep up. After a few minutes, the land widens out and slopes upwards. Glimpses of the sea flash into view through the gaps between the trees on either side. The sky over the water is darker than ever, but here on the island the sun is just about managing to shine through the clouds. Not that it cheers the place up. From the heath, to the trees, to the sea, to the sky, the whole scene is a series of dull greys and browns.

And then, out of the corner of my eye, I glimpse a dark shadow and a flash of red moving through the woods. I turn. Blink. It's gone.

I stop. Miss Bunnock looks round and frowns. 'What is it?'

'I just saw something . . . er, someone.' I point. 'Over there, by the trees.'

Miss Bunnock shakes her head. 'Nonsense, everyone's up at the house. I left the other students with Mr Bradley. Mrs Moncrieff is in the kitchen and Mr Lomax is busy in his office.'

'I'm sure I saw someone,' I insist. 'They were wearing a long dark coat and . . . and something red too . . . at least I think they were.'

'Probably just a trick of the light; the island's known for it,' Miss Bunnock says. 'Come on.'

46

I stand for a second longer, my eyes straining into the trees, but the figure – if it was a figure – has gone. Is Miss Bunnock right that I just imagined it?

Despite the sunshine on my face, I feel spooked to my core.

Six

I follow Miss Bunnock across the heath. Despite looking back several times, I don't see the shadowy figure again. Perhaps it was a trick of the light, as Miss Bunnock said. After a few minutes, we reach another path where the trees to the right thin out and the grey sea stretches beyond.

We hurry down a small mound, through more trees, then up another, steeper hill. Unlike Miss Bunnock, who's as athletic as she looks, I'm panting for breath by the time we round the last bend at the tip of the island and Lightsea House comes into view.

My heart sinks another few inches. It is, without doubt, one of the ugliest buildings I've ever seen: made of stone over three floors, it looks like it's just been dumped here, a horrible granite box, dark grey against the navy sea beyond and steely sky above. Feeling miserable, I follow Miss Bunnock inside. It's no warmer in the stone hallway than it was outside and very bleak: no ornaments, no furniture, no carpets. Even the walls are just concrete with white paint.

A burly man with thick dark hair hurries by as we reach the stairs.

'They're in the library,' he says, rushing past.

Miss Bunnock turns to me. 'You'll meet the others at the welcome meeting,' she says, with a smile. 'But first we need to get you settled.'

She leads the way up the stairs to the second floor where she shows me a white-tiled bathroom with a chipped enamel sink and, next to it, the girls' bedroom: a large, bare room with two tiny windows set into the sloping roof. A steel-frame bed is positioned under each of the windows; a third stands against the wall by the door. All three of them are made up with a neat white cover.

'Open your rucksack, please,' Miss Bunnock orders, pointing to the bed by the door. 'Everything out on the mattress.'

Gulping, I do as I'm told. My heart hammers as I draw out all my clothes and toiletries. The Lightsea rules were very clear, but I don't know how fully they'll be enforced. Before I got here, I'd thought it would be easy to get away with some extra bits and pieces, but, now I'm face to face with Miss Bunnock, I'm not so sure. I've met teachers like her before; they're usually quite fair – but total sticklers for the rules.

I lay my belongings out on the bed. Miss Bunnock chats away as she pores over them, asking questions about my life at home. Then she takes a tightly folded black bin liner from her pocket and shakes it open. My mouth gapes as she shoves all my loose bits of make-up into it, then loads my jeans and two of my prettier shirts on top.

'What are you doing?' I squeak.

'Three changes of plain clothes only, as per the regulations,' she says apologetically. 'I'm sorry, Evie, but the rules are quite clear and Mr Lomax does have good reasons for limiting your focus on fashion and cosmetics.'

'D'you have to take *everything*?'

'Sorry,' Miss Bunnock says again. 'I need to ask for those sandals you're wearing too, please. Oh, and your phone.'

Stunned, I bend down and undo my sandals. Miss Bunnock hands me a pair of my own socks as I straighten up, then the regulation pumps I've brought for indoor use. She lays my boots on the bed – minus, I notice, the BB cream and mascara. Miss Bunnock's black bin bag bulges with my belongings. Tears prick at my eyes again as I hand over my phone. I've been dreading this last restriction for days, but now the time has come it's even harder than I imagined to let go of my only way of contacting the outside world. Even if there is no signal on the island.

'Where are you taking my stuff?' I ask.

'It will be locked away in Mr Lomax's office, ready for your departure,' Miss Bunnock says with a sigh. 'Don't be upset. It's only for a few weeks. I'm sure you can live without mascara until then.'

I'm seriously not sure that I can. My eyes look like tiny pinpricks in my face without any make-up. Another thing I haven't inherited from Irina: big, soulful eyes. Still, the loss of the phone and the lack of a signal are worse.

'Cheer up.' Miss Bunnock clears her throat. 'Remember you're allowed to keep one luxury so long as it's not some sort of electronic entertainment device.' She points to the bed where the small pile of my regulation clothes lies folded at one end. Five items are laid out across the white cover: a photo that Gavin gave me of Irina holding me when I was a baby, another of her dancing, a friendship bracelet that Mina gave me a few years ago, a book about dancing and Irina's old ballet shoes.

I run my hands over the book. I'm tempted to keep it as part of my mission to find out more about my mother's big passion, ballet, but the website said that there's a large library at Lightsea House. The website also said that we will have very little spare time anyway, so perhaps it isn't worth it. The friendship bracelet used to be really important to me, but I haven't talked properly to Mina for ages. I pick up the two photos. These are my favourites from the selection that Gavin gave me. In the picture of Irina dancing, she is smiling, elegantly poised on points. She looks like an angel. In the one where she's gazing down at me, she looks, if anything, even more beautiful, in a blue roll-neck jumper that brings out the intense colour of her eyes. But lovely though these photos are, it's not them that I hold at night when I can't sleep. I put down the photo and pick up the ballet shoes.

Miss Bunnock sweeps the other items into the bin bag, then checks her watch. 'The welcome meeting is in ten minutes. The other girls may be back beforehand to wash up, then it's straight to dinner.' She hesitates. 'Do you have any questions, Evie?'

I want to ask a million things: what we'll be expected to do later, what the other girls are like – and definitely if it will be possible to call Uncle Gavin and tell him that I can't stand it

51

here and beg him to come and rescue me. But there's such a huge lump in my throat that I don't think I can actually speak – so instead I shake my head.

'See you in a little while then.' Miss Bunnock's heavy tread sounds loud across the stone floor. She leaves the room without looking at me. A few seconds later, I hear the glass door at the end of the corridor shutting behind her.

I get up and put my small pile of clothes in the empty drawers next to the bed, then cross the room to the window. I have to stand on one of the other beds to see out of it – but it only shows a patch of grey sky. I get down and go back to my bed. I sit down, Irina's ballet shoes in my hands. The bed is hard, the mattress only about an inch thick.

I have never felt so unhappy in my life.

'Hi there.'

I glance up. A girl stands, grinning, in the doorway. 'I'm Pepper.'

'Evie.' I shove the ballet shoes under my pillow and stand up. The girl is mixed race, about my height, with high, sharp cheekbones and a shock of hair straining for release from its band.

Pepper hands me a scrunchie. 'That woman . . . Buttock or whatever her name is . . . just gave me this for you. Says she forgot to tell you to wear it or you'll have to do Quiet Time, whatever that is.'

'Quiet Time?' I ask, feeling bewildered.

Pepper waves her hand. 'They'll explain later. It sounds stupid, doesn't it? Like this whole place. Still, I guess you get

52

used to it.' She sounds super confident, like she's been living at Lightsea for months.

'Oh,' I say. 'Er, how long have you been here?'

'Coupla hours.' She grins again. 'By the way, you should know that I only ever say what I really think.'

'What you really think?'

'As in: "Buttockbreath, you're a black hole in the universe", that sort of thing.'

'You said that to her?' My eyes widen.

'Nah, not just now, cos that wasn't what I was thinking. I actually said, "I don't want to give the stupid new girl a stupid hairband".' She winks at me.

My head spins.

'Not that I really think you're stupid.' Pepper skips across the room to the bed on the right and flops down. She's dressed in grey sweatpants and a navy sweatshirt. I study her face. She is striking-looking – pretty, but not in a conventional way. And about the same size as me, but somehow more compact than I am; definitely more graceful. 'I've met the boys and they didn't say much so chances are they *are* stupid.'

'Boys?' I stare at her. I'd forgotten that the six teenagers staying at the facility might be a mixed group.

'Yeah, that's probably why Buttockbreath and the rest of them keep stressing over all the stupid rules.' Pepper snorts. 'Like I'd want to get with the boys anyway. Still, Josh says he can pick the locks if there are any, so that's something, I suppose.'

'Josh? Pick the locks?'

Pepper raises an eyebrow. 'OK, now I'm wondering . . . about the stupid thing? Cos you keep repeating everything like you can't understand what I've said and it's not like I'm explaining how to split the atom over here.'

I meet her gaze. Her eyes are full of fun. Suddenly I really want her to like me. 'Right,' I say. 'So what else are you thinking?'

'That you're scared about being here. And that you've got, like, secrets. And that you're scared I'll find them out.'

I gulp, thinking about Irina. I definitely don't want Pepper or anyone else here to know how Andrew and Janet have lied to me about her all my life.

Pepper tilts her head to one side. 'Also I'm thinking that you're pretty, but you don't know it, and that your hair is rubbish cos you've let it grow too long and it bare needs a proper style.'

'Oh,' I say. There's a long pause. I feel the weight of the silence pressing down on me. If I don't get what I say next right, Pepper will judge me for it. The rest of the month hangs in the balance.

'Yeah?' I raise my eyebrows. 'Well, *I'm* thinking that you're bare rude.'

We stare at each other. I hold my breath. Then Pepper roars with laughter and I feel the relief coursing through me. 'What did you—?' she starts.

A beeping alarm cuts through the air. With a groan, Pepper swings her legs off the bed. 'That's the signal for this stupid welcome meeting or whatever.' She sighs. 'No point being late unless there's a party. Which sadly there isn't.'

She bounces up and sweeps out of the room. I sit, feeling like a hurricane's just blown over me.

'Come on, Evie!' Pepper calls from the corridor.

I hurry after her.

Seven

As we turn down the final flight of stairs, I steel myself, ready to meet the other teenagers who are staying here.

'That's Anna,' Pepper says. 'She's the only other girl. There are three boys too.'

I follow Pepper's pointing finger to a pale-faced girl standing alone in the cold stone hall. Anna looks up and sees us straightaway. She gives me a sheepish little wave hello and I wave back, feeling relieved: Anna doesn't look anywhere near as intimidating as Pepper. She has the kind of looks I've always envied, even before I found out about my real mother: petite, like Irina, and smooth-skinned, like a doll, with a soft curly bob and huge eyes. Her cornflower-blue tracksuit hangs off her. Unlike Pepper, who suits her sporty outfit, Anna looks like she's put on someone else's clothes. It isn't hard to imagine why outspoken Pepper might have been sent to Lightsea, but what on earth did Anna do to end up here? She looks like half the girls at my school: a bit shy probably, but perfectly ordinary.

'Hello.' A male voice comes from out of nowhere.

I turn, startled, as a boy walks into the hall. He's dressed in grey sweats and a white T-shirt under which his arms bulge with muscle. He stares at me, his hazel eyes intense with curiosity. I can't help but stare back. Apart from movie stars and celebrities in photos, I've never seen anyone so good-looking up close before. He's only a little taller than me, but very muscular. His chin is square and the way he holds his head makes it jut out, giving him a slightly haughty air.

There's a strange sensation in the pit of my stomach, as if someone is pulling the plug on my guts and all my emotions are swirling around inside. I've liked boys before: I've had dates and kisses with more than a few. But that was mostly because it was what everyone at school expected – and because it used to wind Dad up so much when I told him I had a boyfriend.

The truth is that I've never felt the sensations I'm experiencing right now. Which at this point is frankly the last thing I need.

'I'm Kit,' the boy says, raising his hand in a sort of awkward half-wave.

'Hi.' I raise my hand too, feeling self-conscious. I'm suddenly aware that Anna is standing beside me, her cheeks a deep pink. Kit glances at her, then back to me.

'Hi.' I wonder what he did that got him sent here too. He seems a bit dazed and overwhelmed, much like me and Anna and very much unlike Pepper who oozes mischief and confidence as she swans over to join us.

'Good, you're all here.' Miss Bunnock hurries in, her trainers squeaking on the stone floor. I glance around. Two more boys have appeared while I've been looking at Kit. One seems younger than the rest of us. He's skinny with short sandy hair

57

and glasses. The other is dressed entirely in black. His shoulder-length hair is as dark as mine and he has a guitar slung over his back.

'Leave that instrument in the hall, please, Josh,' Miss Bunnock says with a smile. 'Follow me.'

'Will do, Miss,' drawls Josh in a tone that makes clear he is only obeying the rules because he's being forced to. He puts down his guitar, winking at Pepper as he passes. I sneak a glance at Kit. He's gazing across the room at Josh's guitar.

The six of us traipse after Miss Bunnock into a big, wood-panelled room lined with bookshelves. A trio of large, squashy sofas surrounds a fireplace and there's a snooker table by the window. It's far cosier than anywhere else I've seen so far. Pepper and Josh are whispering right behind me. What are they talking about? It sounds like Pepper is proposing some sort of midnight lock-picking adventure. Can Josh really pick locks? I'm starting to feel intrigued. Maybe Lightsea is going to be more interesting than I expected. I shift slightly sideways to get a better view of Kit. He has a gorgeous profile, all his features perfectly aligned. Butterflies zoom around my stomach as I focus on Miss Bunnock.

'You'll meet the rest of the staff later,' she says. 'For now, I just want to run through a few basics. Lightsea House was built over one hundred years ago and used as an asylum for the mentally ill before being bought by the father of the present owner, Mr Lomax.'

My ears prick up. The older Mr Lomax is the one who was friends with Irina and Gavin's parents, my grandparents.

'They say the island is haunted by nutters,' Pepper whispers under her breath. 'I googled it.'

I shiver, remembering the dark figure outside.

'Do I have your full attention, Pepper?' Miss Bunnock asks, eyebrows raised.

'Course you do.' Pepper grins.

A flash of irritation crosses Miss Bunnock's face, then it passes and she smiles again.

'The older Mr Lomax ran the place as a mental-health facility for young people until his death ten years ago, when the current owner, his son David, took over.'

A little thrill runs down my spine as I remember Gavin telling me that David Lomax might have memories of Irina from when they were kids.

'The current Mr Lomax founded and runs the Lightsea programme for teenagers. This utilises a range of activities from meditation to team-building, all designed to develop the taking of personal responsibility in a supportively holistic environment.'

'In a *what*?' Josh wrinkles his nose.

I glance at Pepper. She rolls her eyes. 'Unbelievable,' she mouths.

'Mr Bradley and I handle all exercise programmes and outdoor chores,' Miss Bunnock continues. 'Meanwhile, our housekeeper, Mrs Moncrieff, will supervise you indoors. There is a rota of chores which all six of you are expected to adhere to.'

'What kind of chores, Miss Bunnock?' Kit asks politely.

'Food preparation . . . cleaning . . .' Miss Bunnock shrugs. 'Now to finish there are just a few rules. We want you to focus on your personal development, hence the restrictions on clothes and make-up and electronic distractions. We also believe in the internalizing of discipline, which is why we insist you all carry out daily chores. However, outside your duties and sessions with staff, you're free to roam wherever you want on the island. I'm afraid swimming is forbidden, for your own safety; the rocks in the sea around the island can be lethal.'

'I wouldn't go swimming in the ocean anyway,' Anna breathes. 'It's far too scary.'

I look down, suppressing the shiver that runs through me at the thought of the cold, dark, dangerous water.

'You also need to be careful of the caves and bays where the tide can easily trap you unawares, and some of the rocks overlooking the sea are dangerous too, sheer drops to the water.'

As Miss Bunnock continues, Kit moves closer so our shoulders are almost touching. The blood pumps furiously against my temples as Miss Bunnock explains that if we refuse to take part in the Lightsea programme the punishment will be Quiet Time, 'a period of solitary and silent reflection undertaken in isolation, usually while carrying out additional chores'.

'Weird, but not the worst, I guess,' Kit whispers in my ear.

I nod as Miss Bunnock talks on. At least if she's droning on, I don't have to work out what on earth to say to Kit.

'Dinner is served at 5.30 pm promptly,' Miss Bunnock continues. 'Though tonight's meal has been delayed until six due to Evie's late arrival.' My cheeks flush as everyone looks at me. Miss Bunnock clears her throat. 'Free time after dinner, then it's bedtime at eight-thirty and—'

'*What?*' Pepper shrieks. 'You're having a laugh, aren't you? And why's dinner so early?'

'Yes, Miss,' Josh adds drily. 'It's so early it's practically breakfast.'

Everyone except Kit and Miss Bunnock giggles.

'Bedtime at eight-thirty with lights out at nine sharp,' Miss Bunnock carries on.

'But . . . but it'll still be *daylight* at 9PM,' Pepper protests.

Beside her, Josh groans.

'Not for long,' Miss Bunnock announces, as if making the sun set earlier is part of her programme for us. 'By next week, sunset in this part of Scotland will be *before* nine. Anyway, you need the sleep; you will be rising early ready for morning meditation at six-thirty. Our aim is to send you back to your parents in a healthy sleeping pattern.'

This time everyone groans.

'The rota for chores is pinned up in the kitchen. So it only remains for me to welcome you and to urge you to make the most of your stay here.' She pauses. 'Any questions?'

Silence. Kit is still standing next to me. I can feel his presence even though I'm not looking at him. As Miss Bunnock walks out, I glance around. He's gazing out of the window. How can I get him to talk to me again? I clear my throat and

61

point to the smart-looking watch on his wrist. It's black, with three interconnecting faces and lots of dials.

'Is that watch your luxury item?' I ask, my cheeks burning.

'It is,' he says. I'm suddenly aware that his accent is very upper class. 'But it's much more than a watch. It has a compass, a heart-rate monitor and it's waterproof as well.'

'That'll come in handy if you fall off the rocks and can't work out which direction to swim back to shore in,' Josh drawls, a big grin on his face. 'Where d'you get it, Scout Camp?'

I smile too – there's something infectious about Josh's grin – but Kit bristles. I suddenly realise the others are watching us. I take in their faces one by one: Pepper, all cheekbones and raised eyebrows, pale, shy Anna and the third, sandy-haired boy whose name I don't yet know. I turn to Josh. He looks cool in his black clothes. Fun. I'm sure he didn't mean to upset Kit.

'The watch was a present from my brother actually,' Kit says with a scowl. He turns to me. 'What's your luxury, Evie?'

All five of them look at me. I gulp, the heat rising in my face. How can I tell them about Irina's ballet shoes? The last thing I want is to explain how Andrew and Janet kept her a secret from me for all those years. But if I mention the shoes it's bound to lead to all sorts of questions.

My mind races over various alternative items, discarding each one as either improbable or impractical. Maybe my clothes? No, I could hardly pretend my sweatpants or pumps are luxuries I've chosen to keep. And I don't have any jewellery.

I'm out of time. And options.

What should I say?

Eight

'Go on, Evie,' Pepper urges. 'My luxury's a picture of my horse and Anna's is her old teddy bear. What's yours?'

Her bright dark eyes sparkle with curiosity. Beside her, Kit's expression is softer, but just as interested.

I take a deep breath. There's no getting out of it. I am going to have to tell the truth. 'Er, my real mum's ballet shoes,' I say.

Oh God, how pathetic does that sound?

'Your *real* mum?' Josh smiles again. He has a narrow face, made longer by his shoulder-length hair, and the palest of pale blue eyes. Is he laughing at me? I don't think so. There's genuine warmth in his expression. I can't stop my eyes flickering over to Kit. He just looks embarrassed.

'Your mum's a *ballet dancer*?' Pepper says with a frown. 'Wouldn't she be a bit old for that? Or did she have you when she was, like, fourteen?'

My insides tighten. 'Er, actually, she *used* to be a dancer. She, um, died in a road accident when I was little. That's why I said my "real" mum. I was actually brought up by my dad and his wife . . .' I tail off. It feels odd referring to Janet as Dad's wife rather than as 'Mum'. Though technically it's the truth.

The others stare at me. I can tell they don't know what to say.

'My mum died when I was a baby too,' Anna stammers, her face as red as mine. 'But she was a secretary. I think it's lovely you have her ballet shoes. My mum died in a house fire so all her possessions were burned with her.'

Another silence. I stare at her. She clearly feels as self-conscious as I do. In that moment, it strikes me that here, where no one knows me, I don't need to explain that Andrew and Janet lied to me for years and that I've only just found out about Irina. Here I can simply talk about her as my mother. Like Anna just did.

'O-kay,' Pepper interjects. 'I think we should stop there, before this conversation gets any more depressing. Can you guys *believe* this place?'

'No, man. It sucks big time,' Josh grunts.

I glance at Anna. She offers me a bashful smile. I nod to show I'm grateful she has shared such a big confidence, that I understand how daunting it is to tell people something so private.

'I think it could be much worse,' Kit says reasonably. 'OK, so there's a crazy bedtime and we have to do chores, but we get lots of free time too.'

'Total Boy Scout,' Josh mutters, though too quietly for Kit to hear.

Another beeping alarm sounds. 'Dinner,' Pepper groans. 'This is like a police state.'

'Yeah, and I bet the food's rubbish too,' Josh adds.

But it isn't. It's delicious – huge plates of tender meat, a tray of perfectly roasted vegetables plus a fluffy baked potato each and a big bowl of salad (no boring lettuce) that has grapes in it. Even better is the massive chocolate cake, oozing with fresh cream, ready for dessert. A grey-haired woman, short and round, like a barrel padded with cushions, is bustling about, setting down plates at the end of a long trestle table as we check out the rota of chores pinned on the wall above. I don't appear to have any jobs tonight, though Pepper announces with theatrical horror that she and I are down to clean all the bathrooms tomorrow afternoon.

'Can't wait,' I sigh as we tuck into the food. We're in the kitchen, another bare-walled, stone-floored room, though this one is as warm as the library with a big oven that blazes out heat.

'There you go.' The woman who has served us steps back. 'I'm Mrs Moncrieff, the housekeeper here. You're to come to me if you need anything house-related and, of course, I'll be overseeing clearing up, cleaning and food prep.'

I glance at Pepper.

'I hate chopping things,' she whispers with a grimace. 'In fact, I hate doing *anything* in the kitchen. When I'm older, I'm only ever eating takeaways.'

'I like baking,' Anna says shyly. She takes the chair between Josh and Kit. Pepper and I sit down opposite, next to the sandy-haired boy.

'I'm Samuel and I like eating,' he says, staring down at his plate. It's the first thing I've heard him say.

'Steady there, Samuel,' Josh chuckles, 'we all like eating.'

'So I'll leave you to enjoy your dinner,' Mrs Moncrieff carries on. She points to the rota pinned to the wall. 'Which of you are Anna and Kit? You're on clearing-up duty tonight.'

Anna raises her hand.

'Yeah, that's me,' Kit says gruffly.

'Very good,' Mrs Moncrieff says. 'Everything you need is by the sink.'

I look down at my food, flashing with a sudden, stupid jealousy that it's not me who's going to be helping with Kit. I blow out my breath, hoping no one has noticed.

Mrs Moncrieff bustles out and the six of us carry on eating. Pepper and Josh do most of the talking . . . their conversation revolves around all the things they hate about Lightsea so far.

'Going to bed before it's dark and all that cleaning,' Pepper moans.

'I'll have no time to play my guitar,' Josh grumbles.

'What kind of things do you play?' Pepper asks.

'Indie stuff mostly, some of my own songs,' Josh says modestly. 'I can play some later if you like?'

He looks at me as he speaks. 'That'd be cool,' I say.

'Yeah, totally,' Pepper says. 'Anything to break the monotony. Can you believe no phones and no Wi-Fi?'

'And no TV,' Josh adds.

'Or even radio, so no sports scores,' Kit says, looking up. A faint line of freckles runs over the bridge of his nose. His hazel eyes are ringed in dark brown.

It's hard to tear my gaze away, his face is so perfect, but I force myself to look at Samuel who is sitting beside me. He hasn't said anything since that rather bizarre announcement that he liked eating. He's holding something small and metallic in his hand, flicking it over and over between his fingers.

I peer more closely. 'What's that?'

Samuel opens his palm to reveal a square silver lighter.

'Miss Bunnock let you keep that?'

Samuel looks at his plate. 'Mr Bradley made me take out the lighter fluid,' he says. 'Fire needs fuel and heat and oxygen.' He pauses. 'I love fire.'

I catch Pepper's eye. She raises an eyebrow. 'Fire *and* eating,' she mouths.

I suppress a giggle.

'Yeah, fire is *awesome*,' Josh says enthusiastically. 'I once made a bonfire that spelled "bite me" on the playing fields at my school.' He grimaces. 'Though technically it's not *my* school any more seeing as I was asked to leave.'

'About five thousand pupils are permanently excluded from schools every year,' Samuel says, looking across the room. He still hasn't made eye contact with anyone.

'Did *you* get sent here for setting fire to something?' I ask, wondering why he's acting so strangely.

'No.' Samuel stiffens, still staring across the room. 'No, I'm here because my parents thought it might help.'

'Help what?' I ask. 'Help how?'

Samuel just shrugs. A minute or two later, he gets up from the table.

'Where are you going?' I ask.

68

'Toilet. An average person pees seven times a day.' He slips away.

The conversation carries on, with Josh and Pepper still doing most of the talking. It turns out Pepper has been sent here for destroying her dad's collection of vinyl records after her mum found out he had an affair with a woman at work. 'He was on my case over *everything* anyway *and* it wasn't his first affair,' she explains darkly. 'My mum's *so* upset, but she refuses to dump him.'

'That's awful,' Anna says in a shocked whisper. 'I don't blame you for wanting to get back at him.'

'Me neither,' Josh says.

'Hey, where's Samuel?' Pepper asks.

I glance sideways. 'He said he was going to the bathroom.'

'That was about two years ago,' Pepper insists.

'Perhaps he went looking for something else to enjoy eating,' Josh suggests. Pepper laughs.

'Or perhaps he just wanted to be on his own for a bit,' Kit says pointedly. It's the first thing he's said since his comment about sports scores. I'm getting the definite impression he hasn't taken a liking to Josh or Josh's sense of humour.

'Oh, do you think maybe he's gone off to do a bit of meditating,' Josh says with a chuckle. 'Get ahead of the game for tomorrow.'

'I'm *dreading* all that stuff.' Anna's lip trembles. 'It sounds *awful,* just sitting doing nothing.'

'Actually, I think it'll be interesting,' Kit says. 'I've done a lot of rugby and we had sessions with a psychologist on handling performance pressures. We did yoga too; it was helpful.'

'I thought you must have done rugby,' I say, then feel my cheeks flushing. Could I make it any more obvious that I've been staring at his muscles?

'You did *yo-gah*, did you, Kit?' Josh says, mimicking Kit's upper-class accent. He grins.

I can't help giggling. Pepper laughs too. It's not really what Josh says that is funny, it's the light, ironic way he says it. Kit's face clouds. He stands up and grabs his plate, then heads over to the sink. A tense silence falls. Josh's expressive face registers bemusement. 'What did I do?' he mouths.

'I think you're being a bit oversensitive, Kit,' Pepper says. I wince. Pepper's mission to speak her thoughts is all very well, but that's too direct.

'Well, *I* don't think he is,' Anna says quietly. She takes her plate and Josh's and joins Kit at the sink.

Pepper rolls her eyes. She turns to me. 'So, Evie, you never said what you're in here for. What did you do? I'm betting you ran away from home once too often, yeah?'

I shake my head, embarrassed that the conversation has come back to me again. At least I'm saved from answering: an alarm screeches out over our heads. As it pierces the air, Miss Bunnock rushes into the kitchen.

She takes one look at us. 'Have you seen Samuel?' she demands.

'Not for a while,' Pepper says. 'Why? What's happened?'

Miss Bunnock's eyes widen. 'He's missing.'

70

Nine

Miss Bunnock ushers us out of the kitchen. She's frowning, anxious. There's no sign of Mrs Moncrieff, but a worried-looking, middle-aged man in worn corduroy trousers is tugging on a jacket in the hallway. As he sees us, his expression softens.

'Mr Lomax, these are the August students,' Miss Bunnock says.

I stare at the man. His face is lined and his hair peppered with grey. So this is the man whose parents were friends with my grandparents. Gavin said David Lomax almost certainly met him and Irina when they were all kids. Does he remember either of them? I expect Miss Bunnock to introduce us, but Mr Lomax already knows our names.

'Ah, welcome, Pepper, Anna, Kit and Josh,' he says, looking at each of the others in turn. He turns to me and it may be my imagination, but I could swear his eyes linger as if he's examining my face, looking for something he recognises. Could he be trying to see if I look like Irina did?

'Hello, Evie, it's a pleasure to meet you.' Mr Lomax speaks slowly and deliberately, his voice as posh as Kit's, but far deeper. 'This is *not* the welcome to Lightsea I had hoped to give you all, but we need to find Samuel before it gets dark.

There are no lights on the island, apart from those in and around the buildings, and though it's fine for you all to explore the island I'm concerned poor Samuel may have wandered too far and got lost.'

'If you ask me,' Pepper says, 'having met him, I'd say there's no knowing what Samuel might do.'

'Indeed.' Mr Lomax smiles, but there's real concern in his eyes. Despite its designer logo, his jacket has a hole at one elbow. Considering he owns the entire island, he surely could afford a new one. Or maybe he just doesn't care about how he looks, like Janet. I'm itching to ask him if he remembers meeting Gavin and Irina, but there's no way in front of all these people.

'Do you think we need to search Easter Rock?' Miss Bunnock interjects, her eyes wide.

'Goodness.' Mr Lomax looks startled. 'I don't think . . . no . . . yes, we should check. I'll take care of it. Why don't you see if he's in the grounds to the back of the house?' He turns to the rest of us. 'Until later, everyone, please don't leave the building. Mrs Moncrieff is currently searching the upper floors again so I suggest you wait in the library.'

'Would you like us to help look for Samuel?' Kit asks earnestly.

Pepper rolls her eyes. 'Ooh, Boy Scout alert,' she whispers.

'No, er, thank you.' Mr Lomax shakes his head distractedly and hurries to the door, Miss Bunnock right behind him.

'What a fuss,' Josh drawls. 'Samuel's probably just gone outside for a cig.'

'I don't think that's very likely.' Anna sounds scandalised.

'No.' I suppress a smile at the idea of Samuel smoking, as we troop into the library. 'Anyway, they took the fuel out of his lighter.'

'Good point,' Josh acknowledges.

'Plus, we were told not to go outside,' Kit says. 'So it would mean breaking the rules.'

'Jeez.' Pepper makes a face. 'Lighten up, will you?'

'Yeah, man, just cos you always obey the rules.' Josh winks at me, then flings himself down on one of the sofas.

I blush. Kit scowls. 'I just meant Samuel didn't seem likely to go against what he was told to do.' He turns away and paces up and down by the bookshelves. His walk is powerful, yet graceful, ridiculously mesmerizing. I can't take my eyes off him.

'What I don't get is *why* they didn't want us to help,' Anna says with a sigh.

Pepper sits down beside Josh and sprawls across the end of the sofa, her arms flung theatrically over the cushions. 'I've got no idea either. This place is weird.'

'They just don't want us outside and unsupervised on our first night,' Kit says, still pacing up and down.

I screw up my courage, ready to sidle over and maybe try talking to him again, but before I can move Anna drifts over to the bookshelves.

'Hey, Kit,' she says. 'Do you think we should get back to the clearing up?'

Kit nods. Without looking round, the two of them leave the room.

Great.

I sit down opposite Josh and Pepper, feeling disgruntled.

An hour passes and the light outside starts to fade. We attempt to explore the ground floor, but only the kitchen and a large, empty, wood-floored room with a pile of blue mats in the corner are unlocked. The rest of the floor is hidden behind a thick wooden door. Josh goes to get his guitar, but it's been taken up to his room and the doors to the bedrooms are firmly fastened. He tries most of the other doors on the way back down and reports that they're all locked too.

'If I had my tools with me, I could open them,' he says, 'but they're in the bedroom.'

'What tools?' I ask.

'Couple of long pins, nothing fancy. They fit down the hem of my rucksack or the side of my boots. Anyway, I'm not leaving the room without them again.'

'It's like an effing prison,' Pepper mutters.

Josh raises his eyebrows. His dark eyes twinkle as he glances from me to Pepper. 'Fancy a prison break?'

Pepper sits up. 'Totally.'

'You mean go outside?' I ask. My heart thuds.

'Yeah, we might even track down Samuel.' Pepper sniffs. She and Josh are already at the door.

My stomach contracts. It's true that we might be able to help find Samuel, but Mr Lomax specifically asked us not to go outside right now and, not only would I prefer to avoid getting into trouble on my very first evening, I also don't want to get on the wrong side of Mr Lomax before I've even had a chance to ask him about Irina.

'Come on, Evie,' Josh grins. 'What's the worst they can do to us? Even if we get in trouble, which I doubt we will, Quiet Time sounds like a punishment for babies.'

This is true. And Josh's cheeky smile is irresistible. I don't fancy him, like I do Kit, but I'm hoping we can be friends. And I don't want either him or Pepper to think I'm afraid.

'Let's go,' I say.

The three of us pad across the hall to the front door. Someone has put a row of boots in front of the bench by the wall. I spot my own pair third from the left.

'See, it's fate,' Josh whispers. 'Our footwear is waiting for us.'

I suppress a giggle. Mrs Moncrieff's soft Scottish tones drift towards us from the kitchen, where she's talking to Kit and Anna. Pepper puts her finger to her lips, then lifts the heavy bar on the front door. It gives a low creak as it opens. I freeze, but the chatter in the kitchen carries on as before. Nobody has heard us. Pepper opens the door a little wider and peers outside.

'I can't see anyone,' she whispers.

'Let's head for the woods.' Josh tiptoes out into the crisp, evening air, Pepper and me right behind. 'I don't know where that Easter Rock is that Lomax and Bunnock were going to, but we're less likely to be spotted if we stay among the trees.'

'Good thinking,' Pepper says approvingly.

'Wow,' I say as we cross the patch of grass outside the house. 'It looks completely different from when I arrived.' Earlier, the sky was grey with dark, glowering clouds that the light struggled to break through. Now the sun is a low orange disc framed by a clear blue sky. Beyond the rocks to the left of the house the sea sparkles like a carpet of diamonds.

Josh and Pepper lead the way into the trees. I follow more slowly, looking around as I walk. There's no sign of any of the adults. Despite the bright sunlight, the way through the woods is dark and shadowy. The air smells damp and salty. Every now and then, I catch sight of the glistening water through the trees. Apart from the wind, there is no sound at all.

Josh and Pepper are moving faster than me. Not wanting to be left behind, I speed up. As I jog along, I catch a flash of red out of the corner of my eye. I spin around remembering the shadowy movement I saw earlier, just after I arrived on the island. A slight figure in a long black coat and a red hat is standing between the trees about twenty metres away. I stop running. Could that be Samuel? The head is bent down, the hat pulled low, so I can't see a face or even tell if the figure is male or female. I take a step forward. In a flash, the figure turns. There's the swish of the coat disappearing into the trees. And it's gone.

My skin erupts in goosebumps. I peer through the branches, straining my eyes to see it again. But the figure has vanished. My heart thuds. Was that one of the adult members of staff? It was surely too short for Mr Lomax and Miss Bunnock, and definitely too slender for Mrs Moncrieff. Anyway, Lomax and Bunnock were wearing short jackets when they went outside. What about Samuel? I hesitate. Josh and Pepper are now out of sight. If Samuel is here, I should try and find him.

I head through the trees towards the spot where the figure

76

was standing. Through the branches beyond, I emerge onto a wide expanse of smooth grey rock. The sea is just a few metres away, waves crashing over the jagged ridges that poke up from the water. Miss Bunnock's earlier warning about how lethal the Lightsea rocks are floats into my head. The sharp ones out at sea do look dangerous, but there's nothing scary about the flat rock that leads to the water's edge. I look along its breadth. There's no way anyone could have run out here within the last minute and not be visible. The only place they could possibly be hiding is on the other side of a high rock that rises up at the far end of the flat expanse, just before the sea. A smallish person could just about conceal themselves behind that.

'Samuel?' I call.

No reply, just the sound of the wind whipping through the trees and the waves smashing against the rocks.

'Samuel?' I call again, louder.

Still silence. This is ridiculous. Whoever ran through the trees *must* be here. And if it isn't Samuel then I want to know who on earth is out here. I test the flat rock in front of me. Not too slippery. Anyway, my boots have a great grip. I take a step.

'Samuel?' I call once more.

No reply. The sun dips out of sight, plunging the area into shadow. The place suddenly feels spooky. I hurry across the rock. My boots keep me steady, though I can feel the ground beneath my feet getting smoother and slippier. I reach the tall stone. Peer around it. It falls away sharply to the sea below. Waves pound against the crags that stick up from the sea.

There's no one here. No way anyone could hide here after all.

And then footsteps sound behind me. I spin around. Too fast. I lose my footing. Stumble back, almost to the edge. The sea smashes against the rocks, loud in my ears.

As I fall, a hand grabs my arm.

Ten

I look up into Kit's hazel eyes. He hauls me to my feet with an angry hiss.

'What are you doing out here?' he demands, letting go of my arm. 'You could have fallen into the water and drowned . . . or been crushed to death on the rocks.'

I glance down to where the grey stone falls away, sheer to the sea, just centimetres away. It was stupid to run over here – and of all the people I don't want to see me being stupid, Kit is currently at the top of the list. The thought that he did see – and is now telling me off because of it – makes me hot with embarrassment.

'I only fell because you startled me. I was trying to find Samuel.' I back away from the edge, my legs trembling. 'I . . . I thought I saw someone creeping through the trees . . . that maybe they came this way. Did you see anyone? Was it you?'

But even as I ask I know it wasn't. Kit is wearing the same clothes as earlier – a white T-shirt over grey sweatpants. Definitely not a black coat or a red hat. Unless he put them on and took them off again.

'No, it wasn't me,' Kit says with an angry snort. 'I only saw *you* creeping through the trees. Which by the way they told us not to do. *And* they *specifically* said not to go on the rocks.'

Irritation rises inside me as the shock of my fall and Kit's sudden appearance wears off. He might be the hottest boy I've ever met, but that doesn't give him the right to order me about.

'I don't see how what I do is any of your business,' I snap. 'Just because you always do what you're told.'

'I don't.' Kit's face flushes a deep red. 'I wouldn't be here if I did, would I? Look, if you're not coming back to the house then I'll see you later.' He turns away.

'Wait.'

Kit turns back. The setting sun behind me is shining on his face. He holds his hand up to shield his eyes. 'What?'

I hesitate, my throat dry. 'What *are* you doing out here?'

There's a long pause. The wind dies down though the waves still crash against the rocks. When Kit speaks, I can only just hear him above the swell and slap of the water.

'I came to find you,' he says. 'I'd just finished in the kitchen and I saw you and the others through the window when you were going into the trees so I came to look for you.'

'Oh.' We stare at each other, then Kit moves slightly closer. My heart hammers. My insides cartwheel madly. Kit's strong, square-jawed face is all I can see.

And then he turns away and looks out to sea.

I gulp, feeling confused. What is he thinking? Is he still mad at me?

'I just wanted to help find Samuel and then, when I was in the wood, I thought I saw him coming this way,' I gabble, eager to explain why I ventured onto the rock. 'The same thing

80

happened earlier on the way here. That is, I think I saw something . . . someone . . . in the trees. Miss Bunnock said it was a trick of the light, but it kind of freaked me out.'

'It *was* probably the light,' Kit says. 'Look.'

I follow his gaze out to sea where the water is calm and the sun, almost at the horizon, is a pure disc of gold. Its light shimmers across the water like a gleaming sheet of yellow silk.

'Oh wow, it's beautiful,' I say, transfixed.

As the sun slowly sets, the tips of the rocks rising up from the sea gleam like needles of bright light. Kit and I stand, side by side, as the sky shifts around us: pearly pinks and soft oranges weaving in and out of the burnished gold.

'It's amazing,' I breathe.

'You can see why the place is called Lightsea.' Kit turns to me, his eyes glowing. 'Evie . . .?'

I wait for him to carry on, but his jaw clenches and he frowns.

'What is it?'

'We should go back to the house before it gets dark.'

I'm certain that isn't what he'd been going to say, but I don't know how to explain that so I just nod, then follow Kit off the rock.

We walk through the trees and back to the house in silence. I have no idea where Josh and Pepper have got to or if Samuel has been found. To be honest, I don't give either thought much consideration. The way Kit looked at me as he moved closer keeps whirling around my head. It was as if he'd been about to kiss me then thought better of it.

81

Nobody is outside the house as we let ourselves in and hurry to the library. Anna is curled up on one of the sofas. She's alone, a large leather-bound book in her lap. Her eyes light up as she sees Kit.

'Hi there,' she says.

'Hi, Anna,' Kit says. 'Where is everyone?'

'I don't know.' Anna blushes, a shy smile on her lips. 'I think Mrs Moncrieff must still be upstairs. I haven't seen anyone else since I came out of the kitchen. Where've you been?'

'Just looking around,' Kit says vaguely. He wanders over to the bookshelves. Anna watches him for a moment, then turns to me. She holds up her book. The title is embossed across the front: *The Haunting of Lightsea*.

'I've been reading about the house being haunted,' she says. 'Apparently, the legends about ghosts began when it was an insane asylum, but this book reckons most of the people here weren't even mentally ill, just different, the sort of people who, with a bit of care and the right meds, would be totally fine today.'

Kit turns around from the bookshelf he's examining. 'That happened a lot in the old days.'

'Does it say anything about the hauntings?' I ask.

'Yeah, it does actually.' Anna tucks her hair behind her ears. She holds out the book to me. 'It was written just after the original Mr Lomax took over the island and set up the Lightsea Institute instead of the old insane asylum that had been here since Victorian times. The old stories said that it's the island that draws the ghosts, like some portal between this life and

82

the next – but the scientists who examined the claims said it was all just a trick of the light. There's a photocopy of a slightly more recent newspaper cutting in the back though, about something from fourteen or fifteen years ago, before the Mr Lomax who's here now took over. Take a look.'

I sit down by the empty fireplace and open the book. It's heavy and smells of damp. The photocopy of the newspaper article is tucked inside the front cover. I glance at it idly, then gasp.

The article features a blurry photograph of a woman in a red wool hat and a long dark coat. The collar of the coat is turned up and the hat pulled down so low that it's impossible to see her face. My heart thuds in my chest. The colour of the hat looks similar to the flash of red I saw earlier. And the swish of the black coat I caught sight of could easily have been made by the coat in the picture. Was *this* who I saw running through the trees? I snatch up the article and read:

An unknown woman is reported to have been pushed – almost certainly to her death – in the early hours of this morning on Lightsea Island, our correspondent writes.

The woman's outer clothes (pictured here on a model) were found on Easter Rock, a lethal promontory that occupies the eastern end of the island. Alan Lomax, head of the Lightsea Institute mental-health facility, claims to have no knowledge of the woman or her presence on the island. The alleged incident was reported by a visitor to the Institute. He remains the only witness, but was only able to give the police a general description of the alleged attacker and the woman who fell. The attacker is believed to be tall with dark hair while the woman was described as fair-haired and of slightly lower than average height and build.

My skin erupts in goosebumps. The woman sounds like Irina. I shake myself. Lots of women could be described in the same way.

This is not the first time tragedy has struck on this particular part of Lightsea Island. Easter Rock was a commonly used suicide spot for inmates of the Asylum that used to stand on the site of the present Institute.

Police are appealing for information from anyone who thinks they may have seen the woman or her attacker in the local area . . .

Heart still racing, I scan to the date of the incident. All the air seems to be sucked out of the room as my brain tries to process what it is seeing.

It is the date of Irina's death.

Eleven

'Evie? *Evie?*'

I'm dimly aware that someone is saying my name, but all I can think is that the woman in the article might be Irina – except of course she can't be. Uncle Gavin would definitely have said if Irina had died on the island. He told me – as did Andrew – that she was run over by a lorry one evening in Nottingham. All the information I found online said so too.

'*Evie?*' Kit shakes my arm. 'Are you OK? You look really pale.'

I force myself to look at him as he sits down beside me, his eyes full of concern.

'I'm fine,' I lie. 'It's just . . . this article is a bit weird.'

'Yeah, I thought so too,' Anna says. She twists her hair around her finger. 'I mean, how come nobody apart from that one guy saw the woman?'

'What woman?' Kit asks.

I pass him the article. He reads it, then gives it back. 'I don't get it,' he says. 'Why is some random woman going missing fifteen years ago upsetting you?'

I pocket the article, avoiding looking directly at his handsome

85

face. I feel too vulnerable to tell him the woman sounds like Irina, but perhaps I can explain just a little bit.

'I think I might have seen her ghost,' I stammer. 'Outside, in the trees . . . running down to the rocks.'

Kit wrinkles his nose. 'Ghosts aren't real, Evie,' he says. 'They're just a stupid, made-up thing to frighten people with.'

'You don't know that,' Anna says. She sits bolt upright, her cheeks flushing bright pink. 'I . . . I believe in ghosts. When I was younger, I was certain my mum was watching over me.'

Our eyes meet. Anna looks self-conscious but defiant, as if she's used to people being sceptical.

'I can understand that,' I say.

Anna nods.

'What exactly did you see, Evie?' Kit asks.

I tell them both about the figure I saw outside, though I still can't bring myself to explain that I think it might have been Irina.

Kit shakes his head, but Anna leans forward, her eyes round with alarm. 'It sounds just like the woman in the article,' she says. 'Wow, Evie, you're being haunted; that's so cool.'

Am I? A chill creeps down my spine.

I really want to explain to her about the connection with Irina, but, before I can find the words to do so, Pepper and Josh rush in, laughing, their faces glowing from the cold air outside.

'Oh my days, we saw Buttockbreath on the way back, had

to run the long way round to get here without her seeing,' Pepper gasps.

'She's quite the speedster,' Josh says admiringly, pointing at Pepper.

In spite of my anxieties, I can't help wondering if Josh likes her. It's easy to see why a boy might. I've never met anyone quite like Pepper before: so open and forthright, so completely unconcerned with what people think of her.

'What happened to you, Evie?' she asks, flopping elegantly onto the sofa next to me. 'One minute you were right behind us, the next you'd vanished.'

'Yeah, we were worried you'd been taken by the same bogeyman who's got Samuel,' Josh adds with a chuckle.

'It's not funny,' Kit says with a frown. 'Samuel could be hurt.'

'I thought maybe I saw him out on a rock past the trees, so I went to take a look.' I avoid Kit's gaze, but I can sense him looking at me. For some reason, I really don't want to tell Pepper and Josh that Kit followed me, that we were out there together.

'Oooh, not the dangerous rocks.' Pepper widens her eyes theatrically. 'Very daring, Evie.'

'Well, we needn't have worried, none of us,' Josh says with a sigh. 'We saw Samuel with Mr Lomax down by this big wooden hut thing at the other end of the island.'

'That must be the boathouse,' Kit says.

'Yeah,' Pepper says. 'It's like a smaller version of the one in our holiday home.'

'You have a holiday home?' Anna sounds awestruck.

'My dad's seriously rich,' Pepper says in a bored, matter-of-fact voice. 'He's still an arse.'

She sounds defiant, but I wonder if she really feels as unbothered as she's making out. Even though I'm angry with Andrew, I don't feel like Pepper clearly does. I can't imagine what it must be like to despise your own father.

'Was Samuel OK?' Kit asks.

Pepper shrugs. 'He looked fine to us, but we didn't hang around.'

'Yeah, couldn't wait to get back,' Josh adds sarcastically.

Outside the twilight deepens, the darkening sky spread with silver and orange swirls. After about half an hour, Miss Bunnock appears. She reassures us all that Samuel is fine after accidentally wandering too far from the house and getting lost and that he has been sent up to bed. It suddenly strikes me that maybe Samuel saw the same figure as me . . . that perhaps it spooked him into running off.

'Is he really OK?' I ask. 'Can we see him?'

Miss Bunnock frowns. 'You'll see him in the morning.'

'He'll be glad to know you care, Evie.' Pepper grins.

'It's not that,' I mumble, feeling embarrassed.

'Anyway, it's bedtime now,' Miss Bunnock says.

'No way.' The grin falls from Pepper's face. 'Seriously, it's not even properly *dark* yet.'

'I know it seems early,' Miss Bunnock says with a smile, 'but you'll get used to it.'

'What if we refuse?' Pepper asks, hands on hips.

'I'm afraid that would mean Quiet Time tomorrow – and you'd still have to go to bed now.'

Pepper opens her mouth as if she's about to protest again.

'Come on,' I urge, tugging at her arm. 'No point in kicking off unless it gets us to a party. Which sadly it won't.'

Pepper flashes me a smile and flounces up the stairs. The rest of us follow. I can hear Josh grumbling to Anna and Kit behind me, but I don't look around until we reach the landing. I'm hoping I'll be able to say goodnight to Kit, but he has already disappeared along the corridor to the boys' bedroom.

I follow Pepper and Anna into our room, feeling miffed. The girls don't notice I'm a bit quiet. Pepper is full of moans about the early bedtime while Anna is still curious about the figure I saw in the woods. Her questions lead to a bigger conversation about whether spirits actually exist and if people and places can really be haunted. I feel for Anna, who is almost breathless in her certainty that it is possible.

'I dunno.' Pepper wrinkles her nose. 'I mean, I like the idea of ghosts, but . . . you only saw what you saw for a second . . . and everyone says how there's a weird light here that plays tricks on your eyes.'

I chew on my lip, feeling irritated. Kit said something similar earlier. And while the light on the sea *is* kind of freaky, easily capable of casting strange shadows, I've seen the dark figure twice now and I'm *sure* I didn't imagine either the red hat or the black coat. Suppose Irina was wearing those clothes on the day she died? Suppose she died here, on the island, after all? I can't see how or why it's even possible, but there was already a connection between her and Lightsea – maybe she came back here the day she died and Andrew and Uncle Gavin never knew.

I clean my teeth and get into bed, determined to talk to Mr Lomax about it all tomorrow. I read the newspaper article one last time, then put it back in my sweatpants pocket. The lights go out on the dot of nine. Which, as Pepper says, is totally crazy. It's not even fully dark yet. The others carry on chatting, but my thoughts drift to Kit. Does he like me? Is that why he followed me onto the rocks? If there is anyone here I feel I can talk to about serious stuff, it's him. And yet, from his earlier attitude to ghosts, I'm certain that he would find the notion that my mother might be haunting me ridiculous.

I reach under my pillow, curling my fingers around the soft, comforting satin of Irina's ballet shoes. I'm never going to sleep for worrying about it all.

Twelve

I wake with a start to find Anna's pale face hovering over mine.

'We have to get up,' she says, her eyes strained with anxiety. 'Bunnock's already been in twice. We have to do meditation in five minutes.'

I groan, then roll over. 'What time is it?'

'Almost six-thirty. And don't forget to make the bed, otherwise you'll be doing Quiet Time.'

I'm still clutching Irina's ballet shoes. An image of the figure in the dark coat being pushed off Easter Rock flashes into my mind's eye as I shove the shoes under my pillow. I stagger to the bathroom to splash some water on my face, weighed down with a sense of dread. Is Irina's ghost haunting me? Was she somehow murdered on the island? If so, how come none of the accounts of her death even suggest that as a possibility?

Pepper is reluctantly dragging on a pair of leggings as I return. Anna, looking worried, tugs her hair into a regulation hairband with fumbling fingers.

'I don't want to be late,' she mutters.

'Stupid rules about getting up early,' Pepper grumbles. 'Who cares?'

'Please, Pepper,' Anna pleads. 'I don't want any of us to get into trouble.'

'Fine, I'm getting dressed,' Pepper says with a sigh.

I yank a sweatshirt over my head, still fretting about whether I can possibly have seen Irina's ghost, and the three of us hurry downstairs just as the clock in the hallway strikes half six. Josh, Kit and Samuel are already in the hall. They all look up as we appear, though I notice that – just like yesterday – Samuel doesn't make eye contact.

Josh smiles. 'Hey,' he says. 'Those beds are rubbish, aren't they? I spent most of the night on the floor; it was softer.'

Anna and Pepper giggle. I glance at Kit. He's standing apart from the others, unsmiling. I sense an atmosphere between him and Josh, as if they aren't speaking to each other. Then Samuel coughs and I remember that he went missing yesterday . . . and wonder again if maybe he saw my ghost.

'Are you OK, Samuel?' I ask.

'I'm fine,' he says. 'Er, Mr Lomax says I should apologise for worrying everyone.'

'No need, man, you've already said sorry about ten times.' Josh grins. 'We weren't *that* worried about you.'

'Good. That's good,' Samuel says earnestly.

Pepper, Anna and I laugh. Even Kit allows himself a tiny smile.

'What made you run off?' I ask, my chest tightening. Suppose Samuel did see the dark figure in the red hat. It's funny, but standing here, waiting for an answer, I'm kind of hoping he didn't. Despite the fact that Samuel seeing the ghost would help prove I wasn't imagining things, I'd rather have my ghost to myself. If Irina's spirit is on the island, I want it to be haunting me, not random strangers.

Which is totally crazy.

'I didn't run off,' Samuel says, pushing his glasses up his nose. 'I just went out to see if there were any killer whales in the sea.'

I stare at him blankly. Is he joking? 'Killer whales?'

'Yes. Did you know killer whales can swim at almost thirty miles per hour?' Samuel asks. 'That's very fast.'

'Hello, everyone.' All eyes turn to Mr Lomax standing silently at the far end of the hallway. He is dressed in faded jeans and a thin grey jumper with fraying cuffs. He smiles at us, his hand smoothing his high forehead. 'This way, please.'

We follow him into the wooden-floored room that Pepper, Josh and I found during yesterday's explorations. I chew on my lip, wondering how I can ask Mr Lomax about Irina. I'm certainly not going to do it in front of everybody. A strange silvery light floods in from the large windows. It's misty outside, the tops of the distant trees hidden by white cloud.

'Sometimes it almost feels like we're in another world, doesn't it?' Mr Lomax says gently, following my gaze. 'Everyone, please take a mat and sit down.'

We each find ourselves a blue mat and, at Mr Lomax's instruction, arrange them in a circle on the floor. Pepper and I keep catching each other's eyes and giggling – the whole thing seems so silly. Kit sits down quietly under the window, but Josh flops onto the mat next to mine with a sigh.

'Nightmare,' he mutters under his breath.

I nod. Pepper positions herself on his other side, then looks horrified as Mr Lomax takes the mat next to hers. I look away to stop myself from laughing out loud. Samuel sits between Mr Lomax and Kit, with Anna between Kit and me.

Anna looks even paler than she did upstairs. I suddenly remember that she said yesterday she was dreading our meditation sessions. Well, I know what it's like to feel anxious. I still have a knot in my stomach over the dark figure from the woods and the newspaper article.

Truth is that Pepper and Josh might be funnier and Kit is, well, insanely hot, but out of everyone here I feel a particular bond with Anna because of our mothers. I reach across and pat her arm.

'I'm sure it won't be that bad,' I whisper, while Mr Lomax busies himself lighting a candle in front of his mat.

She nods gratefully. 'Thanks, Evie.'

'Yeah, I bet you love it,' Kit whispers softly on her other side, with a smile that makes his eyes twinkle and his face more gorgeous than ever. 'It's really not hard, just go with it.'

Anna beams at him and I felt a sudden, sick lurch of jealousy. Does Anna like him? Does he like her back?

'I'm not going to say too much this morning,' Mr Lomax says, his deep voice filling the empty room. I tear myself away from Anna and Kit to look at him. He seems tired; there are shadows under his eyes and his face looks even more lined than it did yesterday.

94

'Welcome to Lightsea and I hope you had a good first night.' His eyes rest for a moment on Samuel, then he clears his throat. 'This is how we will begin each morning – by giving ourselves an opportunity to step back from the cares and concerns of the day.'

I glance at Pepper.

'Insane hippy alert,' she mouths, raising her eyebrows.

I press my lips together to stop myself from laughing again.

'Now I already know that some of you have done a little mindfulness meditation before, but most of you haven't, so we'll save our discussion for afterwards. I'd like you to make yourselves comfortable by lying down on the mats, then close your eyes.'

Once I'm horizontal on the mat with my eyes shut, I try to focus on Mr Lomax's soothing voice. He instructs us to 'feel the pressure' of our weight 'sinking down into the mat', then to become gradually aware of our physical presence. 'Let your mind focus on your toes, your calves, your knees . . .' He takes us through the whole body, then asks us to concentrate on our breathing, counting silently to ten, then starting again. 'If your mind wanders off, just bring it back to the breath.'

I can't hold my mind on my breath at all. Every time I reach three or four, I'm off thinking about Irina again. I don't feel like laughing any more, the meditation is too frustrating. Plus, it seems to go on forever. At last, it's over and Mr Lomax encourages us to 'become aware again' of our bodies and all our senses, then open our eyes.

I look around. How did everyone else find it? Kit seems

very still and peaceful, but Josh has a bored expression on his face, while Pepper is fidgeting like mad.

'How was that?' Mr Lomax asks.

No one speaks for a second.

'Great,' Kit says.

'Amazing.' That's Anna. I turn, surprised by the vehemence with which she's spoken. Her eyes are lit up, the brightest of blues, and the sunlight through the window makes her mousy curls shine like pure gold, softly framing her delicate features. My heart sinks. I'm pleased she's got something out of the mediation, but there's no way I can compete with looks like hers.

'Amazing how?' Mr Lomax enquires.

'Like I was there, but also watching myself,' Anna says, her voice as animated as her face. 'It was so peaceful, just brilliant.'

'Good, that's wonderful.' Mr Lomax smiles. He gazes around the group. 'But not to worry if it didn't feel like that for all of you. Mindfulness meditation is always a fresh experience and sometimes it brings up things that trouble us deeply.' His eyes rest on me and, for a second, it feels like he can tell exactly what is bothering me. I am more determined than ever to speak to him, to find out what he knows about Irina. 'I'm always here if any of you need to talk . . . about anything.'

A few minutes later, after both Pepper and Josh say that they found the meditation really hard and – in Pepper's case – utterly pointless and I haven't spoken at all, Mr Lomax sends us off for breakfast. I hang back, waiting until everyone else has left. Mr Lomax walks over.

'Are you all right, Evie?' he asks.

I look up into his kindly brown eyes. There is something about the warmth of his manner that reminds me of my dad and that, plus my anxiety about whether I saw Irina's ghost yesterday, suddenly makes me feel like crying.

'I'm OK,' I say, holding back my tears. 'I just need to ask you about something.'

'Very well.' Mr Lomax leads me along the corridor to his office. I wait as he unlocks the door then follow him into a gloomy, square room. An overloaded bookshelf lines the far wall. A row of filing cabinets stand opposite. There are two desks, each covered with paper. The desk nearest the door also holds a computer and – I notice – a landline phone.

We sit down and Mr Lomax leans forward, a frown creasing his forehead.

'What would you like to ask me, Evie? Is it something about the meditation?'

'No.' I hesitate, unsure how to begin. 'My uncle told me that you . . . your parents knew my grandparents? That is, my *real* mother's family: the Galloways.'

A wary look crosses Mr Lomax's face. 'I believe that's true,' he says slowly.

I gulp. 'So do you remember meeting my mother – Irina Galloway – or my Uncle Gavin when you were little?'

Mr Lomax shakes his head. 'I'm sorry, Evie, but I don't. The friendship was between the parents – and it wasn't a long-lasting bond as far as I can tell. Once my mother died and my father moved to this island, he lost touch with almost everyone he'd been connected to beforehand.'

My heart sinks. This is very much *not* what I'd been hoping for. 'So you don't think Irina ever came to Lightsea?'

Mr Lomax looks away. I get the strong impression that he's struggling with himself. Like there's something that he wants to say, but doesn't know how to express it.

'I have no recollection of your birth mother at all,' he says at last.

What does that mean?

'So *could* she have come here?' I persist. 'I mean, it's possible, isn't it?'

Mr Lomax frowns. 'Why are you asking, Evie?'

I take a deep breath. If Mr Lomax is into alternative stuff like meditation, maybe he believes in ghosts too. I launch into an account of how I went outside to look for Samuel, stressing how worried I'd felt and glossing over the fact that Mr Lomax had asked us to stay indoors. I tell him about the dark figure with the red hat in the woods. Mr Lomax sits in silence, listening intently. Feeling encouraged, I show him the photocopy of the article that is still stuffed in my sweatpants pocket. I leave out nothing except the part where I nearly fell and Kit arrived and saved me. It isn't fair to get Kit into trouble too.

'So I can't stop thinking that maybe I saw Irina's ghost,' I finish, my eyes filling with tears. 'The red hat and black coat are the same as the woman in the article. So is the date of Irina's death. I know this place is famous for ghosts and I really think she might be haunting me. I want to speak to my uncle to . . . to find out more about how she died. If maybe someone could

98

have made a mistake about the circumstances or the place. Can I call him?'

'Mmm, I see.' Mr Lomax sits back in his chair. I wait for him to go on. I feel better for having told him everything. After a long pause, he taps his fingers together. 'I'm going to overlook your running off last night when I asked you not to, Evie, but only on condition you don't do it again. Deal?'

I nod, wiping my face.

'The thing is, Evie, that when we suffer a terrible loss our brain sometimes struggles to process what has happened. We're liable to look for meanings that aren't there . . . for something to make sense of what, ultimately, makes no sense: why a loving mother should be taken away from her baby. Why that baby should grow up, naturally wanting to find out more about her mother, perhaps even to *be* like her mother.'

I frown, unsure what he's trying to say. 'Are you telling me that I can't phone my uncle?'

'I'm simply saying that I'd like you to examine your thoughts more carefully. For a start, are you *sure* you saw someone in the woods yesterday? As you are bound to have heard already, the island is famous for its light which can play strange tricks on the vision. Peculiar sightings are common here: shadows, bursts of bright white light. At sunrise and sunset in particular, the light seems almost ethereal, other-worldly.'

'I'm sure I saw someone,' I say stubbornly.

'OK.' Mr Lomax sighs. 'Then let's examine the evidence.' He holds up the photocopy of the newspaper article. 'You say the description of the woman given in this sounds like your mother: blonde, below average build and height. Well, wouldn't you also say that could describe literally millions of people?'

'I guess,' I say reluctantly. 'But what about the date?'

'Over a thousand people die in the UK every day. I think it most likely a complete coincidence that your own mother passed on the same day.' Mr Lomax pauses. 'Perhaps my next point won't weigh very heavily with you, but, though I don't remember exactly where I was on that day fifteen years ago, I can't believe a woman could have died here – or a mysterious stranger be suspected of murdering her – without my father mentioning it.'

He points to the article. 'My dad clearly doesn't know the woman, it says so here, so she wasn't an Institute inmate or a member of staff.' He pauses. 'It rather suggests to me that the whole business was probably invented or at least misrepresented by the newspaper. It certainly seems unlikely the unfortunate woman was ever found, which makes it even less likely any kind of crime actually took place.'

I shake my head. 'Maybe your dad just didn't want to talk about what happened.'

'That's as may be, but even supposing this unnamed witness mentioned in the article really did see a woman being pushed into the sea, it doesn't mean that woman was your birth mother.' Mr Lomax sighs. 'Do you not think it's possible that you're simply looking for connections that aren't there? That you are so desperate to feel a bond with your birth mother that you're seeing – or more literally imagining you see – her spirit when it simply cannot be so.'

100

I gulp. The way Mr Lomax puts it sounds so logical and yet I'm sure of what I've seen – and the article is definitely too big a coincidence not to check out.

'Don't you want to know the truth about what happened here?' I ask. 'I know my dad has told you about me not finding out until very recently about . . . about Irina Galloway being my real mum. I've already been lied to about that, so maybe there are other lies too, other secrets.'

A shadow passes over Mr Lomax's face. For a second, his calm expression morphs into a look of guilty confusion. Again, I'm certain that he knows more than he's saying. I fidget in my seat.

'Evie, I've read your file and spoken to your father,' Mr Lomax goes on gently, his face resuming its calm expression. 'I understand that you are in terrible pain. It's an awful thing to have to struggle to become a young woman, without the presence of the very person who is supposed to be here to show you how. I myself lost my own mother when I was a child. She died after a long, slow illness and, although that was nearly forty years ago, the hole her loss left in my life can and will never be filled.'

'Wow, that must have been awful,' I say sincerely.

'It was very hard,' Mr Lomax acknowledges.

I take a deep breath. 'Are there any records that might say if Irina was here, from when your dad was in charge?'

'I'm afraid not,' Mr Lomax says, though he sounds relieved rather than afraid. 'None of the files relating to my father's stewardship of the Institute have survived. The paperwork only

101

goes back ten years, to when I took over the island and set up the Lightsea Young Adult Development Programme.'

'Oh, I see.' I chew my lip. There's no mistaking the 'I've-dodged-a-bullet look' on Mr Lomax's face. He seems determined to block or discredit every single suggestion or idea I come up with. 'I'd still like to talk to my uncle.'

Mr Lomax clears his throat. 'I understand that, but we have the "no contact" rule for a very good reason and we only make exceptions in extreme circumstances which, I think you'll agree, is not the case here where you're basing your request on a series of allegations and suppositions.' He pauses. 'Do you agree?'

I don't. But it's obvious that Mr Lomax is never going to allow for the possibility that I really saw Irina's ghost. I give a tiny nod.

'I also think, if you give the programme here a chance, you'll really find it helpful. Your uncle certainly seemed to think you would.' Mr Lomax sits back. 'What do you say? Are you prepared to let me keep this newspaper article to help you let it fade from your mind?'

'OK,' I reluctantly agree.

'And will you promise to focus on what I believe is really at the root of this: your grief over your mother? Are you prepared to be open to the opportunities Lightsea can offer?'

I stare at the floor. The carpet is as threadbare as Mr Lomax's jumper. His look of guilty confusion from a few moments ago flashes into my mind again.

'I'll do my best,' I say.

'Good.' Mr Lomax offers me a relieved smile. 'Now go and join the others for breakfast, and we'll talk some more in a day or so.' His gaze drifts to the window.

I leave the room, feeling troubled. It is, of course, possible that Mr Lomax is entirely right about what I saw and that the news report did indeed invent or misinterpret what happened here fifteen years ago. It's certainly possible that the woman – even if she was murdered – wasn't Irina.

But my instincts tell me that David Lomax is covering something up.

And I need to find out what.

Thirteen

The others are halfway through a huge cooked breakfast when I walk into the kitchen. Pepper and Josh are deep in conversation, though they both wave at me as I stroll over. Kit and Anna are talking intently too; so intently that they don't even notice me. Does Anna like him? I don't know. It's even harder to tell if Kit's interested in her or just being friendly.

Deeply hoping it's the latter, I sit down at the end of the table beside Samuel. Samuel squints at the sausage on the end of his fork.

'Did you know that a grandmother once found a dead kitten inside her sausage?' he asks.

I forget Kit. 'Er, OK . . . eew, *really*? That's disgusting.'

Samuel keeps his gaze on the sausage. 'They think the kitten must have wandered into the factory where they made the sausages and bits of it got caught up in the machinery.'

I glance down at the bacon and sausages on the table, my appetite vanishing. Everyone else except Anna, who's picking at a thin slice of apple, is munching away. I take a bread roll and nibble at the edges.

Was Irina pushed off Easter Rock fifteen years ago? And, if so, by whom? How on earth am I going to find out?

'OK everyone, I'm Mr Bradley.' The burly young man who rushed past Miss Bunnock and me last night is standing by the door. He scowls, winding his scarf tightly round his neck. His chin is covered with dark stubble, his hair tousled as if he's been out in the wind. 'All those doing outdoor chores need to be by the front door in five minutes.'

Josh and Pepper groan loudly, while Anna heads to the wallchart, offering to check who is supposed to be doing which chore. I pocket the rest of my roll and stand up.

'Where did you get to after meditation?' Kit asks, appearing beside me.

I shrug, my heart giving a little skip that he's talking to me. 'Mr Lomax wanted a word,' I say. 'Nothing major.'

'Oh.' Kit nods. He indicates the wallchart. 'I've already looked,' he says. 'You and me are outside.'

'Oh—' I start.

'What about me?' Pepper demands. 'I know it's toilet cleaning this afternoon, but . . .'

'We're doing food prep in the kitchen this morning, Pepper,' Anna says timidly, turning from the chart. 'Everyone else is outside with Mr Bradley.'

Pepper groans again. Josh pushes himself up from the table. 'At least "outside" is better than peeling veg,' he says.

'But there's food inside,' Samuel says, looking puzzled.

'Come on.' Kit ushers me to the door as Pepper slumps back into her chair.

'I'd even rather do stupid meditation with Loonymax,' she moans as we leave the room. 'At least you can daydream while

105

you're breathing through your arms and legs or whatever it is you're supposed to . . .'

Her loud, clear voice echoes around us, still complaining away, as Kit and I cross the hall with Josh and Samuel trailing in our wake.

'That girl has a definite problem with authority,' Kit mutters under his breath.

I glance at him, unsure what to say. 'Well, no one likes being told what to do,' I venture.

Kit opens his mouth, but before he could speak Josh sidles up between us.

'Depends who's doing the telling,' he says with a wink, then saunters over to the boot rack.

'Hurry up, hurry up,' snaps Mr Bradley who is waiting by the front door.

There is just time to tug on our boots before Mr Bradley chivvies us outside and sets off at a brisk pace. It's still chilly and misty outside, though the sun is already burning through the clouds. But we're walking too fast to feel cold. Even Kit is almost jogging in order to keep up with Mr Bradley, while Samuel is running flat out. Before we are over the first hillock, he starts panting for breath, falling behind the rest of us.

'Mr Bradley,' I call out. 'Please could we slow down?'

'No,' Mr Bradley barks, barely glancing over his shoulder. 'The pace is not excessive. You should all be able to keep up!'

We keep going for nearly ten minutes before Mr Bradley steers us up the hill that dominates the south-west tip of the island. We're all out of breath by the time we reach the top.

It's an amazing spot, especially now the mist has rolled back from the shore. From where we stand, you can see the oval shape of the island and the sea on all sides.

'Orienteering session,' Mr Bradley shouts over the wind. 'That way is north-east.' He points towards the trees and rocks where I saw the dark figure in the red hat yesterday. 'High rocks run along much of the coast. The very tip of the eastern part of the island, opposite where we are now, is Easter Rock.'

I shiver at the mention of the place where the woman in the article was killed.

'The rocks in the sea around that part of the island are particularly dangerous.'

'Yeah, we know.' Josh catches my eye as if to ask: *How many more times are they going to mention it?*

I nod to show I understand.

'Lightsea House is over there.' Mr Bradley points in the direction we've just come from. The roof of the house is just visible beyond another copse of trees. 'The boathouse, jetty and Boater's Cove are along the coast to the south-east. There are many caves dotted around the island that run underground from the sea to the interior of the island. They flood when the tide rises, making them a drowning risk. It's also easy to get trapped in one of the many bays and coves. Water rises, cutting off all routes out and in. Result again: drowning. Understand?'

'Yeah, we get it,' Josh grumbles.

Kit crosses his arms. 'Well, I think it makes sense to keep explaining how dangerous the water can be.'

Everyone except Samuel, currently preoccupied with a

nearby tree, stares at him. Even Mr Bradley looks slightly bemused.

'Quite,' he says. 'Good. Anyway, time to go back down the hill.'

As we jog down the slope, Josh moves closer to Kit.

'Nice job on the sucking-up front, man,' he says with a grin.

I suppress a smile. Kit ignores him.

We reach level ground a few moments later. Mr Bradley directs Josh and Samuel to a patch of trees to gather wood, then turns to Kit and me. 'You two can help me with the boat repairs.'

My stomach cartwheels as we say goodbye to the others and follow Mr Bradley along a winding path. I'm about to spend at least the next hour with Kit. We emerge on to Boater's Cove after about ten minutes. It's a pebble-strewn, horseshoe-shaped beach bounded by high rocks, with a wooden boathouse right on the shore and a huge, covered woodpile lined up against a low fence leading round to the trees. The jetty where Andrew and I were dropped off yesterday is visible in the distance.

'What would you like us to do, sir?' Kit asks.

'Today, varnishing,' Mr Bradley says.

He leads us into the boathouse. I've never been anywhere like this before: a large, square, wooden shed full of boating gear, with one wall open to the sea. A small boat with the name *Aurora* painted along the side bobs on the water inside. Waves from the sea smack gently against its hull.

Mr Bradley hands out tins of varnish and brushes, then

shows us how to apply the varnish properly to the inside of the boat. After checking we know what we're doing, he wanders outside, saying he'll be back in half an hour. Kit and I are alone.

It's nice inside the boathouse: cool and shady, but with the sun shining brightly on the water outside. A gull squawks overhead. We work for a few minutes in silence, then Kit clears his throat.

'I wasn't sucking up earlier,' he says. 'I just don't see the point in making a big fuss about everything like Josh and Pepper do.'

'Right.' I don't quite know what to say. On the one hand, he's right about there not being much point in moaning. On the other, you can't just let grown-ups walk all over you.

There's a long pause.

'What were you talking to Mr Lomax about earlier?' Kit asks. 'Is everything OK?'

I chew on my lip, stumped again. Here in the light of day it seems silly to even consider the possibility of ghosts, but the coincidences still remain. I'm torn between explaining everything to Kit and keeping quiet about my suspicions. In the end, I just tell him that the figure I'm sure I saw in the woods resembles the woman described in the newspaper article who, in turn, sounds like my real mum.

'So it's all seems a bit weird . . . that they look alike, you know . . . blonde, dying on the same day . . .?'

I'm hoping Kit will nod and agree with me. Instead, he frowns. 'Yeah, I can see it's a bit weird, but as a coincidence it doesn't really add up, does it?'

'Oh?' I say, feeling thrown. I keep my voice carefully light: 'Why is that?'

'Well, I don't mean to be nosy, but how was your mum supposed to have died?'

'Everything I've been told or read says she was in a traffic accident in Nottingham, a hit-and-run.'

'Right.' Kit frowns again. 'So if your mum *was* the woman pushed into the sea, why would anyone go to the trouble to retrieve her body and leave it on a road hundreds of miles away?'

'Presumably so that no one would connect her death with Lightsea,' I say.

'OK . . . but how would they make it look like a hit-and-run? I mean she wouldn't have the right injuries on her body.'

I wince. 'The rocks in the sea could leave bruises that might look the same as those from a lorry.'

'What about the fact that there would be water in her lungs?' Kit persists. 'You wouldn't expect to find that if someone had been run over in a road accident. And all those details would be in the post-mortem.'

'Maybe,' I concede, my face flushing. 'But post-mortems can be faked, can't they?'

'I guess, but it seems *really* unlikely.' Kit turns to face me, varnish brush in hand. 'Look, I'm just saying it's strange and . . . and don't take this the wrong way – but . . . well, does it make all that much difference? Your birth mum is gone, which is very, very sad, but knowing exactly how she died isn't going to change anything.'

110

I focus on the patch of wood I'm slathering with varnish, pretending I'm brushing it carefully. Inside I turn over what Kit has said. Like Mr Lomax, he sounds cool, logical and rational. But like Mr Lomax he's wrong. It *does* matter how Irina died. And I can't discount the possibility that her death happened here, just because it can't be explained rationally.

We work on in silence for a few more minutes.

'Evie?' I look up to find Kit shuffling along the boat towards me. He stops about an arm's length away, then puts his hand on an unvarnished bit of wood next to mine so our fingers are almost touching. My heart gives another little skip.

'There's something else,' he says.

My pulse thunders in my ears. Kit looks self-conscious, his cheeks flushing bright red. I hold my breath. What is coming next?

Fourteen

Kit and I carry on looking at each other, the brushes in our hands forgotten. I'm still holding my breath, waiting for him to speak. I could count every freckle on his nose, except that I seem to have lost the power to do anything while he looks at me with those soft hazel eyes.

'I think you're nice. And very pretty,' he says at last. 'Especially your hair. You have really pretty hair.'

'Oh.' I can feel my face burning. What do I say to that? 'Er, Pepper says it needs a style. My hair.'

'Oh.' Kit's cheeks turn a deeper shade of red. I watch helplessly. I've obviously said completely the wrong thing.

'Right, finish up now, please,' Mr Bradley calls from the door.

I jump. Kit turns away and busies himself with his brush.

A few minutes later, we meet up with the others. Josh and Samuel have collected a sizeable pile of wood. Mr Bradley shows us how to bind it into five easy-to-carry bundles, then orders us to jog back to the house, each with a stack under our arm.

Kit picks up his wood straightaway, but the rest of us stare at Mr Bradley in horror.

'What did your last slave die of?' Josh asks, eyebrows raised.

'Quiet,' Mr Bradley snaps.

'I can't carry a whole pile, sir,' Samuel says matter-of-factly.

Mr Bradley glares at him impatiently. But, before he can speak, Kit snatches up Samuel's bundle.

'Don't worry, I'll take yours.' He sets off before anyone can stop him.

Mr Bradley rolls his eyes. 'Well, come on the rest of you.'

Josh catches my eye. It's obvious that if he thinks I'm prepared to back his stand against carrying the wood then he'll keep on refusing. I shake my head. What's the point? I've got much bigger things to worry about than hauling a few sticks across a field. With a shrug, I pick up my bundle. Josh hesitates for a second, then does the same.

We set off together, leaving Mr Bradley and Samuel jogging after us. Josh runs fairly fast, though not as fast as Kit, who is now well ahead. I concentrate on keeping pace with him. It isn't easy, especially with the bundle of sticks under my arm, but in spite of this – and my anxieties about both Kit and the mystery surrounding Irina's death – I enjoy the sense of power in my muscles as well as the feel of the salty wind on my face. Josh talks as we jog, making me laugh with tales of how Samuel came out with a load of bizarre tree facts while they were gathering wood.

'Did you know that the biggest tree in the world is more than one hundred feet around?' Josh asks. 'Or that the manchineel tree causes burns and blisters?'

113

'No,' I chuckle. 'Did you know that some kitten once died inside a sausage?'

'*What?*'

By the time I've explained, we're back at Lightsea House. Mr Bradley directs us to deposit our wood under the porch, then hurry into the kitchen. Mrs Moncrieff, Pepper and Anna are ladling out steaming bowls of fresh chicken soup. I'm starving and gulp down two full bowls along with three of the crusty rolls from the basket on the table. My head is spinning with everything that happened earlier, from my suspicions about Mr Lomax to my confusion over Kit. Luckily, I don't have to say much. Pepper is doing most of the talking, complaining how she thinks it is sexist that she and Anna were made to stay indoors earlier 'doing girly stuff'.

'Well, Evie was outside this morning,' Kit reasons. 'And I'm sure you and Anna will have a turn tomorrow or the next day. It'll all even out.'

Pepper rolls her eyes. 'Jeez, you sound just like Loonymax, Kit,' she drawls.

Kit scowls. He hasn't looked at me since we left the boathouse. I want to tell him that I think he's right about the chores evening out, but when I try to catch his eye he avoids me, sitting down at the opposite end of the table next to Samuel and immediately getting involved in what looks like an intense conversation about the distance of Lightsea Island from the Scottish mainland.

*   *   *

After lunch, Mr Lomax makes us sit in a group and tries to encourage everyone in turn to open up about their situation at home. Pepper does most of the talking, though much of what she says I've heard before: about how her dad is a pig for having an affair and her mum is an idiot for taking him back.

No one else is anywhere near as open: Kit and Josh both say, in different ways, that they don't fit into their families, but Anna clams up, red-faced, when Mr Lomax asks her to talk about her home life and Samuel just seems puzzled at the suggestion he might explain his emotions. As for me, I hint that I feel my parents have let me down about something by keeping a big secret from me all my life, but I don't say what that secret is. I'm aware, of course, that Mr Lomax knows about Irina, but much to my relief he doesn't mention her name or push me to reveal more than I want to.

There are more chores towards the end of the afternoon – Pepper and I are set to work in the first-floor bathroom, and Pepper, who has clearly never cleaned anything in her life, is horrified that this involves having to scrub the toilet. After dinner, we all end up in the library where a roaring fire blazes in the grate.

Josh drags Pepper over to play snooker straightaway. Kit and Anna sit together on the sofa, their blond heads bowed over a book from the library. I grit my teeth. Kit has barely looked at me since that moment on the boat. Why would he tell me I was nice and pretty one minute, then ignore me the next? It doesn't make sense.

I curl up in a corner of the sofa opposite theirs, close to the fire. I stare into the flames, listening to their hiss and crackle. My thoughts drift to Irina again. I need to know the truth about her death, but I'm as far away from finding it as I was this morning.

'You OK, Evie?' Anna looks up from the book she and Kit are examining.

I nod. Across the room, Josh has stopped playing snooker and is holding his guitar.

'Play something, Josh,' Pepper urges. 'Go on, you promised you would.'

'OK, OK.' Josh carries the guitar to the third sofa which is positioned between the other two, directly opposite the fireplace. Kit stiffens as Josh readies himself to perform. Pepper perches on the arm of the sofa next to him.

'Go on,' she says. 'I'm literally dying from not hearing any music. Can you do "Rush of Blood" or any Nightsky songs?'

'Yeah, yeah, hold on to your hairband.' Josh grins. 'I'll take requests in a minute, but this is something I wrote a few weeks ago.'

'Your own song?' Anna asks, sitting forward.

'Yeah, I'm into the whole singer-songwriter thing.' Josh taps his feet for a moment, then starts strumming away.

I settle back into the sofa and tuck my legs under me. I'm very aware of Kit opposite as the first few chords echo round the room. And then Josh starts singing and I forget everything else.

By the look of it, so do all the others. Well . . . Samuel has wandered across the room and is on the floor, reading a book. But the rest of us listen intently, mesmerised by the soft twist

116

of Josh's husky voice and the mournful melody he is singing. The song is about a girl he likes, who's in love with someone else. But it isn't the lyrics that strike me so much as the beautiful tone of Josh's voice.

He finishes the song and there's a moment of total silence before Pepper expresses exactly what I am thinking.

'Wow,' she says, her eyes wide with awe. 'That was *incredible*.'

'Thanks.' Josh's cheeks pink slightly.

'Seriously,' Pepper goes on. 'You could be *massive*. A *star*.'

'You *definitely* could,' Anna agrees.

Josh looks at me. 'It was brilliant,' I say.

Josh smiles.

I glance at Kit. He's staring down at his lap.

'Wasn't Josh fantastic?' I ask.

Kit glances at Josh. 'You've got a nice voice,' he says stiffly.

'*Nice?*' Pepper shakes her head. 'It was *awesome*.'

Kit shrugs. 'I don't know enough about music to judge.'

I stare at him. Why is he being so uptight? Doesn't he realise how he sounds?

'Play another one,' Anna urges.

'Yeah, go on,' Pepper says drily. 'Maybe if you play a bit more it might melt that stick of ice up Kit's backside.'

Anna looks shocked, but Josh laughs. I gaze down at my lap, embarrassed. A couple of tense seconds pass. Then Kit stands up. Without speaking, he leaves the room. Anna follows him.

I half want to go too, but I also feel torn. Kit *was* a bit stiff

117

and awkward. He always is – I suddenly realise – around Josh, and I don't want to make Pepper feel bad by walking out. Plus, I really want to hear Josh play some more. He has already launched into another slightly faster song. I shift in my seat. It would be bad manners to walk out while he's playing. Pepper and I listen in silence as Josh finishes the track. It has a catchy hook and the way he performs it is slick and professional, not just the music, but his habit of glancing up and smiling as he strums and sings.

'That was ace,' Pepper exclaims as he finishes. 'Do another.'

Josh slaps his hand against his guitar. 'In a minute. First I'd like to know what's bothering Evie.' He looks at me. 'You've been upset since this morning. I could see you didn't want to talk in front of everyone, but it's just me and Pepper now.'

I feel my cheeks flushing. I had no idea Josh had noticed so much. For the past few minutes, I've forgotten the newspaper article and my suspicions that Irina might have died here, but now all my earlier fears flood back.

Pepper sucks in her breath. 'It's true,' she insists. 'You've been weird on and off all day. What's up?'

I take a deep breath. 'The thing is, I can't shake this feeling there's someone out there,' I explain. 'There's the ghost or whatever in the dark coat and red hat that I've seen twice now *and* the newspaper article, and they both make me think . . . maybe it's my real mum. I mean, this place is supposed to be haunted. I think, perhaps, that it's my mum who's here, haunting it . . . haunting *me*.'

118

I look up. Pepper and Josh are both gazing intently at me. I brace myself, waiting for them to tell me I've been imagining things.

'I know it's stupid,' I mutter.

'I don't think it's stupid,' Josh says.

'Me neither.' Pepper makes a face. 'But you said before that your real mother died years and years ago; why would she suddenly start "appearing" to you now?'

'Because I didn't know about her until a couple of months ago.' The truth blurts out of me at last. 'Andrew and Janet, that's my dad and my . . . the woman I thought was my mum . . . they didn't tell me the truth. *Ever.* I only found out because Irina – my *real* mum – left me some money which I inherit when I'm sixteen at the end of the month.' I stop. There's no point mentioning the amount. Pepper and Josh are already staring at me with shocked looks on their faces.

'Wow, that's heavy,' Josh says at last.

'Parents.' Pepper shakes her head.

'The trouble is there's no way of investigating here,' I carry on. 'Lomax won't tell me anything, though I'm certain he knows something – and I've got no access to the internet or the newspaper which did the article fifteen years ago. I'd like to call my uncle about it, but his number is on my mobile which is locked away in Lomax's office where the only usable landline is.'

Josh lays his guitar down beside him. 'We'll find a way,' he says.

'Yeah,' Pepper agrees.

'How?' I protest. 'Lomax's office door is always locked. And at night they lock the door to the corridor too.'

A slow smile spreads across Josh's face. 'I think you'll find it's possible.'

I glance across the room. Samuel is still busy with his book and isn't paying us any attention. There's no sign of Anna and Kit. My chest tightens. 'Are you seriously saying you could get me into Mr Lomax's office?'

Josh nods.

'I told you he could pick locks.' Pepper slides off the arm of her sofa and pokes me in the ribs. 'This is awesome,' she says, lowering her voice. 'We're going to break into Lomax's office and you're going to find out everything you want.'

Butterflies swarm in my stomach. Part of me is scared, but I'm excited too. This is a proper opportunity to get to the truth.

'When shall we do it?' I whisper.

Josh leans forward on the sofa. 'Everyone goes to bed here *really* early, so we'll just give them a couple of hours, then it's game on.'

My eyes widen. 'You mean *tonight*?'

Josh grins. 'Hell, yeah,' he says. 'Tonight.'

Fifteen

I hold Irina's ballet shoes, my eyes open to the gloom, waiting as the long hours pass. I'm not remotely sleepy. I can almost feel the adrenalin shooting through my body. The room is dark, but just enough light comes in from the moon outside for me to see that Pepper is also awake – and restless, tossing and turning on her hard, narrow bed. Anna, on the other hand, is clearly fast asleep, her curls like a halo around her head, her teddy bear propped against the wall beside her. The sound of her soft, even breathing carries across the room like the push and pull of shallow waves. It's oddly calming.

At last, Pepper swings her long legs out of bed. As she tiptoes towards me, I throw back the covers. We have kept our clothes on, so there's no need to spend any time in the room. Silently, we creep along the corridor and down the stairs. Josh is waiting at the bottom. We follow him to the locked door at the end of the corridor that leads to Mr Lomax's office.

Josh bends down and begins fiddling with the lock. He's dressed entirely in black as usual. I can't work out what he's doing, though it seems to involve inserting a long pin into the lock at various angles, then twisting sharply. A few moments later and he eases the door open, a big grin on his face.

'Ladies,' he whispers with affected modesty, 'we're good to go.'

'That was amazing,' I hiss.

Pepper touches his arm. 'Thanks, man.'

It's too dark to see properly, but I'm sure Josh's cheeks flush as he turns and leads the way to Mr Lomax's office. The whole house feels asleep. My heart beats loudly into the emptiness as the three of us hurry along the corridor. Josh drops to his knees and begins working away at the office door.

This lock takes him longer than the previous one, causing Pepper and I to exchange several anxious glances. At last, he's through. We hurry inside and I shut the door behind us. Pepper flicks on the wall light. Electricity on the island runs from a generator which is powered down at night, but we know from Mrs Moncrieff that a certain amount is always present.

A dim glow fills the room. It's all exactly as it was when I sat here with Mr Lomax. I take in the two desks and the filing cabinets and the computer. The bookshelves on the wall groan with files. I gulp. It's going to take ages to look through everything and I have no idea where to start.

Josh points to the landline. 'Want to call anyone?'

'Not yet,' I whisper. There's no point ringing Andrew or Janet and Uncle Gavin's number is buried in my mobile which is hidden somewhere in the room.

'Why don't you see if our phones are in any of the cupboards?' I suggest to Pepper.

'OK,' she says.

'What shall I do?' Josh asks.

I indicate the filing cabinet to the right of the desk. 'Would you go through that? See if you can find anything from fifteen years ago, anything to do with the suspected murder or the woman involved?'

'Sure thing.' Josh speeds over to the cabinet and pulls open the top drawer.

I turn my attention to the files on the bookshelves. The front part of each shelf is crammed with photos. I recognise Mr Lomax in a couple of pictures. In one, he's wearing a suit and looks like he's in his late teens or early twenties. The caption says: 'David's graduation'. I put the photo down and begin examining the files on the shelves.

'Hey, there's masses of stuff here on *us*,' Josh calls softly from the filing cabinet. 'Notes and reports on our histories and "personal issues".' He whistles under his breath. 'Says here I'm considered to have a borderline personality disorder.'

'What do they know?' Pepper whispers from the cupboards behind one of the desks. Her voice sounds uncharacteristically bitter. 'None of the therapists I've ever talked to could tell the difference between having a personality disorder and being a bit different.'

'How are you getting on?' I ask.

'No sign of our mobiles.' Pepper sighs.

I gaze at the files on the lower bookshelves. They're mostly full of personal documents to do with Mr Lomax's family. Within a couple of minutes, I unearth his father's death certificate from ten years ago. I turn to the next shelf. My breath catches in my throat. There, lying on top of a pile of papers, is a photo of Irina. She's wearing a long black coat and a red wool hat and is quite clearly standing on the beach outside Lightsea House.

I stare at the picture, too shocked to move or speak. So Irina *was* here after all. And I'm pretty sure that the black coat and red hat are the same as those displayed in the newspaper article *and* identical to the ones my ghost was wearing. Her blonde hair flies out from under her hat as she smiles at whoever is behind the camera.

'Oh my God,' I gasp.

Josh turns from the filing cabinet, pushing shut the drawer he was rifling through. 'What?' he asks.

'Did you find something?' Pepper looks up.

I nod. This is *it*: proof of a connection between Lightsea and Irina *and* between Irina and my ghost. I hurry over to the bank of cupboards to help with the search for our mobiles. I have to find Uncle Gavin's number and speak to him. *Immediately*.

'It's my real mum,' I explain as I bend down. 'I just—'

The creak of floorboards sounds outside, followed by the heavy tread of footsteps. I just have time to stuff the photo of Irina down the front of my sweatshirt when the office door opens and Mr Bradley walks in.

Sixteen

We are in big trouble. Mr Bradley demands to know what the hell we're doing, his eyes popping as he yells that breaking into a private office is a serious offence. Josh tries to bluff it out, saying we'd been hungry and just came down to the kitchen for a snack, but Mr Bradley sees straight through that. He marches us into the library, then goes to fetch Miss Bunnock and Mr Lomax.

Mr Lomax interrogates us. How did we get through the locks on the doors? What were we doing in his office? It's obvious Pepper and Josh are keeping quiet for my sake, which isn't fair on them, so after a few minutes I summon all my courage and speak up.

'This isn't Josh or Pepper's fault; they were just trying to help me,' I insist. 'I was looking for information about the woman who died here fifteen years ago.'

'Oh, Evie.' Mr Lomax shakes his head sorrowfully. 'And did you find anything?'

The edge of the photo I took from his office, still hidden under my sweatshirt, presses against my skin. It is proof that Irina was connected to Lightsea and that Mr Lomax is covering up the connection. But if I challenge him about it now I'll be letting on that I know what he's up to.

'No,' I lie. 'I didn't find anything.'

Miss Bunnock tuts. 'This is unacceptable behaviour. Personally, I feel we need a stronger punishment than an hour of Quiet Time, don't you agree, Mr Lomax?'

Mr Lomax nods, but he seems distracted, saying he'll deal with us in the morning. I'm certain he is more concerned with what I was looking for than interested in how we should be punished. And so we are taken up to bed. Miss Bunnock stands guard while Pepper and I get under the covers. I slip the photo of Irina beneath my pillow, next to the ballet shoes. I don't think I'll sleep a wink, but I'm out straightaway, not waking until Anna shakes my arm exactly as she did the previous day.

There's no time to talk before meditation. Mr Lomax says nothing about our night-time escapade, though I notice his eyes rest on me more than the others as he explains that the point of the session is to learn to be less involved with our thoughts and feelings.

'If you find your mind wandering, just bring it gently back to the breath,' he instructs.

Once again, I struggle with the whole thing. It seems pointless and stupid to be trying to focus on something as basic as breathing with so much at stake. How is it possible that Irina was once here, when everyone says she never came to the island? If she *was* here then it's surely more likely than ever

126

that she was killed here too. But why? And by whom? And what exactly does Mr Lomax know about the whole thing?

My mind skitters about for the entire fifteen minutes or so that Mr Lomax leads us through the session. Afterwards, he asks Josh, Pepper and me to remain behind.

'I'm afraid that last night's unauthorised activities must have consequences,' he says slowly. 'As you know, our ethos here on Lightsea is one of rehabilitation rather than retribution.'

'Say what?' Josh wrinkles his nose.

Pepper rolls her eyes.

'I simply mean that we don't go in for traditional punishments here, but I agree with Miss Bunnock that a single session of Quiet Time isn't enough for such a severe transgression.'

I glance at the others. They look as bewildered as I feel.

'So what does that mean?' I stammer.

'I'm afraid it's got to be an entire day of Quiet Time and solitary chores for each of you, to give you some private space to think about what you did, why you did it and what was wrong with the choices you made.'

'A whole day without talking?' I ask.

Mr Lomax nods.

'This is so unfair,' Pepper mutters.

'Yeah, we wouldn't have needed to break into your office if this place wasn't such a pigging prison,' Josh adds.

Mr Lomax sighs. 'I'd particularly like you to use your Quiet Time as an opportunity to reflect on the need to take responsibility for your actions.'

I grit my teeth. I *am* taking responsibility; I'm trying to find out what on earth happened to my real mother all those years ago.

'Quiet Time at Guantanamo.' Josh shakes his head. 'I can't wait.'

'I hate this place,' Pepper adds.

'I will also be taking each of you in a one-to-one session to discuss why you felt the need to disobey our rules.' Mr Lomax looks at me. 'Evie, we'll start with you.'

A chill runs down my spine. Does he somehow know what I've found out? Has he realised the photo of Irina is gone?

'Pepper and Josh can return to their chores for now,' Mr Lomax finishes.

'Oh, *whatever*.' Pepper turns on her heel and flounces out of the meditation room.

'Sucks, man.' Josh shoots me a sympathetic look, then follows her.

My hands tremble as I put on my boots and jacket and follow Mr Lomax outside. He leads me around the house, down to the shore. We walk in silence past Mrs Moncrieff's walled vegetable garden and down to the stony beach. Waves lap at the pebbles. I stare at the dark water, my old fears of the sea mingling with my anxieties about what happened to Irina.

'This is the only swimmable beach on the island,' Mr Lomax explains. 'All the others, like Boater's Cove by the boathouse, for instance, have treacherous rocks you can cut your legs on just under the surface. That was why the house was built at this end of Lightsea, so that the swimming therapy which was prescribed for the original inmates could take place easily and with supervision. But unfortunately the current proved too strong and, after two inmates drowned, the entire activity was disallowed.' He pauses. 'So . . . swimming was forbidden for a good reason. Do you see that?'

I stare at him. What is he saying? That not letting us get on the phone to our families is for a good reason too? I grit my teeth. The man is *definitely* hiding something.

'I'd like to talk about your birth mother, Evie,' he goes on.

I tense up. The photo of Irina, tucked inside my sweatshirt, flashes in front of my mind's eye again.

'Do you have any actual memories of her?' Mr Lomax asks.

I don't want to talk about Irina to him, but perhaps this is a way of getting him to admit she was here . . . maybe even to explain why.

'No,' I say slowly. 'But I've seen lots of pictures and films. My Uncle Gavin showed me.' I hesitate. Should I tell Lomax that I've seen the photo? I'm itching to challenge him outright, but something holds me back.

'Films of her dancing?' Mr Lomax asks. 'I understand she was a prima ballerina.'

'Yes,' I say. 'There's a DVD of her dancing *Giselle*, but there's lots of short clips on YouTube as well. Uncle Gavin told me what an amazing dancer she was and how hard she studied ballet as a child.'

'Right.' Mr Lomax gazes thoughtfully out to sea. 'What do you think your mother was like?'

I shrug. 'Graceful, talented, passionate – about dance anyway . . .'

'I see,' Mr Lomax says. 'And are those things you want for yourself? Traits you believe your mother hoped you would share?'

I think of the inheritance Irina left me, how when I'm sixteen in just a few weeks I'll get hold of the money and be able to make my own choices like she did.

'I think she just wanted me to be free to follow my dreams,' I say.

I hadn't meant to say quite so much – and feel suddenly self-conscious. Mr Lomax gives me a gentle smile. 'Your birth mother must have loved you very much.'

I nod, unsure what to say. Of course she loved me. Although Andrew refuses to talk about her, Uncle Gavin has told me so many times and, despite the sad lack of any filmed footage of us together, I at least have several photos of me as a baby where she is looking at me with adoring eyes.

'I think she would have been very proud of you too, of the young woman you're becoming: smart and thoughtful and curious about the world,' Mr Lomax continues. 'I wonder if you have allowed yourself to grieve for her loss though?'

I stare at him. What is he talking about? Irina died a long time ago. I think about her all the time. But it isn't exactly grief I am feeling, is it? You can't miss a person you've never known.

'What I'm saying, Evie, is that you lost your birth mother once as a small child, but now you are losing her all over again.'

'You mean because my parents lied about her all that time?' I can hear the bitterness in my voice. 'So I find out about her, but, as soon as I know she existed, I have to cope with the fact that she died.'

I look across the beach, thinking about the picture of Irina on Lightsea again. It strikes me it's possible to say that I've seen it, without giving away where I found it.

'Not exactly,' Mr Lomax says. 'I really meant that now, as a young woman, you are starting to appreciate all the ways in which you and your mother could have related as adults. It's a whole new loss for you and I'd urge you to allow yourself to feel that loss, not to resist it.'

'You said before that you don't think my real mum was ever on Lightsea,' I say slowly. 'But I'm certain that she was.'

Lomax looks away. 'What makes you think that?'

'A photo I think I saw once,' I say, keeping it vague. 'Of Irina on the island. Not when you were kids, but when she was older, maybe just a bit before she died.'

I wait for him to answer, the only sound the waves smashing onto the beach beyond us. But he doesn't speak.

'Mr Lomax, please, I need to know. Could—?'

'No, Evie, you must be mistaken.' Lomax turns to me. 'You have to give this up. Take it from me, I'm certain your mother was *never* here.'

He's lying.

I can see it in his eyes.

The shock is like a slap. Before I can speak, Lomax is already talking again.

'There is no connection between this island and your mother, that's all in your imagination. It's like before . . . you're looking

131

for connections where there aren't any.' He pauses and an expression of concern fills his face. It's a totally fake concern, I'm certain. 'I think perhaps the problem is that you haven't thought about your mum in the right way.'

'Oh?' Fear and anger career around my head. 'And what would the "right way" be?'

'I suspect that since you learned of your birth mother's existence, your parents—'

'You mean Andrew and Janet,' I snap.

Mr Lomax nods. 'Yes, Andrew and Janet have urged you to focus on things other than your birth mother and her life. And while their motives are well-meant I believe that it's entirely appropriate for you to spend some time – maybe a good deal of time – allowing yourself to feel the pain of your birth mother's loss.' Lomax pauses. 'How she died isn't anywhere near as important as how her death makes you feel. Do you see?'

What I see is that Lomax is trying to stop me investigating Irina's presence on the island. Which means he *must* have something to hide. He knows Irina was here. Does he know that she died here too? What possible reason could he have for keeping that from me, other than a desire to cover up her murder?

'Evie?'

I'm suddenly aware that he's stopped talking. I look up at him. 'Yes?'

'I'd like you to spend your Quiet Time for the rest of the day in the walled garden. Please use the opportunity to reflect

132

on your actions and particularly the need to take responsibility for them. You can do that, I think, while you're busy weeding the lettuces and potatoes or whatever Mrs Moncrieff is growing this month. OK?'

'Right,' I say. 'Sure.'

Mr Lomax takes me back up to the garden, fetches a small trowel and a pair of gardening gloves and leaves me working in the sunshine. It's a bit weird being on my own, but at least it gives me time to think. As I weed away – trying to remember everything Andrew and Janet taught me on the few occasions I helped them in our garden at home – a plan forms in my head.

I'm certain now that Irina not only knew Mr Lomax better than he says, but that she was killed on Lightsea Island and Mr Lomax is covering up what happened. And I am going to prove it. My priority is to find a way to tell Uncle Gavin about the photo, which means getting access to a phone again. Once I've spoken to him, Gavin can call the police and then there'll be a proper investigation.

Checking no one else is about, I take out the photo of Irina in the red hat and gaze at it again. Though I hate to imagine her being pushed off a rock into the dark, treacherous water, it's comforting to think that her spirit might be here now, watching over me.

'Hi.'

I spin around, my cheeks reddening as I shove the photo behind my back. Kit is standing by the garden entrance, leaning against the crumbling stone wall. The sun lights up his face, picking out the fine blond streaks in his hair. He looks like a movie star.

'Er, hi,' I say, immediately self-conscious that my hair must look a mess from working outside and that I'm probably covered in earth. 'What are you doing here? I'm supposed to be in solitary confinement or whatever.'

'I know.' Kit grimaces. 'They told us we couldn't speak to you or Pepper or Josh all day. But I'm on kitchen duty and Mrs Moncrieff said you were here and . . . and I was just wondering how you're doing.'

'I'm fine.' My fingers feel clammy on the photo. Has Kit seen it?

'What's that behind your back?' he asks.

Great. Still, I don't have to explain where I got the photo any more than I did to Lomax. Reluctantly, I hold out the picture.

'Please don't tell anyone,' I say. 'I'm not allowed to have this. I've already got my luxury item.'

Kit peers down at the photo. 'It *is* a bit mean only letting us keep one thing. Is this your mother?'

I nod. 'My *real* mum,' I explain. 'The one who died when I was a baby.'

'You look like her,' he says.

I frown. Surely Irina was far prettier and more delicate-looking than me? 'Really?'

'Yeah, really. You've got the same mouth and the same smile.' Kit looks up. 'It's a very pretty smile.'

I gulp, my stomach turning cartwheels. Nice hair and a pretty

134

smile. Is he flirting with me? Or is he about to back off, like he did before?

Kit hands me back the photo and I tuck it inside my sweatshirt.

'You're here because of her, aren't you?' he says.

'What do you mean?'

Kit shrugs. 'The photo, the ballet shoes . . . you talk about her a lot . . . I'm just saying, it's not . . . not, er, how most normal people are about their mums. So you . . . you probably have some sort of, I dunno . . . extra *thing* about her . . .'

My face feels like it's on fire. 'What about you?' I ask, desperate to shift the conversation. 'Pepper and Josh are obviously here cos they keep breaking rules and stuff and Samuel's parents probably just want to help him be a bit less of a misfit. Anna hasn't said, but I'm betting she's here cos she's got some problems back home – so ultimately much the same reason as everyone else: she doesn't fit in and nobody where she comes from knows how to handle her. But you don't seem like you need any help fitting in. And you don't look like you get into trouble much either. So why did *you* get sent here?'

Kit's face clouds. 'If you really want to know, I was set up,' he says with a scowl. 'Or rather my brother was set up and I tried to protect him and ended up getting the blame.'

'For what?' I ask.

'Stealing stuff.' Kit sighs. 'My dad's a lawyer, got it all hushed up. But he and Mum think I'm a delinquent now, hence me being sent here, to work on my so-called *issues*.'

135

'That's so unfair,' I say. 'Thinking you're some kind of bad boy, when you're so not.'

Kit's expression grows darker. 'You mean like Josh is?'

I nod.

'He likes you, you know.' Kit scowls.

'Josh likes everyone.'

'No, Josh *seriously* likes you.'

'Oh.' I'm sure he's wrong. And totally unsure what I'm supposed to say back.

'I'm sorry I acted like such an idiot yesterday, all that stuff about your hair.' Kit rolls his eyes. 'I just didn't know how to tell you.'

'Tell me what?' I hold my breath as Kit moves closer.

'Tell you how much I like you.' Our faces are almost touching. 'I thought you didn't like me back, but then I talked to Anna and she made me realise that maybe I just hadn't been clear.'

'Oh.' So when he was talking to Anna yesterday it was about *me*? My head spins. All I can see are the green flecks in Kit's caramel eyes.

'So I thought I'd ask again. Properly.' Kit's lips hover over mine.

'Ask what?' I breathe.

'If you liked me ba—' But before he can finish we are lost in a kiss.

Seventeen

Kissing Kit.

It's my last thought that night, before I fall asleep, and my first thought the next morning, when I wake up. For the first time since arriving at Lightsea, I'm out of bed before Anna and Pepper. I'm glad of the time to myself, drifting into the bathroom, still reliving that first kiss – and the many that followed – until Kit said he'd better get back to the kitchen before Mrs Moncrieff noticed he was gone.

Kit likes me. A *lot*.

It's amazing, but true. He says he liked me from the first time he saw me, that he was worried I'd fall for Josh, that he didn't know what to say to me.

I've told him I like him too, that Josh is fine as a friend, but I can't imagine going out with him. Kit says he wants to go out with me.

Me.

Yesterday evening, when the long day of solitary chores had at last come to an end, I told Kit how Andrew and Janet had kept the truth about Irina being my real mum from me – and how Uncle Gavin is the only person in my life I can talk to about her. Then I confessed to breaking in to Mr Lomax's office and how I'd found the photo.

Kit was *so* sympathetic about how hard it must have been to find out I'd been lied to all my life. He still doesn't believe that I've really seen Irina's ghost, but at least he agreed that it's *massively* weird Mr Lomax had a photo of her – and that the photo shows she *was* at Lightsea when Lomax says she wasn't. Last night we sat next to each other over dinner and it was soon obvious that all the others – apart from Samuel – were aware there was something going on between us.

In the end, after a few heavy hints, Pepper asked straight out: 'Are you two together or what?'

I blushed from my hair to my toes, but Kit stared straight at her.

'Yes,' he said. 'We are.' And a delicious thrill flowed through me.

The others were all cool about it, even Anna – who I'd suspected had a bit of a crush on Kit herself. Josh was particularly laid-back, which I thought totally proved Kit had been wrong about him liking me.

But none of it helps me find out why Irina was on Lightsea – or what happened to her here. So now, here I am, heading downstairs for breakfast, my heart beating fast as I look forward to seeing Kit again – but my mind focused on getting back into Mr Lomax's office, finding my mobile and, on it, Uncle Gavin's number, then calling him on the landline.

Morning meditation flies past for once, mainly because I spend the entire time planning another break-in. I'm sure Josh will help get me past the locked doors again, but Mr Lomax whisks him off for a one-to-one session, so I don't get a chance to ask, Mr Bradley takes the rest of us outside to tackle a fitness-training course he's set up in the woods. We pair up – I'm with Kit, thank goodness – to teeter our way across logs, clamber over makeshift fences and climb nets that hang from the trees. Kit and I finish the course in record time and spend the journey back to the house holding hands when no one's looking. Frustratingly, I don't get a chance to speak to Josh later as the only time we're together is for our evening meal, which for some reason Mr Bradley eats with us.

That night, after lights out, I tell Anna and Pepper that I'm certain Mr Lomax is covering up what happened to Irina on Lightsea. They are both shocked, though Anna's eyes widen with anxiety while Pepper's narrow with anger. We stay awake for hours after we're supposed to. In the end, I fall asleep with my hand clutching the photo and the ballet shoes, feeling deeply frustrated. Tomorrow I *have* to get hold of Uncle Gavin and get a proper investigation started.

The next morning I'm working with Pepper in the laundry while the others are ordered to undertake various cleaning chores around the house. She's excited at the prospect of us breaking into Lomax's office again.

As soon as we're all alone in the library after lunch, she grabs hold of Josh and explains the situation. Everyone is there apart from Samuel, who is apparently having a one-to-one session outside with Mr Lomax. Josh agrees straightaway to another break-in tonight and I wander over to Kit, who's been chatting with Anna. She melts away as soon as I pitch up, a sad expression on her face. Is she upset because I'm with Kit? Or is it something else?

I don't think about it too much because soon Kit and I are deep in a kissing session behind the bookshelves. I consider inviting him along on tonight's office break-in, but I'm worried he won't approve. Unlike Josh or Pepper, Kit tends to follow the rules – or at least most of them. I enjoy the kissing, of course, but inside I'm all impatient for the afternoon to pass so that we can put our plan into action.

First, however, we troop into the hall ready for outdoor chores with Mr Bradley. As we near the front door, footsteps sound on the stairs. It's Samuel, hurrying down towards us.

'Evie, listen,' he hisses, rushing over. 'I have to talk to you.'

'What is it?' I ask.

'It's . . . I—'

'There you all are,' Miss Bunnock calls from the end of the corridor. 'It's outdoor chores with Mr Bradley.'

'We know,' Josh says.

'We're not late,' Pepper says with a roll of her eyes.

Samuel clutches my arm. 'Evie?' he whispers.

A second later, Mr Bradley himself appears through the front door.

'Sorry, but I need two of them,' Miss Bunnock says with a smile. 'Samuel and Anna, please.'

I glance at Samuel. His forehead is creased with a frown. I'm sure he's just intent on passing on some new fact about trees or animals. To be honest, I'm more concerned with whether or not I'll be paired with Kit this afternoon.

'We can talk later, Samuel,' I whisper.

'OK.' Samuel nods, still frowning.

He and Anna disappear after Miss Bunnock. Mr Bradley takes the rest of us outside. He directs Pepper and Kit to the boathouse, then leads Josh and me into the woods to find suitable stones for his drystone wall project.

I soon forget Samuel's urgent hiss – and the absence of Kit – as Josh and I discuss where our mobiles might be hidden in Mr Lomax's office.

'Pepper already checked through the cupboards behind the desk,' I say. 'But there are lots of other places.'

We discuss our plan a bit more, then focus on the task Bradley has given us. Josh grumbles as we sift earth and twigs in the chilly air, looking for bits of loose rock.

'This is so *not* my idea of fun,' he moans. 'Why can't Bradley find his own pigging stones? What does he need a wall for anyway? It's not like he's got anything to put behind one, like a goat. Or a motorway.'

I laugh. 'It could be worse,' I say. 'He might have wanted us to run back to the house with a sack of stones in each hand.'

'Don't think that isn't coming later,' Josh warns darkly.

We chat as we scour the ground. Josh makes a vague comment about me and Kit being together, adding that he thinks it's great we've hooked up.

'Yeah, it's cool,' I say, equally vaguely. 'What about you? Girlfriend at home?'

141

'Nah,' Josh says. 'Us musicians prefer not to be tied down.'

He's played more songs for us over the past few nights. He revealed the best one last night. It was brilliant; even Kit sounded enthusiastic about it, though perhaps that was because, now we're going out together, he no longer sees Josh as a threat. He knows Josh and I are just friends.

'Do you miss listening to music?' I ask, adding a stone to my pile. It's funny, but talking to Josh is the easiest, most natural thing in the world. And, for a moment at least, I'm not even thinking about Irina or what happened to her here.

'Oh man.' Josh sighs. 'Though actually—' He pauses.

A flash of red streaks past my eyeline.

'What was that?' I ask, my whole body suddenly alert.

'What?' Josh follows my gaze. The woods are empty. 'What did you see?'

I scan the trees. *There.* A figure in a long black coat and a red hat darts between the branches and out of sight again. 'It's her.' A shiver chills through me. Is it really Irina's ghost? This time I have to find out for sure. I drop the stone and run after her. A second later, I realise Josh is pelting along by my side.

'Are you certain, Evie?'

'Yes,' I say. 'Over there.' I point towards the flat rock beyond the trees. This was exactly where I saw the ghost before. I run out onto the smooth stone. It's far more slippery than it was last time, thanks to the earlier drizzle. I stumble to a halt. Why did she run out here? Does she want to show me something?

'Evie, careful!' Josh warns.

I scramble along the rock, keeping far away from the sea.

Just as before, the ghost has disappeared. Or has she? Now I've walked further than I did last time, I can see that the rock slopes down via a series of small steps to one of the stony beaches that are dotted around the island.

'She must have gone down here,' I say, hurrying over as fast as I dare.

'Wait!' Josh calls.

I barely hear him. A light rain starts to fall as I reach the pebbled beach and pelt towards the point where it curves away. The rain grows heavier. By the time I round the curve, it's a drenching downpour.

Where is she?

Another flash of red hat and black coat. The figure disappears behind the next bend. I'm certain from Mr Bradley's orientation session that the trees and the beach peter out into open moorland just beyond.

This time, surely, if I just follow her around the rock and into the next bay, I will find her.

Eighteen

I skid to a stop, gasping for breath. The ghost is nowhere to be seen. I turn right around, rain streaming down my face, making sure I'm not missing her. The stony beach stretches out ahead of me, ending in a point about fifty metres away. To my right is the sea, its waves crashing against the rocks beyond the shore. To my left is the sheer face of the cliff.

There is nowhere the ghost can have gone; she's vanished into thin air.

'No,' I breathe. Loss overwhelms me. How can Irina let me see her, then just run away? The pain of it fills me. I drop to my knees on the pebbles, hardly aware of the sharp cold of the stone. Misery consumes me: the ghost was here, within my grasp, and now she has gone.

For a moment, I'm lost in the heaving sobs that rack my body and then I feel a hand on my shoulder. Josh gazes down at me, eyes full of concern.

'Hey, Evie,' he says, rain dripping from his hair, 'are you all right?'

Shaking my head, I stand and let him hold me as I cry. In the distance, thunder rumbles. We are soaked.

'Let's get out of the rain,' Josh urges.

144

I let him lead me across the beach to stand under a piece of overhanging rock. The cliff face below the overhang has been worn away, leaving a small, shallow cave where we can take shelter.

As we reach the spot, I wipe my face, feeling the sharp pain of my initial misery give way to a dull ache that persists as Josh rubs my arms, then hugs me again, muttering that I must be cold.

Outside our cave the downpour is growing fiercer. Thunder crashes; the waves smash against the rocks, barely visible through the sheet of rain that pounds onto the beach.

'It was her,' I gabble, shivering as I speak. 'It was my mum's ghost. She was right here.'

Josh says nothing. He takes off his sodden jacket and holds it out. 'Do you want this? I'm not sure it'll help, but it's better than nothing.'

'Thanks.' I let him drape the damp jacket over my shoulders. 'I couldn't see where she went,' I say. 'There's no way she could have climbed the cliff and she wouldn't have got all the way along the beach without me seeing . . .' I hesitate. 'Did *you* see where she went? Because I think she was trying to tell me something. Why else would she appear in the first place?'

Josh looks away.

'What?' I ask.

He turns to face me, his expression registering worry . . . and doubt.

'I'm sorry, but I didn't see *anything*, Evie,' he confesses. 'Do you . . . is it possible that you maybe imagined the ghost?'

It's like a punch to the stomach. I back away from him.

'I thought you believed me,' I say, my voice trembling as I realise that, of everybody on the island, Josh was the only one – apart from Anna perhaps – who accepted my ghost story without question. Until now. 'I thought you were on my side?'

'I am.' Josh frowns. 'Seriously, man, I am *totally* on your side. And I'm not doubting that it was your mum who died here or any of that. But . . .'

I turn and walk away, trying hard not to cry again. The space under the overhanging rock is bigger than I'd first thought; it extends back at least ten metres. A proper cave. I walk into the shadowy recess, blinking back my tears, letting my eyes adjust to the dark.

'Evie?' Josh calls.

I say nothing. I know with the logical part of my mind that it is possible I imagined the ghost, but I'm not ready to stop believing Irina's spirit was here.

Except why appear in front of me, only to vanish again?

Outside the storm rages. Thunder cracks the sky. A sudden flash of lightning lights up the back of the cave. I gasp. A cairn of stones has been piled up just beyond the point where I'm standing. In front of the pile, a series of initials are laid out in pebbles.

The first letter is a capital 'I'. I crouch down, the skin on the back of my neck crawling.

'Evie?' I can hear Josh walking towards me. Another crack of thunder is followed by a second flare of lightning. It lights up the rest of the letters:

146

IG DL

'Whoa,' I breathe.

'What?' Josh runs up, kicking the letters as he skids to a halt beside me.

I point to the scattered pebbles. 'I've just realised why my mum's ghost is appearing to me,' I say. 'I think she's been trying to show me who killed her.'

Josh follows my pointing finger. 'What d'you mean?' he asks.

'She arranged the stones to make two sets of initials,' I say. '*IG* for Irina Galloway . . . that's my mum. And *DL* for David Lomax, Mr Lomax . . . her killer.'

Nineteen

The storm rages outside. Another flash lights up Josh's face. The frown creasing his forehead is deeper than before.

'Don't you get it?' I say. 'The ghost came into this cave. She was leading me here . . . to these . . .' I gaze down at the pebbles again. 'My mum *was* here on the island fifteen years ago. And it was *Mr Lomax* who pushed her off Easter Rock. *That's* why he's lying to me about her being here. Those initials prove it.'

Josh clears his throat. 'OK, but . . . but all I can see are a bunch of stones.'

'They were initials before you lumbered over and kicked them away,' I snap. 'I *told* you . . . *DL* for David Lomax and *IG* for my mum, Irina Galloway. The ghost put them there to tell me who killed her.'

'Right.' Josh sounds sceptical. 'You're saying a ghost moved a load of stones? I'm sorry, Evie, but what did she move them with? Ghosts move *through* things, they don't have proper hands.'

A huge roar of thunder is followed by a flare of lightning. All I can see in Josh's eyes is doubt. And pity. My heart sinks. Why won't anyone believe me?

'Haven't you ever heard of telekinesis?'

'Moving things with your mind? Yes, of course, but . . .' Josh tails off.

I turn away and walk back to the cave entrance. The rain is still lashing down outside, the waves bigger than before, pounding onto the beach. A riot of emotion careers around my head: anger that Josh doesn't believe me is mixed with a deep, miserable fear that if he doesn't take what I'm saying seriously then no one else will either.

Most of all I feel desperately alone. Irina's spirit was here and now she is gone. Which is worse than if she had never been here at all. Two hot tears leak out of my eyes and trickle down my cheeks. I wipe them away.

'Hey.' Josh appears in front of me. 'Don't cry. I'm sorry. Look, what do I know? Maybe you're right and your mum's ghost *has* been here, trying to communicate with you. Maybe she only appears to *you*. It would make sense; you're her daughter so there'd be a special connection.' He wipes the tears from my cheeks. 'Anyway, there's definitely something weird going on. Even without your ghost, you found a picture of your mum in Mr Lomax's office, wearing the same clothes as the woman in the newspaper article who died here.'

'Thanks.' I sniff. 'I just feel helpless, with all this information and no way of telling anyone outside the island or getting anything done about it.'

Josh pulls me closer, into a hug. Another crack of thunder is followed by a flash of lightning that whitens the dark, menacing sky over the sea. Huge waves smash, relentless, onto the beach.

'We *will* get something done,' he says. 'We'll break into the office, find our phones and get your uncle's number. And, if we can't get hold of him for any reason, we'll just dial 999 on the office phone and get the police to investigate.'

I nod. 'Come on then, let's go. Mr Bradley will be going berserk wondering where we've got to as it is.'

Josh grins. 'We'll tell him we got sidetracked by some particularly spectacular rocks for his drystone wall, yeah?'

'Yeah,' I giggle, feeling better.

The rain drums on our hunched shoulders as we head out of the shelter of the cave. We've only walked a couple of steps before Josh swears under his breath.

'What?' I ask, shouting over the noise of the storm.

Josh points to the way back, to the bend in the beach which we'd rounded to reach this stretch. Waves are now crashing against the rock face. The beach is covered in water.

It's the same in the other direction. We're trapped by the tide and there's no way out of the bay.

'It's too dangerous to try and get past those waves,' Josh shouts. 'We'll have to wait for the storm to die down a bit.'

He's right. We scuttle back into the cave. I run my fingers through my hair, trying to flick out some of the moisture. It's no good. We're both soaked. I take off Josh's jacket and my own and lay them out at the back of the cave, hoping they'll dry out a bit while we wait. Josh stands in the entrance, staring out at the storm. A new silvery light is shining through the dark clouds over the sea, casting an other-worldly glow over the raging water.

150

'That's a weird light,' I say, joining him at the front of the cave.

'This place is spooky, isn't it?' he says. 'Not just the bay, but this whole island.'

'Sometimes it's beautiful,' I say, remembering the sunset that first evening and how Kit saved me as I slipped on the rock.

'It's not the only thing here that's beautiful.' Josh glances at me, his voice soft and low.

I can feel my cheeks blushing. Does he mean me? I brush my hair self-consciously off my face.

'Hey, d'you want to dance while we're waiting?' Josh asks, his eyes sparkling.

'Dance?' I say, feeling even more awkward. 'To what?'

Josh grins. He digs his hand into his trouser pocket and pulls out a tiny MP3 player, complete with earphones.

I stare at the device, utterly stunned. 'No way,' I breathe. 'How did you get that past Bunnock?'

'Don't ask.' Josh's grin deepens. 'And it was Bradley who checked the boys, not Bunnock. Let's just say he went through the stuff in our bags, but he drew the line at actually patting us down.'

I can feel my eyes widening. 'Why didn't I think of that?'

Josh shrugs. 'Clearly, you don't have a criminal mind like me. To be honest, the MP3 player was nothing; getting the charger in was much more of a challenge.'

I laugh. 'Do the others know?' I ask.

'Samuel does. He and I have a secret hiding place in our

room. And I think Kit must know too, though he hasn't said anything.' Josh peers down at the device, scrolling through the tracks.

'What about Pepper?'

'Yeah, she knows I've got something I can listen to music on.'

So he's told her about his MP3 player. What else have they shared?

'How do you feel about her?' I ask, curiosity getting the better of me.

'We're mates,' Josh says. 'I think she's great. I love that she speaks her mind all the time. No BS like you get with most people. But, er, that's it.'

He holds my gaze.

'I think she's beautiful,' I stammer.

Josh nods. 'She is. And Kit is really handsome. But just thinking someone's cool and good-looking only takes you so far. You've got to feel the chemistry too.'

My heart beats faster. 'Chemistry?' I laugh, but it sounds a little forced. 'What do you know about chemistry? You keep getting kicked out of schools.'

Josh bends over his MP3 player again. 'Everything I know about chemistry,' he says, 'I learned in the School of Life Sucks. *Here*. Let's try this one.'

He reaches forward and tucks one of the earphone buds into my ear. A track I've never heard before fills my head. The singer is a woman with a mournful voice that seems to carry heartbreak with every note. A couple of acoustic guitars weave a tuneful melody around her singing, blending perfectly with each other.

'That's lovely,' I say. 'Who is she?'

'Eugenie See,' Josh says. 'She's brilliant. Hey, we'll hear better if we stand closer.' He moves nearer so we're almost touching. Unlike Kit, Josh is a good bit taller than me. I can feel his breath on my forehead. For a second, I think maybe I should move away. After all, I am going out with Kit. But that's silly. Josh and I aren't doing anything wrong. We're just listening to a song together. And, with just one set of earphones, we have no choice but to stand in each other's space. The Eugenie See track morphs into another faster tune that I recognise.

'Hey, I love this,' I enthuse.

'Good.' Josh reaches for my waist and pulls me closer. He starts swaying. I stiffen, wondering if it's really OK to dance with him. It feels good, moving to the rhythm of the song. I didn't realise until this moment how much I've missed music since arriving at Lightsea. And Josh is clearly totally relaxed about it, his arms around my back. It is only dancing after all.

We listen to another couple of tracks in silence as the rain pours down outside and occasional bursts of thunder and lightning fill the sky. It feels natural to be doing this. Comfortable. Right.

'D'you have any of your own songs on here?' I ask

'Nah.'

'You should record them,' I say. 'I like your music.'

Josh smiles and we dance on, closer than before.

'Man, I don't know how I'd survive if I hadn't brought these tracks in with me,' Josh murmurs, his voice breathy in my ear.

'Why didn't you make it your luxury?' As I ask the question, I remember his guitar. 'Oh, wait. I guess an MP3 player was easier to smuggle in than a huge musical instrument.'

'Yup,' Josh says. 'Anyway, if I had to choose, I'd miss playing music even more than listening to it. Hey, you're a good dancer.'

'Please,' I say, rolling my eyes. 'We're barely moving. How can you tell?'

'I can tell enough to know that you're really sensitive to the music.' Josh shifts position a little, drawing me fractionally closer against him. This time I let myself relax against his chest. 'I guess you get that from your mum. Do you dance, like she did? I mean, classical stuff?'

'I would have,' I say, unable to prevent the note of bitterness that creeps into my voice. 'But I didn't know anything about her when I was younger, and my dad never encouraged me to do ballet.' I sigh. 'Anyway, I'm sure I'd have been rubbish. I'm too tall and . . . too uncoordinated to be a dancer.'

We keep swaying to the music, the storm still raging. It feels as if we're in our own little bubble, like the rest of the world has somehow vanished. I forget about Irina's ghost and the message I'm certain she was trying to leave me with the pebbles. All I'm aware of is the music and the movement and Josh's arms around me.

'I wish you wouldn't do that,' he says softly.

'Do what?' I ask.

'Put yourself down. I just said you were a good dancer *and* really musical and you basically denied both things, adding that you're all uncoordinated. Is that what you really think? Because I've never seen any evidence of you being clumsy or anything, not once.'

'Really?' I ask.

'And even if ballet isn't your thing, so what?' Josh whispers, his mouth right over my ear. 'There are other types of dancing. Everyone gets a bit uncoordinated when they have a growth spurt. I bumped into things every day for about six months a couple of years ago, but it went, and I'm betting you being gawky or whatever has gone now too.' He pauses. 'Being musical's a gift; don't think just cos you're too tall to be a ballerina or whatever that you can't do other stuff. Can you play an instrument? Sing?'

'No, I'm useless at anything like that.'

'There you go again, putting yourself down.' Josh sighs, but when he speaks again I can hear the smile in his voice. 'You know, I like to think of myself as a discerning person with insights into other people's personalities, so I'm kind of bummed that you think so little of my opinion of you.'

'Which is?' I draw away from him so I can see his face.

'That you're interesting and smart and musical and, er, not to sound superficial or anything but also extremely hot.'

I blush, my cheeks on fire. I look down, but Josh catches my chin as I move, lifting it up with his fingertips. He leans closer and I know that he wants to kiss me. I can see it in his eyes.

155

Suddenly I very much want to kiss him back.

Which is wrong. I'm with Kit.

I take a step away. Water splashes at my ankle. The storm and the cave surge back into my consciousness. More thunder roils overhead. I look down as another wave laps at my foot. Outside the cave, the beach has more or less disappeared underwater. In an instant, I forget all about kissing Josh.

'It's the tide,' I gasp. 'It's coming in.'

'Oh man.' Josh meets my eyes. And I can see the panic I feel reflected in his own expression.

We're trapped in the cave with the water rising. And no way out.

Twenty

Josh grabs my hand. 'This way,' he says, indicating the back of the cave.

We race into the shadows, past the little cairn of stones and the scattered pebbles that originally spelled out Irina's and Lomax's initials.

'Suppose the water rises and fills the cave?' I ask, feeling sick with panic.

'We don't have a choice,' Josh says grimly. 'Ever since we got here, they've been going on about how dangerous the water is so there's no way we can try swimming around the bay; the current would drag us onto the rocks.'

I gaze down at the churning sea, my heart thudding loudly in my ears. The tide is still rising. I reach up and feel my way along the cave wall. The stone is cold to the touch. 'Maybe there's a ledge, something high off the ground we can climb on to,' I say.

'Let's hope.' Josh inches his way along the wall opposite. I can barely make him out in the gloom. Rain still lashes down outside and thunder rumbles though the lightning has stopped. The cave smells damp and salty.

Sweat beads on my forehead as I feel up the wall as far as

I can. There's no ledge, nothing remotely big enough to take our weight. I fumble my way across the rough rock. Suddenly my fingers clutch at air. It's a gap in the cave wall.

'Josh,' I hiss. 'Over here.'

I feel the parameters of the space in front of me. It's narrow – about half a metre wide – but tall: a fissure that runs the full height of the cave.

'Where does it lead?' Josh asks, arriving beside me.

'I can't see.' I turn sideways and inch my way between the two walls of rock. Josh follows right behind. My heart beats wildly as I creep along in the darkness, my imagination running riot. Suppose the space in front suddenly closes? Suppose the space behind us collapses? Suppose the ground beneath my feet drops away? I shuffle on, terrified. The seconds feel like hours. And then the narrow gap widens into a proper tunnel just as my eyes adjust to the gloom.

'This could take us inland,' I say, gripping Josh's arm. 'Remember Mr Bradley told us about the caves that run from the shore into the island?'

'Let's hope,' Josh says. 'At least we're away from the water.'

We hurry through the tunnel. What time is it? I have no idea. But it will be obvious we're missing by now. Mr Lomax has probably sent out a search party for us. Kit will be wondering what on earth has happened to me.

I bite my lip, still hurrying through the dark, the only sound now the soft pad of Josh's footsteps beside me.

What would Kit say if he knew I slow danced with Josh . . .

how close I came to kissing him? Still, I *didn't* kiss him. I haven't done anything wrong in fact. And yet I feel deeply guilty, as if I've betrayed Kit's trust in some way.

Maybe it's because I *wanted* Josh to kiss me. Which doesn't make any sense at all. I'm totally into Kit. He's gorgeous and sporty and really smart.

But also a bit uptight, which Josh *definitely* isn't.

'We've been walking for— Hey, can you hear that?' Josh asks, his voice breaking through my thoughts.

I listen intently. The silence is so powerful it's almost a presence in the tunnel.

'I can't hear anything,' I say.

'It's the echo when we speak,' Josh says. 'It's getting louder. And I think the air is getting fresher and lighter too.'

He's right. It *is* easier to see where we're going and, now I listen for it, I can hear that our words are amplified against the walls.

'What does that mean?' I ask.

Josh brushes past me. I feel his hand on my shoulder, and under my top my skin breaks out in goosebumps.

'It means either this tunnel is about to open out into a much bigger cave,' Josh says, striding ahead of me, 'or . . . *yes*,' he says triumphantly. '*That.*'

'What?' I hurry after him, quickly catching up.

Beyond us, a pool of still water stretches for several metres. And beyond the pool the soft glow of twilight glimmers through a narrow opening.

'It's a pool cave,' I breathe.

'And a way out, back to the island,' Josh says. 'All we have to do is wade across.'

I nod, staring down at the dark water.

'Let's see how deep it is.' Josh lowers his arm into the water. His face falls. 'Damn, it's a sheer drop,' he says. 'I can't feel the bottom.'

'Oh.' My stomach clenches.

Josh sits down and let his legs dangle in the water. 'Man, it's cold too. Still, we don't have a choice.' He eases himself into the pool.

'Brrr, it's *freezing*.' Holding onto the side, he looks up at me. 'I still can't touch the bottom so we're going to have to swim across. Hey, what's wrong?'

I stare at him, all the breath sucked out of my chest.

'I can't swim across,' I say. 'I can't swim at all.'

Twenty-one

Josh looks up from the water, horrified. 'You *can't swim*?' he exclaims.

I shake my head. 'I had lessons when I was little, but I hated getting water on my face and . . . and then I got scared cos I couldn't do it . . . so I started refusing to go. I've never actually swum more than a couple of strokes without putting my foot on the bottom.'

'Well, we can't go back.' Treading water, Josh gazes up at me and grins. 'Swimming's a breeze anyway. And it's not far. Come on, get in. I'll help you across.'

I sit down at the edge of the water and put my hand below the surface. My heart pounds. 'Jeez,' I say. 'You're right, it's freezing.'

'Tell me about it.' Josh's teeth are already chattering. 'Get your arse down here.'

I slide my legs out from under me and into the water, then turn and ease myself gently over the edge. I gasp as the cold reaches my waist, then my chest. Josh swims up so he's right beside me. I grip the rock, memories of Saturday morning swimming lessons rushing into my head. Old fears flash through me: Andrew's anxious face on the other side of the pool, the other kids all splashing about, me too scared to take my hands away from the edge.

'You're fine, Evie.' Josh's voice in my ear is calm and soothing. 'You can do this.' He puts one arm around my middle. 'We're going to swim together. I'm going to hold you up; you're going to kick hard and pull with your hands. OK?'

'OK,' I say. 'Don't let go.'

'I won't,' he says. 'I promise.'

I give a swift nod, then let go of the side. I start to sink down into the water, but Josh's arm keeps me up.

'Kick with your feet,' he urges. 'Pull with your hands.'

I do as he says. Immediately, I rise in the water. Josh tightens his grip on me, then pushes off from the side. We swim shoulder to shoulder. Well, Josh does most of the actual swimming. With one arm and both legs, he propels us across the cave pool, towards the light. I scrabble with my hands, desperately trying to keep my face above water.

'You're doing great,' Josh pants. 'Keep going, keep kicking.'

I move my feet like flippers, as fast as I can. I realise I'm holding my breath and take in a mouthful of air. Water splashes up my nose. I splutter it out, coughing madly.

'Keep going,' Josh gasps, 'Nearly there.'

I look up. The light across the water still seems very far away. Too far.

'Come on, Evie, you can do this.'

On we swim. The cold seeps into my bones; my arms and legs ache from the effort of pulling them through the water.

And then, just as I'm thinking I can't swim another stroke, I feel the hard ground at my feet.

'I can stand,' I pant. 'We can stand.'

We stop swimming, our toes resting on the bottom. The light is closer now. I can just make out the outline of trees against the dark grey sky outside.

'It's not far now,' Josh urges. 'Come on.'

We half wade, half swim the rest of the way. Josh keeps his arm around my waist the whole time, until the water is only at our knees. Then he lets go and we make our way to the narrow cave opening, where the water finally peters out into a muddy puddle.

We stagger onto dry land. Well, dryish. The worst of the storm seems to be over, but it's still drizzling and the wind is fierce. We've come out close to the start of the trees where we were working before, just a few minutes from Lightsea House. The light has almost totally faded from the day. In a few minutes, it will be pitch-black. I shiver in the cold gusts of air. Josh peers across the scrubland ahead of us. It's strewn with branches that must have been torn from the trees beyond in the storm. 'The house is that way,' he points, his teeth now chattering so fast he can barely speak.

Relief and gratitude fill me to my toes. I fling my arms round his neck.

'Thank you,' I breathe. 'You saved my life.' I hug him hard.

'Steady.' Josh laughs. 'You saved your own life, I just helped.'

'No you *did*.' I kiss his cheek, then draw back. Our faces

163

are so close, our eyes locked. Water drips from Josh's hair, from his nose. His eyes gleam in the twilight as he leans forward and brushes my lips with his.

It's like electricity thrilling through me. I reach up to kiss him again, forgetting everything else.

'Evie! Josh!' Miss Bunnock's distant shout cuts through the air.

Josh and I draw apart, our eyes still intent on each other. He smiles at me and something in my chest flips over and over as I smile back.

'They're looking for us,' I say.

'Yeah.' Josh raises his eyebrows. His face is alive with fun. 'Shall we let them find us?'

'Race you there.' And I turn and speed away, across the moorland towards the house. As I run, Josh flying beside me, an image of Kit flashes into my mind's eye. Guilt settles over me like a cloud.

You didn't do anything, I tell myself. *It was just a thank-you kiss, nothing more. You're bound to feel emotional, a bit different than before – Josh saved your life – it doesn't change anything between you and Kit . . .*

Night has well and truly settled and it's hours past the normal Lightsea bedtime by the time Josh and I are showered and changed and sitting in the kitchen. Mrs Moncrieff flaps around, offering us hot rolls and bowls of steaming chicken-noodle soup that we eat in about ten seconds flat, then Miss Bunnock ushers us, tight-lipped, into Mr Lomax's office.

'What on earth happened?' he asks. 'Where have you two been?'

Josh and I glance at each other, then we both start talking at once.

'One at a time, please,' Mr Lomax says. He looks tired and stressed, with dark shadows under his eyes. 'Evie, you first.'

I take a deep breath and tell him everything: how I saw my ghost again, how I followed her through the trees, across the flat rock and along the stony beach to where she vanished.

Mr Lomax listens attentively, leaning forward over his desk, his fingertips pressed together.

'Then it started raining and we sheltered in this cave and at the back of the cave were these stones that spelled out my real mum's initials – IG.' I hesitate. 'And DL which are *your* initials.'

Mr Lomax's head jerks up. He stares at me for a second, then his gaze switches to Josh. 'Did you see these stones too?'

Josh shifts uncomfortably in his seat. 'Er . . .' He shoots an apologetic look at me.

'He kicked them over because it was dark when he ran up and he didn't see them,' I explain.

'Right, I see.' Mr Lomax gives a weary sigh.

'I think it was my mum's ghost trying . . . trying to show a connection between you and her.' I tail off, unable to accuse him of what I'm more and more certain is the truth: that the carefully-spoken, middle-aged man in front of me killed my mother.

There's an awkward silence. Josh stares at the floor. Mr

165

Lomax wrinkles his brow. 'Isn't it more likely the stones just formulated themselves into shapes that *looked* like letters? After all, an "I" is basically just a straight line.'

'No,' I say.

Josh says nothing.

'They were *definitely* letters, all four of them, and they can't have been there very long,' I argue. 'The tide would have washed them away otherwise. It was coming up fast when we were there; we found a gap . . . a tunnel . . . that took us inland.'

'Yes, there are a lot of those on the island,' Mr Lomax says.

'The tunnel turned into this underground pool inside the cave,' I explain. 'We had to swim through it to get out.'

'And there are a lot of pool caves too.' Mr Lomax sighs. 'I can see why you were soaked when you got back here.' He shakes his head. 'I'm very disappointed in you, Evie. You promised me you wouldn't run off again and yet that is exactly what you appear to have done today, this time dragging Josh into danger as well as yourself.'

'No one dragged me,' Josh says, bristling. 'I make my own decisions.'

'Fine, then you're both equally to blame. Not that blame is helpful here . . .' Mr Lomax sits back and crosses his arms. 'What I'm trying to say is that your lack of responsibility has only led you into life-threatening danger. And for what? For *nothing*.'

I sit back. Clearly, Mr Lomax has no intention of admitting to any involvement in Irina's time at Lightsea fifteen years ago, let alone her murder.

166

'Josh, would you leave us?' Mr Lomax asks.

Josh shoots me a sympathetic glance, then leaves the office.

Mr Lomax leans forward. I shiver. He may appear all reasonable and mild-mannered, but if he really did kill my mother he is a murderer. The thought chills me to the bone.

'Evie, I'm very concerned about your behaviour today. I hoped that our programme here of structure and discipline, with regular chores and plenty of opportunity to talk through your feelings, might help you come to terms with your recent discovery about your birth mother. But instead you seem to be becoming more obsessed than ever. This last incident is the most worrying yet – getting trapped by the tide because you think you see a ghost, then hallucinating about a set of stones that—'

'I *didn't* hallucinate them,' I protest, furious. 'I *know* my mother was here on Lightsea and I think she died here.' I stop, still wary of actually accusing him of killing her.

'And why on earth do you think that?' Mr Lomax asks.

'Well, for one thing there's the photo I found *here* in your office,' I blurt out.

'*What?*' Mr Lomax's eyebrows shoot up. 'There isn't – *wasn't* – a picture of your mother in this office.'

I look away, cursing myself for letting that detail slip.

Mr Lomax taps his fingers together. Once. Twice. Very slow and deliberate.

'Show me, Evie,' he says. 'I'd like to see this photograph. Will you fetch it?'

I hesitate for a second. I hadn't meant to challenge Lomax like that, but maybe it will prove to be a good thing. Perhaps once he sees proof that Irina was here on Lightsea he'll stop denying all knowledge of her.

'It's up in the girls' bedroom.' My heart thuds.

'Very well.' Mr Lomax calls Miss Bunnock in and asks her to escort me upstairs, where Pepper and Anna are asleep. Anna's hair gleams in the light from outside the house while Pepper is starfished across the top of her bed. She's still dressed. I'm guessing she was trying to wait up for me, but couldn't stay awake.

I scuttle over to my bed and reach under my pillow. I left the photo underneath Irina's ballet shoes. My hands find the shoes straightaway, but nothing else. I lift up the pillow. Behind me, Miss Bunnock sucks in her breath.

Because the photo is gone. And in its place is a knife.

Twenty-two

Miss Bunnock orders me downstairs. Back in Mr Lomax's office, she lays the knife from under my pillow on his desk.

'What's this?' Mr Lomax asks.

'The photo has disappeared,' I say, my voice shaking.

'I see,' Mr Lomax says, in a voice that suggests he doesn't believe it was ever real.

'But we did find this under Evie's pillow where she said the photo would be.' Miss Bunnock points to the knife.

Lomax sighs. 'Oh, Evie.'

'I have no idea how that got there,' I insist. My head spins. Who switched the photo with the knife? And why? Did Mr Lomax know the knife would be there? Is that why he sent me for the photo?

Mr Lomax rubs his forehead. 'Please, Evie, this puts everything in a very different light.'

I look up. What does that mean?

'I agree.' Miss Bunnock meets his eyes. 'Clearly, a danger to herself or others . . .'

'*What?*' I glare at her. 'I'm *not*. I already told you, I don't know anything about the knife.'

'There's no history of violence,' Mr Lomax muses, more

to himself than to me or Miss Bunnock. 'Evie, I need to ask you something very serious,' he continues. 'Did you take the knife because you've been . . . having thoughts about hurting yourself?'

'No. I *didn't*, I *don't* . . .' I suck in my breath.

'I'm just asking about your feelings,' Mr Lomax asks gently. 'Are you sure this knife isn't really a cry for help?'

'No.' I clutch the arm of my chair. Is it possible Lomax put the knife there himself to make it look like I'm going crazy?

Mr Lomax sighs again. 'I think you should get a good night's sleep, Evie, then we'll talk again in the morning.' He stands up. The silence in the room, the whole house, presses down on me. I glance at the window. It's stopped raining, but the earlier downpour has left tracks all along the dark glass.

'I'm not lying!' I insist. 'Someone else put the knife there. And right now I'm thinking maybe it was you.'

Miss Bunnock tuts. Mr Lomax's eyes widen with horror.

'Of course it wasn't me,' he says. 'Evie, I'm seriously concerned about you.'

'Well, you don't need to be.' My knuckles are white on the chair arms. Clearly, Lomax isn't going to admit to any wrongdoing. I turn to Miss Bunnock. 'He's making it up about me wanting to hurt myself.'

Miss Bunnock averts her gaze.

Lomax taps his fingers together. 'OK, Evie, off to bed. I'm going to permit you to lie in tomorrow morning. Miss Bunnock will make sure the other girls don't wake you. Then I'd like to talk with you again, once you're rested.'

'Oh.' I think fast. After everything that's happened this evening, there's no way I'm going to get a chance to find my mobile and retrieve Gavin's number tonight – but maybe there's another way to reach him. Mr Lomax is clearly trying to make out I'm mad to stop anyone taking what I'm saying seriously, so perhaps I should play along a little, use the situation to my advantage.

'Maybe in the morning you might let me call my uncle,' I suggest. 'I know it's against the rules here, but I do feel . . . er, confused now . . . and Uncle Gavin has a way of explaining things that might help me accept what you're saying.'

Mr Lomax studies my face. I return his gaze, feeling my cheeks flush. I'm sure that if I can explain everything I've found out to Gavin I can get him to take me off this island *and* look into the circumstances of Irina's death again.

Mr Lomax nods. 'I think perhaps in your case we do need to speak with your family. As soon as the phones are working, you can make a call. The storm brought down our power lines so we're operating on backup electricity and have no way of contacting the mainland.'

'You mean we're cut off?' A shiver snakes down my spine.

'Well, the storm looks like it's abating, which means Mr Bradley will be able to take our boat to the mainland tomorrow morning, bring back someone to do the necessary repairs. I'll . . .' he smiles at me, '. . . we'll *both* be able to talk to your uncle by tomorrow afternoon, I hope.'

'Provided the storm goes away,' I say.

'Yes, I'm afraid if the storm comes back as forecast then there's no way any boat will be able to get through.'

'Thanks.' I stand up.

A few minutes later, I'm back in the bedroom. At least – storm allowing – I'll be able to talk to Uncle Gavin tomorrow. I lie down on my bed, pull the covers over my head and hug Irina's ballet shoes to me. Soon I should have answers. Soon.

The next thing I know it's daylight. I sit bolt upright, forgetting for a moment where I am. Anna's bed opposite is empty, the sheets folded and smoothed under the pillow. Pepper's bed is also deserted, and the covers drawn up, though far less neatly. I tuck Irina's ballet shoes back under my pillow, shuddering as I remember the knife that was left there last night.

The sun outside is already high in the sky, though partly hidden behind a bank of cloud. The nearby trees are bending and swaying in the wind, but there's no sign of the predicted storm. Which means Mr Bradley is probably already on his way in the boat to fetch someone to repair the phone lines. And soon I'll be able to speak to my uncle.

I hurry into my clothes, then race downstairs. I'm starving, so I head straight for the kitchen. The hall clock says it's just past ten, so I'm assuming the kitchen will be empty, with everyone doing chores around the house and in the grounds. But to my surprise all the others except Samuel are still sitting around the table, talking in low voices as I rush in.

'Hey, Evie, they wouldn't let us wake you!' Pepper jumps up, eyes wide with excitement.

Kit and Josh have their backs to me. They turn as Pepper says my name.

I skid to a halt. The sight of them side by side is like someone throwing a bucket of ice water into my face. Kit smiles, as good-looking as ever in a tight blue T-shirt. Josh raises his eyebrows. His quizzical look sets my heart racing.

I'm with Kit, I think.

But it is Josh whose face I linger on.

Twenty-three

I stand, frozen in the kitchen doorway, my eyes still fixed on Josh.

'Are you OK, Evie?' Kit asks.

'Yes, I'm fine.'

'Josh says you got trapped by the sea and had to swim out of a cave,' Pepper declares with relish.

Josh gives a tiny shake of the head to let me know that he hasn't said anything about the ghost or the stones in the cave; that he knows I wouldn't want everyone discussing those intimate details. I try to convey my thanks with my eyes.

'Evie?' Kit asks. 'Are you really all right?'

I look at him at last, then at Pepper. 'Course,' I say. 'Though Josh basically saved my life yesterday.'

Josh leans back in his chair, trying to look modest.

'Wow,' Anna breathes, shooting him an admiring glance.

Pepper's eyes grow wider. She digs Anna in the ribs. 'I *knew* it. Tell us all the details.'

I can feel Kit's eyes on my face.

'Er, maybe later. Um, is there any breakfast left?' I ask, hoping to change the subject. It isn't just that I don't want to talk about Irina's ghost in front of everyone ... there's something in that intent look of Kit's that's making me feel very uncomfortable.

'I think there are some rolls,' Anna says vaguely.

'If Josh and Kit haven't eaten them all,' Pepper drawls.

I scuttle over to the bread bin and pick out a roll.

As I sit down at the end of the table, Kit clears his throat. 'Sounds like you guys were stranded for hours.' His voice has a definite edge to it. 'With just each other for company?'

I nod, feeling a blush start to creep up my neck. I focus on spreading butter on my roll. 'We mostly spent the afternoon telling jokes,' I say.

'Yeah and listening to music,' Josh adds.

'Right.' Kit's lips are pressed tightly together. What on earth is the matter with him?

I turn to Pepper. 'Where's Samuel?' I ask.

'No idea,' she says.

'He wasn't in our room when we woke up,' Josh says.

'He's probably having another one-to-one with Mr Lomax,' Kit adds.

'But Loonymax didn't turn up for morning meditation . . .' Pepper drawls, '. . . so we don't actually know what's happened to him or Samuel or anyone else.'

My chest tightens as I remember Samuel's anxious face the last time I saw him. He said then that he had something important to tell me. I hope he's OK.

'The only person we've seen is Mrs Moncrieff,' Anna adds, chewing at one of her fingernails.

'Yeah, batty old bird told us to stay here, said someone would be in to talk to us soon.' Pepper yawns.

Silence falls. I take a bite of my roll, carefully avoiding both Kit's and Josh's gaze.

'Hello, everyone.' Miss Bunnock appears in the doorway.

I turn in my seat. Miss Bunnock's hair is tousled and she's frowning, her expression anxious and distracted.

'Where's Samuel?' I ask.

'I'm afraid that Samuel has run away from the island,' Miss Bunnock says.

Everyone stares at her. I stop chewing.

'What?' Josh's mouth gapes.

'What do you mean he's *run away*?' Pepper asks. 'How is that even possible on an island?'

'He's taken *Aurora*, the motorboat from the boathouse.' Miss Bunnock purses her lips. 'Mr Bradley found signs he'd been there, that lighter he carries with him was on the floor.' She holds out her hand to show us.

'Samuel took the boat?' Anna asks, wide-eyed. 'Oh my goodness.'

'You mean he went to sea?' Pepper sounds more shocked than I'd ever heard her.

'During the storm?' Kit looks incredulous.

'Well, we don't actually know when he left,' Miss Bunnock says. 'At first, we thought he must have gone looking for killer whales at sea again, just as he did on his first evening here. But then Mr Bradley found the *Aurora* missing late last night

176

after you returned. I'm afraid there's really no other explanation: Samuel has run off.'

'Ho-ly cow,' Pepper says with slow emphasis. 'I had no idea Samuel had it in him to steal a boat and take it to sea in a storm. That's not easy.'

'It's not something to be proud off,' Miss Bunnock tuts.

I lay down my roll, thinking of Mr Lomax's plan to send Mr Bradley to fetch an engineer to repair the phone lines. 'But if the boat has gone that means no one can leave the island.'

'Indeed,' Miss Bunnock says. 'Though we're hoping someone on the mainland will send a boat to check on us. They normally do if the telephone lines go down.'

'Hoping?' Kit asks with a frown.

'The sun might be shining now, but another storm is brewing,' Miss Bunnock explains. 'Looks like it might be even worse than yesterday and, if the weather makes the journey treacherous, no one on the mainland will risk sending a boat.'

'So what do we do now?' Anna asks, winding a strand of hair anxiously round her finger.

'Have a musical interlude?' Josh suggests hopefully. 'I could play my guitar, take everyone's mind off the situation?'

I smile in spite of my worries. So does Pepper.

'You'll be getting on with your chores of course.' Miss Bunnock consults the wallchart. 'But nothing outdoors until Mr Bradley has fully assessed the storm damage outside.' She glances at me, her expression softening into one of soothing concern. 'How are you feeling this morning, Evie?'

'Er, fine,' I mumble, a blush heating my cheeks.

Miss Bunnock looks around the kitchen. 'Mmm,' she continues, 'we'll have to change things around a bit as Samuel isn't with us . . .'

'Evie and I would like to work together, please,' Kit says.

'I'm afraid that isn't possible.' Miss Bunnock sounds distracted. 'You and Pepper are cleaning bathrooms this morning. Anna, you can join them. Josh and Evie are on kitchen duty, but no chopping or carving; we've removed the knives.' Her concerned gaze rests on me for a moment, then she looks away.

'You *what*?' Pepper asks.

My blush deepens. Have the staff done that because they're worried I might hurt myself?

'Why have you taken the knives away?' Pepper persists.

Miss Bunnock ignores her. 'Right then, Mrs Moncrieff will be in shortly to give you instructions.' She sweeps off.

Kit turns to me, his expression as full of concern as Miss Bunnock's.

'Are you sure you're all right?' he asks. 'I don't want to leave you.'

I stare at him. 'Honestly, I'm *fine*. Why won't anyone believe me?'

'You know why,' Kit says quietly. He moves closer, whispering in my ear. 'Miss Bunnock told me about the knife.'

'That had nothing to do with me,' I whisper back. 'As far as I'm concerned, Lomax probably planted the thing under my pillow, to make it look like I was . . . unbalanced or something.'

'What are you two talking about?' Pepper demands.

Kit chews on his lip. 'Guys, we need to keep an eye on Evie, make sure she's all right today.'

For goodness' sake. I'm starting to feel irritated. 'Seriously, I'm OK.'

'Of course you are,' Kit says, his voice oozing sympathy.

'Sounds like you're the one we need to keep an eye on, Kit,' Josh says. 'You're acting like a right weirdo.'

'I wasn't talking to you.' Kit clenches his fists, suddenly mad.

'Ooh, testosterone surge alert.' Pepper rolls her eyes. 'Come on, Kit, let's get your muscles working on the first-floor toilets.'

Kit gives a low growl, then turns away as Pepper ushers him and Anna out of the kitchen. Josh and I are alone.

'Hey.' He glances at me and smiles, looking suddenly self-conscious.

'Hey yourself.'

'Right . . . I've apples for you to peel, then crumble mix to make and peas to shell.' Mrs Moncrieff bustles in.

Josh rolls his eyes. 'Great,' he says. 'Bring on the fruit and veg.'

For the next few minutes, Mrs Moncrieff sorts us out with the equipment we'll need. We're given two blunt peelers to do the apples with; no knives. Mrs Moncrieff says she'll core the fruit later.

'Now are you quite all right, Evie dear?'

'Great, thanks,' I mutter.

'Good, good,' she says with a smile. 'I'm afraid I have to leave you as the storeroom is flooded. We moved what we

179

could yesterday, but I want to go through what's there, see what's ruined and what can be saved.'

She hurries out of the room and Josh and I get on with our work, applying our peelers to the huge pile of apples Mrs Moncrieff has set in front of us.

'I saw that look Bunnock gave you earlier,' Josh says as soon as we're alone. 'What was all that about the knives?'

I take a deep breath and tell him. Josh shakes his head.

'Something very weird is going on.' He falls silent.

Relieved he isn't buying into Lomax's self-harming story, I focus on finishing my apple peeling. I wonder if Josh is remembering our brief kiss. I'd like to find out what he thinks, but my head feels too confused because of Kit to talk about it, so I keep the conversation focused on Samuel's dramatic departure from the island.

'I hope he's OK.' I chew on my lip. 'Why d'you think he ran off?'

Josh makes a face. 'Dunno, but he's kind of strange and he knows lots of things, so I wouldn't be surprised to hear he could handle a motorboat even in a storm all the way to the mainland. He obviously remembered exactly how to pick the lock on the corridor door and I only showed him how to do it once, using a bit of wire, which is much harder than with my long pins.'

'I see,' I say.

Josh sighs. 'Samuel's smarter than you think – and he definitely knows stuff your average person doesn't.'

'That's true,' I say, remembering Samuel's story about the

dead kitten inside the sausage. 'You know, he said he had something important to tell me yesterday, but when I asked what it was he just said he'd tell me later and of course, by the time we got back, he'd run off.'

'That's certainly odd.' Josh lays down his apple peeler. 'But, again, Samuel *is* odd. D'you think he just wanted to tell you another strange fact?'

'At the time I did, but now . . .' I frown. 'Now I'm thinking that the way he was talking was different from when he tells you about trees or animals or whatever. He looked worried, like it was a seriously big deal.'

'If it was such a big deal, why not tell you there and then?' Josh asks.

'I don't know, but he did get called away,' I say.

'Mmm . . . do you think what he wanted to say had anything to do with the knife being put under your pillow?' Josh asks. 'Maybe Samuel saw whoever did that.'

I shrug. 'Maybe.'

'Hey.' Josh looks up, his eyes widening with excitement. 'Perhaps Samuel wrote down whatever it was.'

I wrinkle my nose. 'Why d'you think he'd have done that?'

'He writes down lots of stuff in this notebook. He keeps it up in our room, in that hiding place I told you about. It's worth a look, don't you think?'

'Yes.' I stand up. 'I know they lock the doors up there during the day, but could you get us into the boys' bedroom?' I ask.

Josh stares at me. '*Now?*'

'Yes,' I say. 'I remember that after our first day you said

you'd carry stuff for picking locks at all times . . . or was that a joke?'

A slow smile creeps across Josh's lips. 'No joke,' he says. 'Let's go.'

The boys' bedroom looks just like the girls' with three beds, each set with a simple white cover.

Josh kneels down at the far end of the room and pulls away the small armchair that sits in front of the wall.

'Is that the hiding place?' I ask.

'Yeah, under this floorboard,' Josh explains. 'I found it on the first night. Samuel and I were using it for our contraband.'

I wrinkle my nose. 'I can't believe Samuel had contraband.'

'He didn't really, just his notebook and a bit of food we smuggled up from the kitchen. Here . . .' Josh curls his fingers under the edge of a patch of floorboard about seven centimetres long, then lifts it up. Underneath I can see his little MP3 player, plus the charger, then the edge of a piece of stiff white card.

'What's that?' I ask, pointing at the card.

'Dunno. I didn't notice it last night when I put the player back.' Josh kneels down and puts his hand into the gap. He feels along the dusty plank of wood and draws out the white paper. He turns it over.

It's my missing photo of Irina, the one from under my pillow.

I gasp. 'This is mine,' I say. 'It's the picture I found in Lomax's office, the one that got swapped for the knife. What's it doing here?'

Josh shakes his head. 'Maybe Samuel switched them.'

I frown. 'Then why did he want to talk to me so badly?'

Josh doesn't answer, he's staring down at the photo. 'This is your birth mum?' he asks. 'You don't look much like her.'

'I know.' Something shrivels inside me. Kit had seen a similarity or at least he'd said he did. 'She was really pretty, much prettier than me.'

'Nah, to be honest, she looks too thin, like unhealthy-looking. You're way better-looking,' Josh says matter-of-factly. 'How come Samuel has it?'

'No idea,' I say, my face burning. Does he mean that about me being better looking than graceful, beautiful Irina? 'Last time I saw it, it was under my pillow.'

Josh frowns, then reaches into the hole again. 'Let's see if the notebook is here.' His fingers probe under the floorboards. 'Yeah, look.' He draws out a small notebook with a black cover, opens it and squints down at the first page.

'What's in it?'

'On this page, Samuel facts,' Josh says wryly. 'Written in the tiniest writing you've ever seen.' He hands me the notebook. I scan the open page. Every millimetre is covered with minute sentences:

one quarter of the bones in your body are in your feet, people have on average seven million breaths every year, everyone has a tongue print as well as ten fingerprints, the northern leopard frog pushes its food down its throat with its eyes, when a glacier melts it fizzes

And so on.

'You'd think he'd have taken this with him.' I flick through the pages to the final few entries. I read the last line and my jaw drops.

'Have you found something?' Josh asks, edging closer.

I nod, unable to speak.

'Show me.'

I shove the notebook at him, but even as I hand it over the final entry stays imprinted on my brain:

I just found Lomax's gun and I know why it's there. It's to kill Evie.

Twenty-four

Josh looks up at me. His expressive face is etched with a deep frown.

'D'you think this is for real?' he asks.

'Yes, I do.' A chill settles inside me. 'I'm already sure Lomax killed my mum on this island and somehow covered it up. Samuel must have found out that he wants to kill me to stop me from revealing what he did. The knife under my pillow must have something to do with it too.'

Josh's frown deepens. 'D'you really think that . . .?' He pauses. 'What about your mum's photo?'

'Maybe Samuel found the photo at the same time as he found out what Lomax is planning.'

'Or maybe someone else put the photo here,' Josh says thoughtfully. 'Kit knows we keep stuff under this floorboard, nobody else does.'

I stare at him. Could Kit be involved?

'Think about it, Evie; he's been acting really oddly, like all aggressive and stuff.'

I chew on my lip. What Josh says is true. Kit *was* aggressive earlier, at least to Josh. Plus, he has dismissed my belief that I've seen Irina's ghost – or that she might have been murdered here – *and* he's going along with the idea that I put a knife under my pillow so I could hurt myself.

On the other hand, Kit has no possible reason to want to hurt me. If anything, the last time I saw him he was over-the-top concerned that I might want to hurt myself.

'It's not him,' I say. 'It's got to be Lomax. Anyway, none of this explains why Samuel felt so desperate that he stole the *Aurora* and left the island instead of waiting to talk to me later.'

'Maybe he got scared when we went missing,' Josh suggests.

'You mean he thought I was already dead? *That's* why he took the boat, to get away from Lomax? Get to safety himself?'

'Exactly. Oh man, this is heavy.' Josh replaces the floorboard and draws the armchair back into position. 'What do you want to do?'

'We have to tell—' I start.

'What are you doing in here?' Kit stands in the doorway, a big scowl on his handsome face.

I spin round, instinctively hiding the notebook and photo behind my back.

'Nothing,' Josh says.

Kit glares at him. 'I wasn't asking you.' He turns to me. 'Evie, why are you here? You're not supposed to be in this room.' He jerks his thumb at Josh. 'Especially not with him.'

'Oh, chill out, for goodness' sake,' Josh snaps. 'I was just trying to help her.'

'Yeah and I know exactly how you'd like to do that,' Kit spits, clenching his fists and storming towards Josh.

'Calm down,' I say. 'Both of you.'

Kit reluctantly stops, though he's still glaring at Josh.

'Are you OK, Evie?' he asks. 'I've been worrying about you all morning.'

'I'm fine,' I say. I draw the notebook out from behind my back. 'I'm with Josh because he helped me find this. It's Samuel's. Look.' I point to the entry we've just read.

Kit takes the notebook and scans the page. 'OK, I can see this looks alarming,' he says, 'but you have to remember who wrote it. I mean, Samuel's probably imagining things.'

'He *doesn't* imagine things. You know that as well as I do,' I say, my chest tightening.

'OK, then he's got it wrong.' Kit peers down at the notebook again. 'Even if he found some sort of gun, it's probably not real or, if it is, it's used for killing rabbits or something. You shouldn't be worried about it anyway.'

'This isn't about me being *worried*, it's about Lomax wanting to kill me because I've found out he murdered my birth mum.'

'What?' Kit's eyes widen. '*That's* what you think? Is that why you hid that knife?'

'I told you a million times I *didn't* hide the knife. I don't know anything about the knife.' My voice rises.

'OK, OK.' Kit raises his hands, patting the air as if to calm me down. 'But . . . well, don't you think all this . . . a knife, a gun . . . it's all a bit too much of a coincidence? And, even if any

187

of it is true, what would be the point of risking everything to kill you when you don't even have any evidence against him? Plus, there's no way Mr Lomax is capable of committing a murder.'

'He *is* capable of it,' I argue.

'And of covering it up for fifteen years,' Josh adds darkly.

'Why on earth would Mr Lomax have killed your mum anyway?' Kit goes on, pointedly ignoring Josh. 'It doesn't make sense.'

'Maybe he liked her and she rejected him,' Josh suggests, an edge to his voice.

Kit glares at him.

'Yes, perhaps he fell in love with her and invited her to the island.' A lump lodges in my throat as I imagine Irina, her eyes sparkling as she happily agreed to visit Lightsea, only to find out when she arrived that Lomax had darker intentions. 'Maybe he tried it on and my mum said no because of me back at home.' I gulp. 'And then Lomax pushed her off Easter Rock out of jealousy.'

'For goodness' sake,' Kit mutters.

Ignoring him, Josh turns to me. 'What do you want to do, Evie?'

I consider for a moment. 'We should tell Mr Bradley,' I say. 'He's the only adult physically strong enough to confront Mr Lomax.'

'Evie, please.' Kit reaches for my hand. 'I'm so worried about you. You're being paranoid . . . I think maybe you're seriously ill.'

I take a step away from him.

'Telling Bradley's a good idea.' Josh makes his way to the door. 'Coming, Evie?'

I look at Kit. His expression is furious, but I can see the hurt in his eyes too.

'I'm not ill.' The words spill out of me. 'Why won't you believe me?'

Kit frowns. He says nothing. Josh waits, watching us from the door.

I walk out of the room without looking back, then follow Josh down the stairs. The photo of Irina and the notebook are still clutched in my hand. Josh doesn't speak as we hurry down both flights of steps. My heart feels heavy in my chest at Kit's refusal to trust me, but as we reach the entry hall fear overrides my misery. I point along the corridor towards Lomax's office, then put my finger to my lips.

'Lomax could be here,' I mouth.

'OK, then we need to find Bradley urgently.' Josh glances up and down the deserted hall. 'He's probably still checking for storm damage outside.'

'Where do you think he might have—?' But, before I can finish my question, Mr Bradley himself strides into view.

'Where are the others?' he demands.

'Cleaning bathrooms, I think,' I say, rushing over to him. 'Please, Mr Bradley, I really need to talk to—'

'Get the others and meet me outside in two minutes,' Mr Bradley orders, marching over to the front door. 'There's a big mess outside the boathouse that needs clearing up before the storm starts up again.'

189

'But sir—'

But Mr Bradley has already gone, slamming the front door shut behind him.

'Let's get the others, *fast*,' Josh says. 'It'll be easier to make him listen then. I'll fetch Kit, you find the girls.' He sets off, racing up the stairs two at a time. I follow him as far as the first floor. Pepper's voice booms out of the bathroom along the corridor. I run towards it.

'How are you doing that without barfing?' she's saying as I rush into the room.

Anna is peering into the toilet bowl. Pepper stands over her, a disdainful expression on her face.

'Hey, Evie,' Pepper says, glancing over. 'Anna reckons the plumbing is about to blow up.'

'I didn't say that . . .' Anna looks up, blushing furiously. 'I just said it was a bit inefficient.' She catches sight of my anxious face. 'What's the matter?' she asks.

There's no time to explain. I have to get out of the building, avoiding Mr Lomax at all costs, and tell Mr Bradley everything I've discovered.

'We've been ordered outside. *Now.*' Without waiting for either girl to react, I turn on my heel and run back downstairs. I grab my boots and attempt to tug them on, but the laces are stuck in a tight knot, presumably from where I pulled them off yesterday. Swearing loudly, I try to drag the boots on anyway. It's no good, the knot just tightens. As I fumble to unpick it, Kit and Josh appear and collect their own footwear. Kit says nothing. I glance along the corridor towards Lomax's closed office door. Is he inside? Does he know I'm just out here? As the three of us sit in silence, Pepper strolls into the hall, Anna trotting at her side.

'Why d'you run off, Evie? Hey, what's that?' Pepper asks, pointing to Samuel's notebook on the seat beside me.

I frown, hoping that if Lomax is in his office he hasn't heard her say my name.

'Oh, don't tell me,' Pepper says with a loud groan. 'It's Loonymax's latest brilliant idea: he wants us to keep notebooks recording our mental state. I'll be writing: "bored and disgusted by toilets" in mine. What'll you put in yours, Evie?'

I look up, an icy shiver crawling down my spine. If Lomax is here, he will almost certainly have heard that.

Except . . . I shake myself. Lomax isn't going to try to kill me in front of everyone. I need to focus on getting my boots on and going outside to talk to Mr Bradley.

'Evie?' Pepper asks impatiently. 'What's up?'

'I'll tell you later,' I whisper, turning back to my laces.

'OK, woman of mystery.' Pepper grins.

I concentrate on my boots again. Despite all my efforts, the knot is getting worse.

Kit stands up. 'I'm going out,' he says.

'At least I don't have to stay in that bathroom,' Pepper says, peeling off her rubber gloves and sitting down with a theatrical flourish. 'I don't think I could have stood any more of that blocked toilet.'

'It wasn't blocked,' Anna says with a sigh, fetching her boots and sitting beside her. 'It's just a really old system.'

191

Anna ties her bootlaces in a neat bow, then follows Kit outside, while Pepper tugs her own boots on with a sigh. Josh shuffles from foot to foot, impatient as he waits for us. Cursing again, I redouble my efforts with the knot. Pepper keeps up a steady stream of grumbling chatter beside me, but I hardly hear a word. Thoughts career around my head:

Lomax murdered my mum on this island, then covered it up.

Her ghost was trying to warn me. And so was Samuel. And now he has run away and gone for help because he knows that Lomax is trying to kill me.

'Need a hand?' Josh kneels down and picks expertly at the knot in my lace. It undoes in seconds.

'Thank you.'

Pepper, whose boots are now also done up, bounces around me on the balls of her toes.

'Come *on*, Evie,' she drawls. 'Before pigging Bradley gives us pigging Quiet Time.'

'I'm done.' I stand up and rush outside, struggling to hold the door against the wind. I'm determined to go straight to Mr Bradley and show him the notebook, but to my horror he's already halfway across the moorland, Kit jogging at his side. Anna trails in their wake.

'Oh no,' I say as Josh and Pepper appear.

'Are you OK?' Josh asks.

'Yes, Evie's fine.' Pepper rolls her eyes. 'And, oh, let me see, um, yes, I'm fine too, except for the stink of toilet cleaner on my hands, thanks for asking.'

'I didn't mean—' Josh starts.

'I'm only joking,' Pepper says. 'Jeez, you've got it bad, man. It's written all over your face.'

Flushing, Josh turns and hares off after the others.

Pepper and I start running too. What exactly did she mean by that? Underneath my overriding need to speak to Mr Bradley, a secondary set of worries about Kit and Josh is building up. I have to sort out whatever is going on with both of them. I glance at Pepper, whose long limbs are stretched in a graceful run as she keeps pace beside me. Does she mind that Josh has just asked about me rather than her?

'Josh was just a bit worried about me,' I explain. 'We found this . . . this note Samuel left. He thinks I'm in danger . . .'

Pepper's head whips around. 'Because you've been digging up stuff on your birth mum's death?'

I nod.

Pepper lets out a low whistle. 'I thought there was more to it.'

'More to what?' I ask, feeling confused. The ground beneath our feet is soggy from the rain, but the air smells amazingly fresh. 'What do you mean?'

'Just that you're obviously in a state because Kit and Josh are both totally into you and hate each other's guts because of it.'

I stop running, so shocked by her words that I forget all about my urgent need to find Mr Bradley. Pepper halts beside me. I look into her deep brown eyes.

'Do you really think that's true?' I gasp.

'Course it is,' Pepper snorts. 'And, before you ask, I'm

totally cool with it. I know you think I like Josh, but only as a friend. I could have, like, ten boyfriends at home if I wanted so I seriously don't need another mooning all over me.' She pauses, tilting her head to one side. 'But who I like doesn't matter. The question that counts is which of them do *you* like? Kit or Josh?'

Twenty-five

I stare at Pepper, all thoughts of Irina's ghost and the threat against my life vanishing. I didn't see it as a direct choice before. But now Pepper has put it into words I realise that's exactly what I'm facing:

Kit or Josh.

'I'm going out with Kit,' I say, blushing furiously.

'Yeah, right.' Pepper rolls her eyes. 'So you might be, but you spent most of yesterday with Josh who, er, let's see, *saved your life* like some action-movie hero. Plus, I saw the way you two looked at each other this morning. More to the point, so did Kit. *That's* why he's been in such a bad mood all morning.'

'Oh, Pepper,' I wail. 'This is such a mess. I like Kit, really I do. He's *gorgeous*. But Josh is great to talk to and . . . and there's just something about him . . .'

'Yeah, he's all about the charm.' Pepper puts her hands on her hips. 'Well, don't look so miserable, most girls would *love* having two hot boys after them.'

'Pepper and Evie, unless one of you has actually broken your leg, will you *please* hurry up.' Mr Bradley's yell makes me jump.

My fears about Lomax – and my need to talk to Mr Bradley – flood back and I set off running across the moorland again, faster than before. Pepper keeps pace by my side. Thoughts tumble over and over in my head. For a minute, I seriously expect my brain to explode. There's just too much for me to get my head around. Josh and Kit are both up ahead. They're standing apart, clearly not talking. Kit holds himself stiffly. Even at this distance, it's obvious he's angry. Josh is looking out across the treetops, the wind tousling his dark hair.

I follow his gaze to the steely clouds that are massing over the sea. It might be sunny on the island right now, but it looks as if Miss Bunnock is right that another storm is brewing. I focus on Mr Bradley in the distance. Never mind all the confusion of Kit and Josh, what really matters is telling Mr Bradley that my life is in danger.

I speed across the uneven ground, leaving Pepper behind. Mr Bradley and the others are waiting at the end of the path that leads to the boathouse. As I race up, Mr Bradley scowls, a look of impatience on his face.

'I need two volunteers to—'

'Please, Mr Bradley, I desperately need to speak to you,' I interrupt.

Mr Bradley glares at me. 'What is it, Evie?'

I glance around. The others are all staring at me. 'It's about Mr Lomax . . .'

I hesitate, unsure how to begin my explanation.

'*What* about him?' Mr Bradley is almost radiating impatience. 'Because I was only just able to get inside the boathouse when

196

I was looking for Samuel earlier, and there's a huge mess of rubbish outside. I've made a start at clearing it up, but if the job isn't finished before the next storm begins then it might be completely impossible to access the building. Plus, there's a fallen tree blocking the jetty, which I need to remove. I'm guessing we have about two hours until it starts raining again, so there's no time to—'

'It's really important,' I insist as Pepper runs up.

She bends over, her breath coming in jags.

'You have to listen,' Josh urges.

'Go on then, quickly,' Mr Bradley snaps.

Everyone except Pepper – who's still doubled over – is watching me. Kit is shaking his head, a look of disbelief on his face. Anna wears a bemused expression. Josh is the only person offering any sympathy. It's there in the warmth of his eyes.

I take strength from that.

'I found a note Samuel left,' I say. 'It adds up with a whole bunch of other stuff . . . I think Mr Lomax is trying to kill me.'

'*What?*' Mr Bradley's eyes bulge with surprise. Beside him, Anna's mouth gapes open.

'Seriously,' I say. 'Mr Lomax murdered my real mother fifteen years ago and now he wants to kill me.'

'Enough,' Mr Bradley snaps. A look of concern, similar to the expressions worn by Kit, Miss Bunnock and Mrs Moncrieff earlier comes over his face. 'Evie, are you feeling all right? Mr Lomax said you might be—'

'I'm fine,' I interrupt.

'There's no need to get hysterical, Evie. I'm—'

'I'm *not* hysterical. I'm telling you the *truth*.'

'She really is,' Josh says, throwing me a reassuring look. 'Evie's found out that Mr Lomax killed her birth mum and somehow covered it up and now we think he's after Evie herself.'

'Because that's not melodramatic or hysterical at all,' Kit murmurs under his breath.

'Oooh, he went there.' Pepper shoots Kit a mocking look, her brows arched high.

'You're not helping, Pepper.' Kit turns to me. 'This is ridiculous, Evie.'

'Back off,' Josh says, squaring up to him.

'Make me.' Kit shoves him in the chest.

'Hey, stop that.' Mr Bradley pulls Kit away. 'For goodness' sake, I've got enough to deal with without listening to delusional ravings *and* breaking up fights.'

'I'm *not* delusional,' I insist.

'But it doesn't make sense. Mr Lomax wouldn't cover anything up,' Kit says. 'He might be a little out of the ordinary, but—'

'"A little out of the ordinary"?' Pepper snorts. 'He's a total hippy whack job who lives in the middle of nowhere, giving meditation tips to supposedly dysfunctional teenagers.'

'Quiet,' snaps Mr Bradley.

'Anyway, you don't know what Lomax is capable of doing.' Josh glares at Kit who glares furiously back.

'I said *enough*. Mr Lomax is *not* a murderer.' Mr Bradley pauses. 'Now what did Samuel actually say in his note?'

'That . . . that he found a gun and that Mr Lomax wants to kill me,' I stammer.

'Right, I see.' Mr Bradley sighs. 'And where did he find this supposed gun? What did he do with it?'

'I don't know, but—'

'And what makes you so sure that Samuel is right that your life is under threat?' Bradley goes on. 'Or that Mr Lomax is the one who supposedly wants to kill you?'

'I told you, because Mr Lomax killed my real mum and wants to stop me telling everyone.'

Bradley sighs. 'I don't suppose you have anything approximating to evidence of any of this?'

I hesitate. I can just imagine how he'll react if I tell him about Irina's ghost. I focus on something more tangible.

'There was an article,' I say. 'We all saw it, Mr Lomax has it now. An unknown woman was pushed off Easter Rock on the very same day that my mum died.'

'It's true. There was an article about a suspected murder,' Pepper says. 'You should listen to Evie.'

I shoot her a grateful glance.

'It does all seem really suspicious,' Anna stammers.

I squeeze her arm, grateful that even if Kit doesn't believe me my other Lightsea friends are prepared to back me up.

Mr Bradley rolls his eyes. 'I'm afraid this is all completely fantastical,' he says. 'Especially as Mr Lomax isn't even on the island.'

199

'What?' I stare at him.

'He left half an hour ago. A boat came from the mainland to check on us,' Mr Bradley explains.

I exchange a glance with Josh. So a boat got through earlier. And Mr Lomax has gone. Which makes me safe for now. That's something at least.

'Did the person who brought the boat also fix the phone lines?'

'No, it wasn't an engineer,' Mr Bradley says. 'They weren't here long enough to look at the storm damage. Mr Lomax wanted to leave straightaway so he could call Samuel's parents from the mainland and let them know he's missing. But he'll send another boat back as soon as he can, I'm sure.'

With a sick lurch, I wonder if Mr Lomax's real intention in leaving the island was in fact to follow and find Samuel – then to stop him before he could speak to anyone.

I meet Josh's eyes again. He looks as concerned as I feel.

'When will Mr Lomax be back?' he asks.

'This afternoon, I hope.' Mr Bradley glances at the darkening sky. 'Though once the next storm arrives there's no way any boat will be able to make the crossing so there's a chance he won't get back until early tomorrow morning. In the meantime, we really need to get on.' He points at Kit and Anna. 'You two with me. I need you to help me shift the branches blocking the jetty.' He turns to me. 'Are you really feeling all right, Evie?'

'Yes,' I insist.

'Then I want the rest of you to start clearing the debris from around the boathouse. I'll be back soon.' And, without another word, he turns and marches away.

Kit doesn't look at me as he follows Mr Bradley across the remaining patch of moorland, but Anna throws me a sympathetic smile before turning and trotting after them.

I stand, staring after them, numb with fear. Mr Bradley doesn't believe me, didn't even really listen to me – he has totally bought into Lomax's line that I'm mentally unstable. And, though Lomax himself isn't on the island, the situation is even worse than I thought. Samuel is probably now in terrible danger too. But at least he's escaped from the island.

I, on the other hand, am trapped here.

Twenty-six

Kit, Mr Bradley and Anna disappear into the trees. I turn towards the path that leads to the boathouse, my eyes stinging with tears. Josh puts his hand on my shoulder.

'Don't worry, Evie,' he says. 'We'll talk to Bradley again when he comes back.'

'Yeah, all three of us will,' Pepper adds. 'And I am personally going to make sure that Kit stops being such an arse too.'

'I don't know why he's behaving like that.' Josh looks into my eyes as he speaks. 'He seems to think I'm a bad influence, like I'm encouraging you to believe a whole load of nonsense, like . . .' he makes his voice posher, more like Kit's, '. . . like I'm an unscrupulous cad, don't you know.'

I laugh. It's impossible not to with Josh's eyes twinkling right in front of me. 'It's also that Kit is worried about me,' I say.

'If he's really worried about you, he should support you,' Pepper says. 'If Kit's your boyfriend, he should stick up for whatever you say.'

Is that true? On the one hand, it must be: loyalty is surely important in a relationship. On the other, being honest about how you feel is vital too. Isn't it? I give up. I can't work out how I feel about Kit any more . . . or Josh.

'At least Lomax is off the island,' Josh says. 'You'll be safe for a bit.'

I nod, a fresh idea occurring. 'If we can't make Mr Bradley or the other adults believe what I'm saying before the boat gets back, I'm going to wait for it to come, then, once Lomax gets off, I'll sneak on board and go back to the mainland on it.'

'Yes!' Pepper fist-pumps the air. 'Me too.'

'And me.' Josh grins, then his face falls. 'That's if the boat manages to get here in the first place.'

I glance over the tops of the trees. The sky is grey with low clouds, but there's no sign yet of the storm Mr Bradley predicted.

'Hopefully, the boat will make it back this afternoon before the weather gets too bad,' Josh says. 'We can keep a lookout for it down at the boathouse. You can see the jetty from there.'

'OK.' Feeling better at this thought, I follow the others across the moorland and down through the trees to the boathouse. There is, as Mr Bradley said, a terrible mess outside, with fallen branches blocking the area between the boathouse and the trees. We can only just get through to the door which is hanging off one of its hinges, with much of the equipment and tools from inside scattered beside the entrance. The side of the jetty is just visible in the distance.

'Wow, the storm did *all this*,' Pepper says.

'Samuel must have felt really desperate to have taken the boat when he did,' I say, my anxieties rising up again. 'I hope he's OK.'

'Maybe he didn't run off in a panic, maybe he went to get

help,' Josh suggests. 'Help that could be on its way back here already.'

'Yeah, with Samuel boring the helpers to death with bizarre facts all the way.' Pepper sniffs, then starts dragging a length of stray tarpaulin away from the door.

I bend down to pick up a can of paint. 'If anyone is coming to help us, I hope they get here before the storm comes back.'

'You're not alone, you know, Evie,' Josh says quietly. 'I can see it's what you're used to thinking, but it's not true, not any more. You've got friends.'

I smile gratefully up at him. He isn't as obviously fit as Kit, but he's just as attractive in his way, with his laughing eyes and easy manner. The more time I spend with him, the more I like him. *Really* like him.

Josh and I work at clearing the area around the boathouse door for about ten minutes while Pepper keeps watch in case a boat appears – though we all know it's highly unlikely anything will arrive for another few hours at least. By the time we've piled all the rubbish next to the mess of felled branches that line the space between the boathouse and the trees, the sun has clouded over and the wind is far stronger than before.

'Bradley was definitely right about the storm,' Josh says.

'Yeah,' Pepper says, wandering over. 'There's still no sign of any boats from the mainland, just a load more rubbish on the beach.'

'We could pick some of that up too,' I suggest. 'It might make Bradley more likely to listen to us if he thinks we've been helpful.'

'Good idea,' Josh says.

Pepper doesn't look wildly impressed with this plan, but she follows us down to the shore. After yesterday's high waves, the sea here in Boater's Cove seems tame and gentle, especially now the tide is out, but across the water a bank of dark clouds is massing, threatening rain. I take a bin bag and follow a trail of splintered wood, picking up the smaller pieces and kicking the larger ones to the back of the beach. Behind me, Pepper shrieks as she spots a washed-up jellyfish.

'Ugh, look at that!' she exclaims.

'Oh man,' Josh says, sounding part fascinated, part disgusted.

I keep walking, relieved to have a moment to myself. Boater's Cove beach ends in a line of high, sheer rock. I know, from one of Mr Bradley's previous sessions, that at high tide the water comes right up to the edge and it's impossible to pass. Despite the fact that the tide is as far out as it can go, the thought that it's possible to get cut off from the rest of the island here, just as Josh and I were yesterday, on that other beach, sends a shiver down my spine.

The rock face looks bleaker than I remember along this stretch, with bushes uprooted by yesterday's storm lying scattered across the pebbles. And then I see it – a cave set into the rock. I peer closer. A tin of varnish bobs on a puddle just inside the cave. Except . . . it isn't a puddle. It's the start of a cave pool, similar to the one we found yesterday. A strong gust of wind blows the tin of varnish across the water, further into the cave. It disappears from sight.

Some instinct draws me closer to the entrance. I peer inside.

The cave opens up into a much larger space than I'm expecting, light flickering off the uneven walls. A dark shadow is cast over the water at the far end. I strain my eyes into the gloom, trying to work out what is in here.

My breath hitches in my throat as I realise what is moored just a few metres away in the shadowy depths of the cave. Deliberately hidden from view is the *Aurora*, the island's missing boat.

'Josh! Pepper! Look!' In seconds, they stand beside me. I point into the cave.

'How did that get there?' Josh demands, his eyes wide with shock.

'Well, it didn't just drift,' Pepper exclaims. 'It's been properly moored by someone who knew what they were doing.'

'More to the point,' I say, 'if the boat that Samuel supposedly ran away in is here then where on earth is Samuel?'

Twenty-seven

The *Aurora* bobs about in the depths of the cave pool. Josh, Pepper and I stare at each other. Around us the wind is picking up, tearing through the nearby trees. The sea is louder too, the distant waves crashing onto the stony beach.

'Samuel didn't take the boat to the mainland,' Josh says, his voice hollow.

'Well, somebody moved the *Aurora* from the boathouse to here.' Pepper frowns. 'Do you think that was Samuel?'

'No.' My heart thuds. 'That's not what happened.'

'No,' Josh agrees. 'Samuel wouldn't muck about like that.'

I glance at him, a terrifying thought hitting me like a brick. Could Josh himself have moved the boat? Or Pepper? Or Kit? I gulp. No. Josh saved my life yesterday. Anyway, he and Pepper are my friends. So are Kit and Anna. None of them would want to harm me. This must all be part of Mr Lomax's plan.

'The only possible explanation is that Lomax hurt Samuel because he found out Lomax wants to kill me, then Lomax put the boat here to make it look like Samuel took it.'

'To cover up the fact that he's hurt Samuel,' Josh adds.

'Just like my mum's murder was covered up.' My heart thuds.

There's a long pause. Each of us is lost in our own thoughts.

'Samuel might be worse than hurt.' Pepper digs her hands into her pockets. Her eyes are dark with fear.

The wind whips across my face. Is she right? Is Samuel dead? Could Mr Lomax have killed him?

I follow Josh's gaze to the boat. 'Do you think . . .?' I can't bring myself to ask the question: could Samuel's body be hidden inside the boat.

Josh's face pales as he grasps my meaning.

'I'm going to take a look,' he says, his face grim. He pulls off his outer clothes and slides into the water. He swims across to the *Aurora*. My eyes have adjusted to the gloom enough to see that the boat's engine has been carefully covered with a piece of tarpaulin. Pepper is right: whoever moored the boat knew what they were doing.

'I think the boat's been left here so that whoever stole it can leave the island at high tide,' Pepper said, looking out to sea. 'When the tide comes in, this beach is covered with water. You could sail the boat right out of the cave and off to sea.'

'If you know how to handle a motorboat.' As I speak, a new, terrible realization chills me. 'Mr Bradley must be in on the whole thing,' I say.

Inside the cave pool, Josh reaches the boat and grips the sides with his hands.

Pepper turns to me in horror. 'You're right. Bradley's the expert on boats, plus, he's the one who searched the boathouse and told everyone it was missing,' she says. 'Maybe Loonymax is paying him to carry out your murder. That would explain why he refused to listen to you earlier.'

'And poor Samuel got in the way,' I say. My throat tightens.

Across the pool, Josh hauls himself out of the water far enough to see properly inside the *Aurora*.

'The boat's empty!' His voice echoes around the cave.

'I guess that's something,' Pepper says uneasily.

I shake my head as Josh swims back to the cave entrance. Just because Samuel's body isn't inside the boat doesn't mean he isn't lying dead somewhere else on the island.

I turn away from Pepper, tears pricking at my eyes. This is all my fault. By trying to find out the truth about Irina's death, I've put not just myself but all my friends in terrible danger. I sink down onto the cold pebbles, consumed by guilt and fear.

'Evie?' Pepper gazes down at me, concern in her eyes. 'Are you OK?'

I shake my head as Josh races over. His outer clothes are back on, though he's still shivering, hugging his arms around his chest. I look up at them both.

'We need to get back to the house,' he says.

'But there's no one we can trust,' I say. 'No one who can help us.'

'What about Moncrieff and Buttockbreath?' Pepper argues. 'I think we should tell them everything.'

'No.' Josh and I speak together.

'Why?' Pepper demands.

I stand up. 'If Lomax is paying Bradley, he could be paying the others too,' I explain.

209

'Exactly,' Josh adds. 'I think we should keep quiet to all the staff about finding the *Aurora*.'

'But tell Kit and Anna?' I ask.

He nods.

'Then what?' Pepper looks unconvinced.

'We wait for the storm to pass, then get on the boat from the mainland when it arrives, just like we planned.' Josh's voice is clear and strong over the sound of the wind. 'Once we're away from the island, we can go to the police. Tell them everything.'

'We have to look for Samuel first,' Pepper says. 'He must be somewhere on the island.'

'Yes,' I agree.

'But we need to stick together,' Josh adds. 'No one on their own at any time. Especially Evie, it's too risk—'

The end of his sentence is drowned out by a huge clap of thunder. It makes all three of us jump.

I peer out to sea. The waves are higher than earlier, their white edges curling and smashing against the navy water. The smudged grey lines on the horizon mean it's raining hard out at sea.

'That looks like a *massive* storm,' Pepper says. 'Coming directly for us.'

'Which means no boat from the mainland today.' My heart sinks. How on earth are we going to survive another twenty-four hours here?

'Don't worry,' Josh says. 'We'll get through this.'

I nod, but inside I don't feel at all confident.

We hurry back to the boathouse as the first fat drops of rain began to fall. Mr Bradley, Kit and Anna arrive just as we reach the pile of rubbish we collected earlier. Mr Bradley is brusque, ordering us straight back to the house – though he does comment that Josh, Pepper and I have done a good job tidying up.

I try to catch Kit's eye on the way back to the house. I want to tell him about finding the *Aurora* – and our plan to escape the island. But he avoids my gaze, striding on ahead with Mr Bradley. At least Pepper is walking arm in arm with Anna, whispering a warning in *her* ear.

Why is Kit being so horrible? He got all cross this morning, then sneered when I tried to tell Mr Bradley my suspicions. Now he's back to ignoring me, like he did when we first arrived on the island. I glance at Josh. He's hurrying along the moorland beside me, hunched over against the rain. He senses me looking and smiles. It's a lovely smile – not full-lipped and gleaming-toothed like Kit's, but warm and friendly. Well, not just friendly . . . there's something about the way his lips turn up in that slightly crooked way that is, if I'm honest . . .

No, I'm not going to think that.

We reach Lightsea House. I'm afraid Mr Bradley might ask about my suspicions again, but he doesn't mention the conversation we had earlier, simply muttering something about checking the storm drains and disappearing around the corner.

The rest of us go inside and take off our damp jackets and boots. Rain teems against the windows; low rumbles of thunder sound in the distance. As I shove my boots against the wall, Kit comes over.

'Evie, can I talk to you?'

I look into his hazel eyes. I expect his expression to register anger or maybe a repeat of his earlier scepticism. But all I see is misery. I stare at him, feeling confused. But before I can say anything Mrs Moncrieff is bustling into the hall to tell us that lunch will be ready in twenty minutes.

'We're a bit behind, so I need Pepper, Josh and Kit in the kitchen,' she says. '*Now*, please.'

'*Later*,' Kit mouths. I nod.

'What about me and Evie?' Anna asks.

Mrs Moncrieff frowns. 'I suggest you make sure that all the windows on the ground floor are properly fastened against the storm, then come into the kitchen yourselves for lunch.'

She bustles off with Kit. Pepper follows them, grumbling loudly.

'Stay with Anna,' Josh says. He gives me an anxious look. 'Don't go anywhere by yourself. And don't stay out here too long.'

'Don't worry,' Anna says. 'Miss Bunnock is outside with Mr Bradley. I just saw them through the window. We'll be OK for a bit.'

Josh nods, but still hesitates.

'Go on,' I urge him. 'I'll be along in a minute.'

As Josh leaves, Anna gives a nervous cough. 'Pepper told me about you finding the *Aurora*. I can't believe it, I'm so worried about Samuel.' Her face is pale. 'I definitely want to come with you when you get off the island. If we haven't found Samuel by then, we need to call his parents . . . and the police.'

I glance out of the window. The trees are going berserk in the wind. 'Good, but it's not going to be today,' I said. 'There's no way any boat will get through from the mainland in this weather.' Panic rises inside me again. What on earth have Lomax and Bradley done with Samuel? How are we all going to stay safe until we escape?

Anna clears her throat. 'Er . . . Mrs Moncrieff said we should check the windows, remember?' she stammers. 'I know Josh said to stick together, but we'll be faster if we split up.'

I nod my agreement though, in truth, I'm hardly following what she's saying. Properly fastened windows seem a very low priority right now.

'Why don't you do the windows in the two rooms closest to the kitchen, so you're near the others?' Anna suggests. 'I'll do the rest, then join you.'

'Will you be OK?' I ask.

'Course I will,' Anna says. 'It's you who needs to be careful.'

She throws me a nervous smile, then scuttles away along the corridor. I hurry in the other direction. The two rooms nearest the kitchen are, for once, unlocked. I dart in and out of an old, unused dining room, complete with worn wood table and chairs that were once probably plush, but whose upholstery is now as faded and threadbare as one of Mr Lomax's jumpers. I check all the windows are properly fastened, then move next door. This room looks like it was once some kind of parlour from, like, a hundred years ago, with two stiff-backed armchairs set on either side of an empty fireplace.

'Evie?'

I spin round.

Kit's is standing in the doorway, an expression of unbearable hurt on his face.

'Hi,' I say, immediately flustered. 'Er, aren't you supposed to be in the kitchen?' Panic seizes me. Is it possible Kit is in on the whole plot to kill me after all?

'I snuck out.' Kit moves across the room until he is right in front of me.

I back away, my heart racing.

'I had to see you,' he says. 'I'm so sorry I was such an idiot earlier.'

My mouth gapes. His expression is full of remorse. I'm certain he doesn't mean me any harm. Relief washes over me as he reaches for my hand. I let him take it.

'Josh just told me you found the *Aurora* which means something really weird is going on and no one knows where Samuel is, but obviously he hasn't left the island so that's bad and . . . and I shouldn't have been so dismissive about it all earlier.' He draws me closer and the blood pounds in my ears. 'I was jealous,' Kit goes on. 'I can see you like Josh, and he's cool and talented at music which you love, and all I can do is run fast and help win rugby matches, and I don't know what you'd see in me because I'm useless at talking, especially about things that really matter – which you do, Evie, you really matter to me, but I've screwed everything up and did I say that I'm sorry for being an idiot?'

He hugs me. I close my eyes, feeling safe for the first time

214

in hours with his strong arms holding me tight. Kit's face is centimetres from mine.

'Please still be mine,' he whispers.

I reach up and let our kiss flow through me. For a moment, all I am is in that kiss, then we pull apart and the turmoil in my head surges up again.

'I don't know what else to say,' Kit mumbles. 'I hate myself for not knowing what to say. I'm just really, really sorry and—'

'Shh.' I put my finger on his lips. 'I think you said it all very well.'

'Do you?' Kit's face brightens. 'So are we OK?'

I think of Josh and his crooked smile and the way our lips brushed together after yesterday's escape. And I think of Pepper's question: *Which of them do you like? Kit or Josh?* And how I haven't been sure about the answer. And then I look up into Kit's beautiful, eager eyes, at the green flecks and the dark lashes. And I know that right now I want him just as much as I wanted Josh earlier.

Which makes no sense.

'We're OK,' I say.

Kit beams, then kisses me swiftly again. 'I'd better get back to the kitchen,' he says. 'And don't worry. Lunch is in, like, ten minutes and after that I'm not letting you out of my sight.'

He disappears. I turn back to the window and absently reach for the catch to check that it's locked. Rain lashes against the glass. Somehow the storm outside reflects the turbulence inside my head. I gaze through the window across the scrubby grass to the patch of woodland beyond. The rain is thick, driving into the ground, the wind tearing through the trees. All of a sudden, a flash of red appears between the branches. I freeze. As I strain my eyes, desperate, a figure in a long black coat and a red hat darts onto the moorland. She spins around, head bowed, so I can't see her face.

It's the ghost. Something dangles on ribbons from her outstretched hands. My chest constricts as I realise what she is holding, what she must have somehow taken from under my pillow:

Irina's ballet shoes.

Twenty-eight

For a few seconds, I watch, frozen to the spot, as Irina's ghost dances from side to side in front of the distant trees. Her back is turned to the window and, thanks to the length of the black coat, I can't make out her shape, but she moves elegantly, toes pointed, just like in the *Giselle* DVD.

Rain pounds against the window and onto the grass outside. In front of the trees, the ghost rises up on tiptoes, arms outstretched, the ballet shoes swinging in the wind. She darts into the copse, running from one tree to the next. For a moment, she disappears and I lean forward, pressing my forehead against the cold glass, desperate for another glimpse. *There.* I can just see the red hat – and the twirling of a ballet shoe. She's still there, between the trees.

She is waiting for me, I'm sure of it.

I turn and race across the room. Out into the corridor, along the hall. I grab my jacket – there isn't time to put it on. Still wearing my thin pumps, I throw open the front door and pelt outside. The rain drives into my face, huge, fierce drops on my back and legs, the stone paving rough through my thin soles. I tear across the grass towards the trees where I saw the ghost. There's no sign of her. My heart is in my mouth, all thoughts of Samuel's disappearance and Mr Lomax's plot against me buried deep inside, all my confused feelings about Josh and Kit forgotten.

All I can think about is finding Irina's ghost . . . finding my real mother at last.

'Where are you?' I dart into the trees. A flash of red to my left. I hurry after it, tugging on my jacket as I run. On through the woodland. I'm sheltered from the worst of the rain in here, but my feet are battered and bruised from the stones on the ground. I don't dare stop.

If I stop, she might think I don't care enough to go after her.

I follow the ghost blindly, through trees, across patches of scrub, round bushes. I lose all sense of where I am on the island. My feet are frozen lumps of ice on the ends of my legs. Every time I think I've lost her, she appears again, winding her way further and further away from the house.

'Irina!' I call. '*Mum!*'

But she never turns around.

On I run. I have no idea for how long. The ghost is always ahead of me. Uncatchable. I race through a thick clump of trees then all of a sudden burst out on to a wide expanse of rock.

It's wet from the rain and the spray that shoots up from the sea below. The ghost is here. Right in front of me. As I dart towards her, she slips. Falls. Two more steps and my feet in their slippery pumps give way too. I lose my balance and crash with a painful thud onto the hard stone. The ghost rises. I hurl myself at her. Push her down.

My heart hammers, my throat is tight with fear.

I can feel her arm through the black coat.

This is no spirit.

Panting, I force her to turn round. I stare and stare at her face.

Not Irina. Not my long-lost, beautiful birth mother. Not a ghost at all.

It's Anna.

I get up. She stands shivering, buffeted by the wind and the spray, the red hat soaked through, the dark coat flapping about her legs.

I can't believe it.

Not Irina. Just a pale-faced, anxious-looking Anna. I'm still staring at her, my mind reeling, as she pulls off the hat, letting her soft curls tumble onto her shoulders. The rain hammers down. Neither of us speak. My hair is plastered to my face, my feet numb with cold, my clothes damp against my skin. The edge of the rock is a few metres away. The water below rages and crashes against vicious crags that poke up from the waves. Anyone who fell from here would either be dashed to death or swept out to sea in an instant. I have never been here before, but I recognise the place immediately from Lomax's and Bradley's descriptions.

This is Easter Rock, the most dangerous place on Lightsea Island.

This is where Irina died. This is where she was pushed into the sea.

'You,' I gasp.

Anna hangs her head. She takes Irina's ballet shoes from her pocket and holds them out to me. She doesn't meet my eyes. 'I took them from under your pillow,' she says. 'I'm sorry.'

Dazed, I take the shoes. The wind drives the drizzle into my face, stabbing at my skin.

'What do you think you're doing, dressing up as my mum's ghost? Oh . . .' I suck in my breath as the full realization strikes me. 'Oh . . . it's been you *all along*?' Anna looks up. She says nothing, but the guilty look in her eye tells me it's true.

'*Why?*' The word sounds strangled.

'It's just an experiment . . .' Anna begins.

'*What?*'

'Girls.' Miss Bunnock's voice echoes towards us. She emerges through the trees. 'What on earth . . .? Get over here now.'

Anna turns and walks towards her, shrunk down inside the black coat. I follow, still barely able to process what has happened. Irina's ballet shoes dangle from my hands. Misery roils inside me, great waves of it.

There is no ghost. My mother's spirit hasn't come to me.

I have lost her before I even found her.

The pain of it fills me.

'I don't understand,' I gasp, ignoring Miss Bunnock.

'Get back to the house, Anna,' Miss Bunnock orders.

I barely register how tense Bunnock looks or how odd it is that she's only sending Anna away. I'm still trying to deal with what has just happened.

'I don't understand,' I stammer again, tears pricking at my eyes.

Miss Bunnock opens her mouth, then shuts it again.

'I'm sorry,' Anna says, her voice barely audible over the crashing waves. I assume she's talking to me, but when I glance across she is looking up at Bunnock.

Why is she apologizing to her?

'Go,' Bunnock orders.

Without looking at me again, Anna races off, into the trees, the black coat streaming out behind her.

Bunnock grabs my arm. Before I know what's happening, she has dragged me out onto the rock. The rain is fiercer out here, away from the shelter of the trees.

I stumble, resisting. 'What are you doing?'

'Shut up,' Bunnock snaps. 'Get over to the edge.'

What? I stare at her, shocked out of my piercing misery. Rain streams down around us; the roar of the wind and the waves fills the air. 'You *knew* Anna was pretending to be my mum's ghost,' I breathe. 'You *knew* she's been tricking me since we arrived here?'

'Yes.' Miss Bunnock meets my gaze. Her eyes are like steel pellets. 'Of course.'

My mouth gapes.

'I got Anna onto the Lightsea course. She was instructed to fool you, just as she was told to appear open to the idea of ghosts when the subject came up and to make sure that you saw the photocopy of the newspaper article that I mocked up and left in the back of the library book.'

'That was *made up*?' My stomach feels like it's falling away. 'You went to all those lengths to make me think my

221

mum was here as a ghost, that she died on the island? For some stupid experiment? *What* experiment?' A sob rises inside me. '*Why?*'

'I'm afraid I'm not at liberty to explain why and there weren't really so many lengths,' Miss Bunnock says with a sigh. 'Apart from the article and Anna's appearances as the ghost, all I did was hide a photo of your mother in Mr Lomax's office when I knew, thanks to Anna overhearing you and reporting back, that you were going to break into it and look for clues.' She pauses. 'Your imagination and desire to make contact with your dead mother did the rest.'

'What about the knife?' I demand. 'Did you put that under my pillow?'

Bunnock nods.

'Why?'

She tightens her grip on my arm, ignoring my question. 'Move,' she orders.

I try to pull away, but she yanks me back, closer to the edge of the rock.

'What are you doing?' Panic fills me. 'Let me go.'

Bunnock grits her teeth. She hurls me round, pushing me right to the edge. I teeter on the stone, my pumps slipping. And in that moment it suddenly makes sense: the knife left to make it look like I might want to hurt myself, the encouragement to believe in Irina's ghost, the story about her dying right here, at Easter Rock.

For reasons which I don't understand, Miss Bunnock wants to kill me, and make it look like I have committed suicide by falling from the place where I believe my own mother died.

My mouth opens to accuse her and she gives me a final shove. My arms windmill. My hands grasp air.

With a scream, I lose my balance and fall backwards.

Twenty-nine

For a single, terrifying second, I think I'm going to fall off the rock and into the dark sea beneath. Then my fingers latch onto the cloth of Bunnock's jacket. I grip it with a strength I didn't know I had. Roaring, I haul myself up, push Bunnock away from me and run. Across the rock, my feet threatening to slide out from under me with every step. Then into the trees.

I'm gasping, wet through, as I race through the wood. I can hear Bunnock calling out behind me.

'Come here!' she yells.

I run on. Anna darts out from behind a tree. What is she still doing here? Furious, I try to duck past her to get to the path.

'No, Evie," she whispers. 'This way. Bunnock will see you on the path.' She turns and heads into the dense bushes opposite.

She's right, though I hate to admit it. I hesitate a second, then hurry after her. We're instantly hidden from view. I can hear Bunnock stomping over the fallen twigs and leaves that are strewn across the ground.

Anna puts her hand to her lips.

'Evie!' Bunnock calls out.

I hold my breath. Rain drums down.

Bunnock's footsteps crash about, then fade away. She's gone, for now.

'I swear I didn't know she wanted to kill you,' Anna whispers, her face pale and her eyes wide and scared. 'I honestly thought it was some kind of experiment, to see how you'd respond if you thought your birth mum was haunting you.'

'That's some sick experiment,' I hiss at her, fury rising inside me. 'Josh and I nearly died when we followed you along the beach. And anyway . . .'

I can't put into words just how cruel a trick it has been.

'I know.' Tears fill Anna's eyes. 'I'm so, so sorry.'

'I bet your mum isn't even dead, is she?'

Anna shakes her head.

'Bitch.' The word shoots out of me. 'Why did you do it?'

'Miss Bunnock said it was part of my "Lightsea experience" and that I'd be in trouble if I didn't,' Anna says.

I stare at her. Is that true? Anna certainly looks genuinely upset. It doesn't matter. *Nothing* justifies making me think Irina's spirit was here, trying to contact me. *Nothing* makes up for the desolation of knowing that there never was a ghost. Which means there is no history of my mother on the island.

I frown. In which case, there is no cover up and I must have been wrong about Lomax wanting me dead.

'Are you sure Bunnock never said why she wants to hurt me?' I ask.

'I told you, I didn't know she *did* want to hurt you.'

I stand up. There's no sign of Miss Bunnock, though the

225

rain is falling as heavily as ever and the wind is picking up too. 'I don't believe you,' I say.

I crawl away, out of the bushes. Anna follows.

'Go away,' I tell her.

'Where are you going?' Anna asks. 'Let me help—'

'Go away,' I repeat.

'But—'

I turn and run into the trees. I run hard, quickly leaving Anna behind. I don't know where I am on the island. Or where I should go next. I run blindly on, thoughts careering around my head: about the ghost, how I was fooled, why on earth Bunnock wants me dead, that Samuel tried to warn me.

I stop dead.

Samuel. He must have found out what Bunnock was planning – some of it at least; that's how he knew I was in danger. Rain trickles down my face. In a daze, I wipe it out of my eyes.

Without warning, a hand grabs my arm.

Yelping, I tug away. It's Bunnock. Her grip on my forearm is fierce, like a vice.

'No!' I shout.

'Quiet!' she orders. She twists my arm. A sharp pain shoots through me. 'Now move!' She gives me a hard push.

A cold shiver trickles down my spine as I stumble on. Could Bunnock have hurt Samuel? Her grip on my arm never loosens as she hurries me through the trees. Another few seconds and I recognise where I am: just a few metres from the boathouse where Josh, Pepper and I were clearing up earlier. We reach the edge of the wood. Rain lashes down, soaking me through. My damp clothes cling to my skin, my hair sticks to my face.

Pain from my arm sears through me. I stagger onto the boathouse path. Footsteps sound behind us, crunching over the twigs and stones. Without warning, I'm yanked sideways, hurled to the ground. I fall heavily, damp earth on my face . . . in my mouth.

Spluttering, I scramble to my feet. Pepper is here. Josh too.

'Stay back,' Josh urges. He and Pepper rush at Miss Bunnock. Which is when I see the gun in her hand.

'Stop right there,' she snaps.

Josh and Pepper freeze. I stare at the gun. It must be the same one that Samuel saw. Which makes it even more certain that Bunnock has done something to him. Before I can form this thought into words, Bunnock grabs hold of Pepper and swings her round, twisting her arm so high up her back that Pepper screams in pain.

'Another step and I break her arm.' Bunnock's voice is ice-cold. I have no doubt that she means what she says.

Josh and I exchange a look, then he backs away.

'Over there.' Bunnock points her gun towards the boathouse. 'Inside!'

Josh and I hurry along the path, Miss Bunnock and Pepper right behind. Josh's hair and jacket drip with rain.

'What the hell is going on?' he murmurs in my ear. 'I thought it was Lomax who was after you. What is Bunnock doing? D'you think that's the same gun Samuel wrote about

227

in his notebook?' He pauses. 'Evie, d'you know what's happened to him?'

I shake my head.

'Hurry up!' Miss Bunnock barks.

'You can't do this,' Pepper insists. I can hear the pain in her voice. 'You can't kidnap people at gunpoint. Why are you—?'

'Shut up.' There is something so cold, so menacing about the way Miss Bunnock speaks that Pepper instantly falls silent.

'How did you and Josh find us?' Miss Bunnock asks angrily as we reach the door. I snatch a quick glance behind me. She's still twisting Pepper's arm high up her back, the gun tightly gripped in her other hand. There's no way Josh and I can overpower her without risking Pepper's life.

'We were looking for Evie,' Pepper says.

'And when we don't go back everyone at the house will notice,' Josh adds.

Bunnock doesn't react to this at all.

I bite my lip. Suppose *all* the adults are in on the plot? Just because Lomax isn't covering up a murder doesn't mean he isn't somehow in league with Bunnock over wanting me dead.

'Inside,' Bunnock orders.

Josh opens the boathouse door. I follow him through, out of the rain. The boathouse smells damp. Across the room, the expanse of water that lies open to the sea is choppy. I stare at where the boat used to be, where Kit and I worked together. Water slaps at the walls, echoing around the room.

'What have you done to Samuel?' I demand.

Bunnock ignores me. 'Through there.' She points to an

228

alcove beside the big store cupboard where I've seen Mr Bradley store tins of varnish and brushes. Before it was covered with old cloths. Now these have been pulled away, revealing a trapdoor set into the wooden floor. The iron ring that opens it is padlocked to the ground.

I glance anxiously at Bunnock. She lets go of Pepper's arm, but keeps a tight hold of her gun. She tosses a set of keys at me. 'Undo the padlock and go down the steps.'

I crouch down and fit the key into the padlock. It turns with a click. Hands shaking, I remove the lock and lay it on the wooden floor at Miss Bunnock's feet.

'Help her lift the door,' Miss Bunnock orders.

Josh bends down and together we haul the trapdoor open.

A ladder extends into a gloomy cellar. It's totally dark down there. Once the trapdoor shuts over our heads, we won't be able to see our hands in front of our faces.

'You can't send us down there without any light,' Pepper insists.

'What about food? Or water?' Josh adds.

'And you still haven't told us what you've done to Samuel,' I say.

'Enough,' Miss Bunnock snaps.

I swing my leg over the hole and feel for the top rung. My palms are sweating as I descend into the darkness. I reach the stone floor at the bottom and look around. It's a large room, empty as far as I can see, apart from a table near the ladder set with a candle lamp. Beside the lamp are a box of matches, a large bottle of water and a loaf of bread.

My fingers shake as I take a match and light the lamp. It casts ghostly shadows over the walls which flicker as Josh and Pepper climb down. As Pepper reaches the ground, the trapdoor shuts with a thud. Above our heads the padlock is clicked into position.

'What the hell is Bunnock *doing*?' Pepper exclaims.

'She's going to kill me,' I say flatly. 'She used Anna. I think someone is paying her. Possibly Lomax. Maybe all of them.' I'm trying to sound brave, but my voice trembles.

Pepper shakes her head. 'I don't get it,' she says. 'If they're *all* in on it then why the subterfuge? It doesn't make any sense.'

'It doesn't make sense anyway,' Josh points out. 'Why do they want Evie dead?' He takes the lamp and walks across the cellar, lighting each corner in turn.

It's soon obvious that apart from the table and its contents the cellar is empty, save for a heap of tarpaulin in one corner. The lamp casts sinister shadows as Josh sets it down on the table.

'What was that?' Pepper grabs my arm.

I follow her pointing finger to the tarpaulin in the corner.

'Oh man,' Josh says.

'What?' I ask.

And then I see it myself: the tarpaulin is moving.

Thirty

The three of us jump back, away from the tarpaulin. Josh puts out his arm, his hand reaching for mine. Even in the midst of my terror, I feel a glow that his first thought is for me, to make sure I'm safe.

'Who's there?' Pepper demands.

And then the tarpaulin rears up and Samuel emerges.

My whole body sags with relief. Josh squeezes my hand. I squeeze back, then remember Kit and let go as Samuel scrambles to his feet.

'Man, you gave us a fright,' Josh says.

Samuel nods. 'I was hiding under the covering,' he says unnecessarily. He's shivering – though with cold or fear I can't tell. He has always seemed younger than the rest of us. Now he looks about six years old. I rush over and put my arms round him. He stands, letting me hug him, though not hugging back.

'Miss Bunnock wants to kill you, Evie,' he squeaks, his teeth chattering. 'I tried to warn you. I found out, but now she wants to kill me too.' He peers over my shoulder at Josh and Pepper. 'She'll want to kill you as well. That will be at least twice the average number of UK murders in one day.'

'I don't understand,' Pepper snaps. 'What the hell is

Buttockbreath doing with a gun, ordering us into a pigging cellar and trying to kill us?'

'Let's sit down,' I suggest.

Josh nods. He helps me lead Samuel back to the tarpaulin. I settle Samuel in the corner, drawing the rough tarpaulin over his shoulders. Josh brings the bottle of water and the loaf of bread. Neither looks as if it's been touched, yet Samuel has been missing for nearly a whole day.

'Have you been down here since last night?' I ask. 'Have you eaten anything?'

'Yes to your first question and no to the second,' Samuel says solemnly. 'Did you know you can survive three days without water and three weeks without food?'

Josh tears a chunk off the loaf. He hands it to Samuel. 'Never mind three weeks, you need to eat. Now tell us what happened,' he says. 'From the beginning.'

Samuel settles himself back against the wall with a sigh. 'OK, well, the first thing – one – was that I found a gun yesterday morning when I was coming back from my one-to-one with Mr Lomax, along with a picture of a woman who looked like Evie.'

'That was the photo Bunnock switched with the knife,' I explain. 'The photo of my birth mum.'

'Yes, I worked that out,' Samuel says proudly.

'*Bunnock's* gun?' Pepper wrinkles her nose.

'Yes,' says Samuel.

'We found your notebook, Samuel,' I say, exchanging looks with Josh. 'You don't say it's Bunnock's gun there.'

232

'I didn't know it was her gun then.' Samuel pauses. 'You said to start from the beginning.'

'OK, sorry, go on,' I say.

'So I found the gun and the photo, and I remembered Josh and Kit arguing about Evie and her ghost and how she thought there was this cover-up of her mum's murder, so I thought about it logically and if the two things were connected then the gun must be to kill Evie to keep her quiet.'

'Which was true,' I said.

'But then I thought the gun was Mr Lomax's because *that's* who Evie said was covering up the murder.'

'Which was wrong,' Josh says.

'Right,' Samuel says.

'What did you do next?' I ask, my eyes intent on Samuel's face, pale in the lamplight.

'I came to warn you.'

'So that was what you meant when you saw me in the hall yesterday morning and said you had something important to tell me later?' I ask.

'Yes, but then Miss Bunnock called me for chores before I could say anything, so instead I decided to explain to her, so that she would understand and come and warn you herself. That was "two".'

'But instead she kidnapped you?' Pepper snarls.

'Not at first,' Samuel says. 'Miss Bunnock made me show her the gun and she said it was just a pretend one that didn't even work and that she didn't know who the photo was of but it couldn't be anything important and that she'd ask Mr Lomax about the gun and that I shouldn't say anything to anybody about it as it might frighten them. And she stayed near me the whole time, except once when Mr Lomax called her away for something which was when I snuck the photo upstairs and wrote in my notebook and left them both in the hiding place in the bedroom. And I still would've told Evie, but—'

'But we'd gone missing by then,' Josh says.

'Exactly. And then later, after going-to-bed time, when everyone was asleep, I woke up and Miss Bunnock was pressing some bit of cloth down on my face, and it smelled odd, and then I don't remember anything until I woke up here, in the boathouse. Which was "three".'

'Whoa,' Pepper whistles.

Josh shakes his head. Hearing Samuel explain everything so matter-of-factly somehow makes it sound even worse. I feel in my jacket pocket for the shoes. In all the turmoil, I forgot I have them back now. It's reassuring to touch their soft leather.

'Wait a minute!' Pepper's eyes widen and she throws up her arms. 'You must have been here while we were outside this morning . . . me, Evie and Josh, clearing the rubbish from the storm outside the boathouse door.'

'Yes, I could hear you, but I was tied up so I couldn't shout or anything. That was "four". Miss Bunnock came down after you went and untied me so I could eat. She said that now I know about her being involved she can't kill Evie the original way . . .'

'By luring me to Easter Rock, pushing me off and making it look like I jumped,' I mutter. 'That's why she put the knife

234

under my pillow, so that Mr Lomax and everyone would think I wanted to top myself.'

'Anyway, now she's probably going to find a new way to kill you,' Samuel continues. 'And she's going to kill me at the same time.'

'Oh man.' Josh lets out a long, jagged breath. 'What do we do now?'

'We have to get out of here.' Pepper jumps to her feet, a look of determination on her face.

Josh looks around the cellar. 'The only way out is through the trapdoor.'

'That won't work,' Pepper says. 'Did you see the size of that padlock?'

'So . . .' I take a deep breath. 'Our situation is that we have no weapons, no tools and no way of getting out of the cellar.'

'Yeah, thanks for putting such a positive spin on it,' Pepper grumbles.

'We've got to shout,' I say. 'Think about it. The others are going to wonder where we are soon. They'll come looking for us.'

'Suppose Anna or Buttockbreath tells them some lie about where we are?' Pepper says.

'Suppose the others are in on it?' Josh adds darkly. 'Bradley is probably involved, maybe even Moncrieff. And we can't be sure about Kit either.'

'Kit isn't involved,' I say.

'How do you know?' Josh asked.

My thoughts drift to the way Kit looked at me earlier, the

way he kissed me. He's surely the last person who would want me to come to any harm. I look up, into Josh's enquiring eyes. My cheeks burn. 'Kit just wouldn't,' I say.

'Even if no one else is involved, it's possible Buttockbreath will hear us before anyone else does.' Pepper groans. 'Then she'll gag us on top of everything else. What a cow. I never liked that woman.'

'All that's true, but as shouting is our only chance we might as well give it a try,' Josh says.

No one can think of anything to say to that, so I clap my hands together to get us started.

'Everyone together,' I urge. 'One . . . two . . . three . . . HELP!' I yell as loudly as I can, the others joining in.

'Again.' Josh scrambles to his feet, pulling me up beside him. 'One . . . two . . . three . . . HELP!'

The four of us shout until our lungs burn with the effort. But no one comes.

'We should time it, space it out,' Josh says. 'Otherwise, we'll have no voices left. Every couple of minutes or so, we yell.'

'I'll keep the count,' Samuel says. 'I'm good at counting in my head.'

An hour or so passes. Then another. And another. It's hard to keep track of time, though from the sounds of wind and rain that reach us through the walls it's obvious the storm has been building up again. The sea will be at high tide now. I can just picture huge waves crashing against the cliffs and over the dark rocks that stick up out of the water.

The candle burns about a quarter of the way down inside

236

the lamp. In spite of Josh's plan to stagger our yells and Samuel's careful counting, we're all growing hoarse and the bread and water are gone.

'It must be night by now,' I muse. 'Do you think there's any chance a boat's made it here from the mainland?'

'No way,' Pepper says. 'The storm's too bad. I've done a lot of sailing on my dad's yacht and there's no way any ordinary boat would set out in a sea like that unless it was a total emergency.'

'Oh man.' Josh catches his breath. 'Bunnock could be back any second.'

There's a long pause.

'I don't want to die,' Samuel says.

'Me neither,' I say.

Into the silence that falls, a set of footsteps sounds above our heads. Josh and I exchange worried glances. Is that Miss Bunnock coming back for us?

I hold my breath as the padlock releases with a click and the trapdoor slowly opens.

Broken Dawn

Thirty-one

Kit's face appears in the trapdoor opening: glistening with rain, as handsome as ever.

'Evie?' He squints into the gloom of the cellar.

'I'm here,' I say, rushing out of the shadows so that I'm directly under the trapdoor. 'We're all here. How did you find us?'

'Anna told me everything,' he says.

'What?' I freeze.

'Where is she?' Pepper peers up at Kit.

'We can't trust her,' Josh adds.

'I'm here.' Anna's voice echoes down the ladder.

Josh and Pepper look at me in alarm.

'We *can* trust her,' Kit insists. 'She told me where you were and about pretending to be the ghost. *And* she helped me get the key to this padlock from where Bunnock keeps it. I can't believe what Bunnock—'

'We can talk later. Come on, guys, let's go.' Pepper is already on the ladder. She clambers up and disappears through the hole above our heads as Josh ushers Samuel to the bottom rung. Samuel slowly, anxiously makes the climb.

'You next, Evie,' Josh says. He puts his hand on my back

and my heart gives a little skip. Then I remember Kit is at the top of the ladder and a wave of guilt washes over me. Pushing it away, I hurry after Samuel.

Kit is kneeling by the trapdoor. As Samuel scrambles out, Kit reaches for me, helping me up the last step and onto my feet. He pulls me into a huge hug. His arms are strong around my back, his damp cheek cool against mine. Outside the wind howls, louder here than it was in the cellar. Rain lashes on the boathouse roof. There's a huge crash as something heavy thuds to the ground.

'Sounds like a tree falling,' Anna says, looking worried.

Kit pulls me tighter. 'Thank goodness you're all right,' he breathes into my ear. 'Anna was practically hysterical when she found me, said Miss Bunnock was about to kill you. What's going on?'

'I'm so sorry, Evie.' Anna is hopping up and down beside me.

I extricate myself from Kit in order to look at her. Her pretty face is creased with misery, her eyes red-rimmed from crying.

'Please forgive me,' Anna babbles on. 'Miss Bunnock said it was like . . . like a psychological experiment and . . . and I didn't think it would mean anything. I had no idea she was going to try and kill you or Samuel.'

'She's trying to kill *all* of us actually,' Pepper says with feeling.

'And she could come back at any moment,' Josh adds as he climbs out too. 'We need to get out of here.'

242

'He's right,' I say.

'Let's go then,' says Kit.

The wind whips round our heads as we emerge into the fading light outside. Rain tears at our faces. The path ahead of us is completely blocked by a fallen tree.

'Oh no!' Anna whimpers. 'That's the tree we just heard.'

'Try and get past it,' Pepper urges.

But the way through to the rest of the island is completely cut off. The rain pounds down as the six of us pull at the branches, trying in vain to clear the track.

'It's no good,' Kit says, panting with the effort.

'Maybe we can go along the beach.' Josh sets off, the rest of us following. We squeeze past the debris we collected earlier, down to the pebble-strewn beach. The white-tipped waves smash and suck at the stones. It's instantly obvious that the beach with its high cliffs is as impassable as the path.

'We're trapped,' Pepper says, her voice hollow.

Rain teems down, plastering our hair to our heads and our clothes to our skin.

'At least if we can't get out then Bunnock can't get through to us either,' Kit reasons.

'She'll just go back and fetch Bradley to help her cut through the branches so she *can* reach us,' Pepper says bitterly.

'Yeah, and if Bradley isn't in on the whole thing she'll kill him along with the rest of us,' I add.

'Surely, when she realises we've disappeared, Mrs Moncrieff will do something,' Anna says. 'I'm certain she doesn't know anything about—'

'No way.' Pepper snorts. 'Even if she's not involved, Mrs Moncrieff would be about as much use against Bradley and Buttockbreath as one of her cucumbers.'

'So where do we go?' Kit asks.

Josh peers along the beach, now covered with water, to the cave where we found the *Aurora* earlier. He turns and meets my gaze.

'What about the boat?' he suggests. 'We found it hidden along the beach earlier. We can swim round, sail it out of the cave and get to a safer bit of the island. Then we moor the boat and hide until the storm passes.'

'Yes!' Pepper's eyes light up. 'Genius.'

I gulp, thinking of the dangerous water between us and the cave and my own inability to swim.

'But the storm is *really* bad,' Kit says doubtfully. 'Plus, none of us know how to handle a motorboat,' he adds. 'Unless Samuel actually does, like they said?'

Everyone looks at Samuel. He shakes his head.

'I went out in a rowing boat once,' I say uncertainly. 'But there's no way I could operate something like the *Aurora*.'

'Don't worry about it,' Pepper drawls. 'I've been in boats like that millions of times. My dad *has* one for goodness' sake. I've watched him sailing it loads of times. How hard can it be? I'm sure I could do it.'

Kit looks at me. 'What do you think, Evie?'

I glance from face to face, at Anna, riddled with shame and fear, at Samuel, cowering against the boathouse wall, at Pepper, chin jutting out, defiant and confident, and at Josh, whose eyes meet mine with an intensity that makes me shiver. Then I turn back to Kit.

'If we stay here then Bunnock and Bradley will find us. I think using the boat is our only chance,' I say. 'So we'd better take it.'

Thirty-two

'You're saying we have to swim to the cave with the boat?' Anna asks, paling.

Rain streams down my face. I'm already trembling at the prospect of having to attempt the crossing.

'It's not too dangerous if we stay close to the shore,' Pepper says. 'The underwater rocks are all further out to sea; we just have to be careful of the current.'

Josh looks at me. I can tell he's remembering that I can't swim.

'We don't all need to go,' he says softly. 'Two of us will be enough. We can bring the boat back for everyone else.'

'I'll go with Pepper.' Kit crouches down and begins undoing his bootlaces.

'No, I'll do it,' Josh says. 'I'm a good swimmer and I've been there before.'

'But I'm stronger than you,' Kit argues. 'I won the two hundred and the four hundred-metre freestyle races at my school and—'

'This isn't a pigging race,' Josh snaps. 'And it isn't about showing off either.'

Kit stiffens. Clenching his fists, he moves right in front of Josh. 'I'm not showing off, I'm just—'

'Enough!' Pepper shouts. 'We can't afford to waste time on some macho who-can-impress-Evie-the-most contest.'

My cheeks burn. The rain stings my face as I turn away into the wind.

'I say Josh comes with me because he knows exactly where we're going,' Pepper goes on, ignoring my embarrassment. 'We'll pick up the rest of you in the boat.'

I sigh with relief.

'But—' Kit starts.

'Shut up, Kit,' Pepper snaps. 'Just be a hero and help the others swim out to where we'll pick you up.'

Swim out? I glance at Josh.

'Can't we bring the boat up to the shore?' he asks. 'Or round to the boathouse?'

Pepper stares at him as if he was mad. 'It'll take twice as long to get to the boathouse and it's too shallow to bring the boat close to the shore.' She points to a spot about three metres out into the bay. 'The others will have to meet us there, in the water. It's not far and there aren't any hidden rocks, you just have to be careful of the current.'

I gaze out to sea. Even in the bay, the waves are choppy and restless. My blood chills as I imagine the cold of the sea, the way the tide might suck me under. I look up. Josh is watching me, his eyebrows raised.

I give a quick shake of the head. 'I'll be fine,' I say.

'Come on, Josh, let's go,' Pepper says.

For one horrible second, I think Josh is going to tell everyone that I can't swim. Instead, he simply steps forward and whispers something in Kit's ear. A few moments later, he and Pepper are both in the water, fighting hard to stay on course against the current which keeps drawing them away from the shore.

Kit watches them, a worried expression on his face. 'The tide has turned, it's going out,' he says, wiping his dripping hair out of his eyes. 'Soon we won't be able to get the boat out of the cave.'

I strain my eyes as Josh and Pepper make their slow, agonizing way through the water.

'Evie?' Anna sidles up beside me. 'I just wanted to say again how sorry I am. I honestly thought it was a proper experiment. I would never have—'

'You made me think my mum's spirit was here, trying to communicate with me.' I meet her gaze. 'Even if you really thought it was just some stupid experiment it was cruel . . . and wrong. Josh and I nearly died in that cave where you left the initials. That *was* you, wasn't it?'

'Yes,' Anna admits, tears welling in her eyes. 'Miss Bunnock told me to do that. She told me about the passageway out too. I'm so, so sorry.'

I study her face, feeling torn. I can't bring myself to forgive her, but I can't help feeling a bit sorry for her too. 'Well, we've got more important things to worry about now.'

'Oh, Evie.' Anna bursts into sobs and flings her arms around me.

248

I stiffen, then pull away. Over Anna's shoulder Samuel looks alarmed at this sudden display of emotion. I smile at him and he carefully forms his lips into a curve and offers me a smile back.

Kit clears his throat. 'Josh says you can't swim,' he says. 'Is that true?'

Samuel and Anna stare at me. I nod, feeling my cheeks colouring again. 'OK, well, I'll help you get to the boat,' Kit says.

I hang my head. It's stupid to feel embarrassed about something so minor as not being able to swim when all our lives are in danger. But I would still rather have kept it a secret.

Across the water, Pepper and Josh are clawing their way through the waves. Josh reaches the cave first. He waits, treading water, until Pepper joins him, then together they disappear inside.

Kit glances anxiously at Anna and Samuel. 'How strong swimmers are you two?'

'I'm OK,' Anna says with a shrug.

Samuel makes a face. 'In one lifetime, the average person produces enough spit to fill two swimming pools.'

Kit and I exchange worried looks.

'Er, that's fascinating, Samuel,' I say, 'but how are you at swimming yourself?'

'I can do doggy-paddle,' Samuel says solemnly, 'in an indoor pool.'

'Great.' Kit blows out his breath.

'Look, here they come.' Anna points.

We follow her finger in time to see the motorboat chugging out of the cave. It rocks madly on the waves that smash against the cave wall, but it's moving steadily forward.

Pepper sits at the back, her hair whipping across her face, her hand on the tiller. Josh is at the front of the boat. He points ahead of him to the spot in the sea that Pepper indicated earlier.

'It's time,' I say.

'OK. 'Kit rubs his hands together. 'Take off anything that will weigh you down. Then into the water.'

I'm trembling as I slip off my pumps. I keep my jacket on, the pocket containing Irina's ballet shoes carefully zipped. I'm not losing those again.

Kit ushers Anna into the water, then turns to Samuel. 'Off you go. I'll be right behind.'

Obediently, Samuel wades into the sea after Anna. He is soon out of his depth, paddling furiously with his hands.

'Now us.' Kit puts his arm around my waist. 'It would be easier to do this on our backs, but we wouldn't be able to see the boat and the tide could easily take us off course, so . . .'

'We'll be fine,' I say, though inside I feel terrified.

'Course we will.' Kit gives me an anxious smile.

We walk into the water. It is seriously cold. My trousers stick to my legs. I can already feel the current tugging at my body, trying to draw me away.

'Put your arms under,' Kit orders. 'And pull.'

We wade through the water, buffeted by the waves. After a few steps, we both lose our footing and Kit starts swimming, holding me up as he goes. This is far harder than when I was with Josh in the cave pool, where the water was calm and there was no current surging at my legs. Kit keeps a tight hold of me, all the muscles in his arm working furiously to keep me beside him. Trying to resist the fear that fills me, I kick and pull as hard as I can.

It takes forever. Water splashes against my mouth, but I remember how easy it is to choke if you swallow and keep my lips tightly pressed together, taking only shallow breaths through my nose.

I lose track of time, only aware of Kit's arm around me, my own aching body and the bobbing of Samuel's head in the water alongside us. Just ahead, Anna reaches the boat. Josh is yelling, hauling her out of the water, as Pepper keeps the motor as steady as she can.

'Samuel!' Kit cries.

My head snaps round. Samuel has drifted away from us, he is nowhere near the boat.

Kit swears under his breath. I can feel him pushing himself on, fighting the waves. The cold chills me to the bone. A huge wave smacks us both in the face. Spluttering for air, we press on. At last, my hand touches the hull of the motorboat. Relief courses through me. Josh holds his arm out to pull me in, but I'm looking across the water, searching for Samuel. He's flailing, his arms only just visible above the waves, further away than ever.

'Look!' I shriek.

Kit follows my gaze as Samuel disappears under a particularly vicious wave.

251

'Go!' I yell.

As Kit dives away from me, I reach for Josh's arm.

Wham! A huge wave knocks me sideways. I sink, water covering my face, filling my lungs. I scrabble for purchase with my hands, but the current is too powerful.

I can't find the surface.

I can't reach the air.

Panic shoots through me. This is it. I am drowning.

Thirty-three

A strong hand grips my arm. Hauls me up, out of the water. Cold air slaps at my face. Josh's terrified eyes are right in front of me. He gives a huge roar as he yanks me over the side of the boat. More hands, Anna's, pull at my legs and waist, helping me inside.

'Hey!' Pepper's cry carries over the storm. 'Stop rocking it!'

I land with a thud on the damp wooden bottom of the boat. I cough over and over, spitting out water.

Josh's pale, panic-stricken face appears in front of mine.

'Are you all right?' he gasps.

'Yes.' I kneel up, my whole body trembling.

We hold each other for several long seconds as the storm swirls around us. Wind and rain drive against our bodies. The boat bucks madly under our knees.

'You saved my life,' I gasp. 'Again.'

'I just—'

'Help me!' Anna shrieks.

Josh and I spring apart, turning towards her voice. She's at the very back of the boat, reaching out over the side to Kit and Samuel who are still in the water. Beside her, Pepper sits grim-faced and hunched over the tiller, clearly struggling to hold us in position.

'He's too heavy!' Anna yells again. She's trying to grab hold of Samuel while Kit pushes him up and into the boat. Josh and I hurry over to help.

'No!' Pepper screams. 'Just one of you!'

Josh and I freeze.

'If we're all at this end of the boat, we'll capsize,' Pepper shouts over the storm. 'Evie, go to the other end.'

I scrabble backwards across the boat, watching as Josh and Anna haul first Samuel, then Kit over the hull. As soon as they're both inside, Pepper lets the boat turn and we zoom out to sea. The waves grow bigger and stronger, splashing over the sides, but at least the boat isn't rocking and tipping so badly.

Kit struggles to his knees. His face is grey and strained from exhaustion. Samuel lies spluttering on the boat's damp boards.

'Oh God, oh God, we're going to drown!' Anna cries. A huge wave crashes over us.

'Shut up and get the water out!' Pepper yells.

There is nothing to use to scoop up the water except our hands. Soon all of us except Samuel are bailing furiously. I kneel at the front, Kit beside me. Josh and Anna tip out water at the other end. Samuel is still prostrate on the wooden boards.

'Is he OK?' I ask Kit.

'He's swallowed a lot of seawater,' Kit shouts back.

I gaze anxiously down at Samuel as I chuck another handful of water back into the sea. All at once, Samuel rears up, clutches the side of the boat next to me and pukes into the water.

As if he's pressed some sort of vomiting button, Kit and Anna are immediately sick too. Josh and I stare at each other.

'Keep bailing!' Pepper shrieks from the stern.

I redouble my efforts. Soon Kit is back, next to me, tipping water over the side as fast as he can. I lose all track of time. I exist only in this moment, numb with cold, slapped by waves and stabbed by rain, the storm roaring around me, desperately trying to bail out the seawater that threatens to sink us all.

And then, all of a sudden, the waves subside and the rain eases to a drizzle. In the distance, a ray of sunlight pierces through the clouds. I scoop a few more handfuls of water over the side, then lean back against the small wooden seat in the bow. Kit shuffles over and sits next to me. He puts his damp hand over mine.

The others stop bailing too. Pepper takes her hand off the tiller and rubs at her face. Directly in front of her, Anna and Josh kneel on either side of the boat, panting for breath, while Samuel hunches over the wooden seat that bridges the boat's middle.

'So much for trying to sail to a safer place on the island,' Pepper says darkly. 'We're miles away. I don't even know which direction it's in.'

I look around. The sea surrounds us, vast and grey.

For a moment, nobody speaks. Then Samuel raises his head.

'Did you know that if you try to stop yourself from puking by closing your mouth it will just come out of your nose?' he says.

I laugh. So does Kit beside me. Suddenly we're all laughing.

255

I stop, but the bemused look on Samuel's face sets me off again. By the time we've finished, the rain has dried up completely, though thick banks of cloud remain, the wind has dropped and the air is warmer than before. The sudden silence feels strange. Everyone's faces are etched with the strain of what we've been through, salt-encrusted hair plastered against heads, clothes wet and heavy on exhausted bodies.

After a while, Kit clears his throat. He looks at Pepper.

'Do you have *any* idea where we are?' he asks.

'If we're miles from Lightsea, we could be quite close to the mainland,' Samuel suggests hopefully.

'I've got no clue,' Pepper admits. 'I lost complete track of which direction we were going in about an hour ago and it's too cloudy to work out where the sun is, so . . .'

'So . . .' Josh says. 'We're lost at sea, with no food and no water, and no idea how to get to the mainland.'

'Yup.' Pepper gives a mirthless chuckle. 'That pretty much sums it up.'

Silence falls over the boat again. Anxiety twists in my stomach. Samuel said human beings can survive three days without drinking water, but I can't see the six of us lasting half that long. I wonder what time it is. The light is already fading. I don't want to think about what sort of state we'll all be in when the pitch-black of night falls, or if another storm whips up.

I glance down at Kit's hand on the hull next to mine. I point to his watch, a vague memory of our first proper conversation flitting into my head. 'Didn't you say . . .'

'You're right!' Kit straightens up. 'I completely forgot. My watch is a compass.'

Josh whistles. 'I take back everything I said about you being a Boy Scout.'

Kit snaps the clasp off his wrist and hands it to Samuel, who passes it back to Pepper. She squints down at the screen, then sets it on the bench beside her.

'OK,' she says, 'according to this, we're pointing north, but we need to be . . .'

'. . . heading east,' Kit says.

'South-east,' Pepper corrects.

'That's right,' Josh agrees.

'You're saying if we go south-east then we'll end up on the mainland?' Anna asks.

'Yes,' Pepper says.

Kit beams and hugs me. I glance at Josh. He's watching us with a resigned expression on his face. He catches my eye and looks away.

I try to wriggle back from Kit, but before I can stop him he takes my face in his hands and kisses my mouth. It isn't an intimate kiss, more a big, happy smack of one, but I still feel bad that Josh has to witness it.

My chest tightens. Truth is I wish it were Josh I was kissing. But I've chosen Kit. And Kit will be devastated if I pull away from him now.

I put my head in my hands. It's stupid to be worrying about Kit and Josh. All six of us could be dead by morning if we don't find dry land soon.

'So what's this all about, Evie?' Pepper asks as the boat motors on.

'Yeah, if Lomax isn't covering anything up, who on earth would pay Bunnock to try and kill you?' Josh adds.

I shiver.

'Do you have to bring that up?' Kit snaps at him.

'No, Josh is right,' I say, not looking at either of them. 'I need to know what this is all about. I mean, why would anyone want me dead?'

'Do you have any enemies, Evie?' Pepper asks, raising her eyebrows dramatically.

'No,' I say.

'Of course she doesn't,' Kit says with a scowl. 'Everyone likes Evie.'

Pepper rolls her eyes.

'No,' I say. 'That's not true. For example my parents . . .' I hesitate. 'That is, my dad and the mum I grew up with . . . I don't think they like me very much since I found out about my real mum and that they'd been lying to me for years.'

My mind goes back to home and the many rows of the past two months. Those fights suddenly seem silly. After all, maybe Andrew and Janet did keep the truth – and my grandparents and uncle – away from me, but I can see now that one lie could easily have led to others and that there probably never seemed like a good time to tell me something so momentous.

In my heart, I know that Andrew and Janet have only ever wanted the best for me. I think of their stricken faces when Mr Treeves revealed the truth about Irina. Sitting here, cold and hungry and wet through, it occurs to me that perhaps they were keeping their secret not to protect themselves, but to protect me. Because they love me. I suck in my breath, suddenly aware of how much they both care about me.

And how often, over the past two months, I have thrown their love back in their faces.

'To be honest, my parents have good reason not to like me right now,' I say quietly.

Kit gives me another hug. 'How could anyone not like you,' he says. 'You're so pretty and nice.'

Across the boat, Pepper makes puking noises.

I wince, extracting myself. As I turn to look out to sea, I catch Josh's eye. His eyebrows are raised – just a slight tilt, but enough for me to see that he knows Kit's reply shows that Kit doesn't understand at all.

'Prima donna,' Josh mouths, his eyes sparkling with affection.

I blush, turning away. Josh is right. Andrew and Janet should have told me the truth far, far sooner than they did, but I was selfish too, only thinking about what I wanted. And it all stemmed from my idolizing Irina, a genuine prima donna, a prima ballerina. But Irina earned her status as an amazing performer: she had style and grace and talent.

I'm just a kid with two left feet and a dream of being special that is never, ever going to come true.

A hard lump lodges itself in my throat. I swallow it painfully down, fighting back the tears that threaten to trickle down my cheeks. The boat chugs on. After another hour or so, the sun finally comes out from behind the clouds, lowering gently towards the horizon, and it's now clear that we are, as Kit's compass indicates, definitely heading south-east.

'How much further?' Anna asks.

'No idea,' Pepper says.

'Did you know that seventy-per-cent of the earth's surface is covered by water?' Samuel asks.

'Good to know,' Josh says with a sigh. 'It can't be much further. The original boat trip over to the island only took about half an hour. We've been out on the water for much longer.'

'Yeah, but we don't know how far north we drifted before we started steering south-east,' Kit says.

We all fall silent again, the only sound now the occasional squawk of a seagull and the monotonous drone of the boat's engine.

And then the engine's steady chug sputters and stops.

'What's happening?' Anna asks.

Pepper bends over the engine, pulling something, pressing something else. I hold my breath as she straightens up and surveys the rest of us. She throws her hands up in that theatrical way of hers. But despite the overly dramatic gesture there is real worry in her eyes.

'More good news, guys,' she says. 'We're out of fuel.'

Thirty-four

Hours pass. Night falls and the sky is scattered with stars. A cold wind blows across the boat and the six of us lie inside it, top to tail. We're freezing. My clothes are damp against my skin, I'm dirty, my hair is matted and, like the others, I am desperate for a drink of water.

On either side of me, Kit and Anna are fast asleep. Josh, Pepper and Samuel lie at the other end of the boat, but, as there isn't room for us to stretch out, our legs are necessarily touching. Pepper's salt-stiffened trouser bottoms rest against mine. Cramped though it is, the limited space on the boat at least means we are unlikely to die of hypothermia. I know about that because Janet's auntie who I never met died of it one winter. Janet was so upset. I found her crying and felt bad, but didn't know what to say so crept away without saying anything.

For as long as I can remember, Janet has been telling me she loved me. With a flush of shame, I realise I've never said it back. I huddle down in the boat, memories shooting through me – of us all laughing as we spun on the teacup ride at some funfair a million years ago, Janet holding my hair off my face as I was sick from a stomach bug that kept me off primary school for a week.

Andrew was right. In spite of everything, she is – and has always been – my mum. Up until a few days ago, all I wanted was to get away from them both. And yet, now, all I find myself wanting is to see them and call them Mum and Dad again.

'Evie? Are you awake?' Josh whispers from across the boat.

I sit up and the boat rocks as I move. Beside me, Anna gives a groan and Kit snuffles, turning over onto his side. Josh is already sitting upright. I glance at Samuel, lying with his eyes closed and his mouth open, face up to the night sky, and at Pepper between him and Josh.

'Are you OK?' Josh whispers.

'You mean apart from the worry that we're all going to drift out to sea and die of exposure or thirst or another storm?' I ask.

'I mean that you looked so upset earlier . . . I'm guessing that was about all this stuff, your mum . . . things at home . . . wishing you hadn't made your family mad . . .' Josh hesitates. 'I hope I didn't upset you with the "prima donna" thing?'

'No, you didn't, you were right,' I say. 'I was a pain in the butt back home.'

'Yeah, I've been thinking that maybe I was too.'

'Really?'

Josh nods. 'It was something Lomax said after we got stuck in that cave, how making jokes is a defence mech— Anyway, it doesn't matter now.' He frowns. 'I was just wondering if, on top of dealing with all the danger, maybe you were sad that your mum's ghost wasn't real.'

I think about it. 'At first, I was sad,' I say. 'But actually now it doesn't make a lot of difference. Irina died a long time ago. Even if I *had* seen her ghost, it wouldn't have changed that.'

'Right.' Josh peers out to sea. The horizon is just visible, the sky a few shades lighter than the dark navy sea beneath. 'It'll be dawn soon.'

I nod. The boat drifts on. It's incredibly quiet without the storm or people talking. The only sound is Samuel's deep breathing and the occasional smack of water against the hull of the motorboat. Josh and I sit in the silence, watching the stars above us spread wide across the navy sky.

'It's beautiful,' I breathe.

'It is.' Josh hesitates. 'And, in case there isn't another chance to say it, I'm happy for you if you're happy with Kit.'

I shoot a look at him, but before I can speak Pepper is scrambling to her knees, pointing across the sea.

'Look!' she cries. 'Land! We're heading for land!'

I scan the horizon. A dark ridge rises up over the sea, its uneven edges just visible against the deep velvety blue of the sky.

'Are we really going towards it?' I ask anxiously.

'Yes,' Josh says. 'But we can still help the boat along.' He reaches into the water and, using his arm like an oar, propels the *Aurora* forward. I join him, forgetting my parched throat as I pull at the gentle waves. Pepper is shaking the others awake. Soon everyone is up, kneeling three on each side of the boat, helping to steer it towards land.

263

In less than half an hour, we're scrambling ashore. Everyone jumps out of the boat and pulls it onto the dark beach.

'Where the hell are we?' Josh asks.

'Could be anywhere along the coast, I guess,' Kit says. 'I can't see any lights.'

Shivering in the cool night air, the six of us trudge along the beach. There are still plenty of stars in view, but the moon is a soft smudge behind the night clouds and, as Kit says, there are no electric lights of any kind.

'This place is deserted,' I say.

'Wait, what's that?' Pepper asks.

I follow her pointing finger to an old brick house. No lights are on inside, but I can just make out the slope of its roof and a row of boarded-up windows along the first floor.

'It's shelter,' Kit says grimly. 'Of a kind.'

'But there's obviously no one inside,' Josh points out. 'Shouldn't we keep moving, find a road, maybe flag down a car? Get help?'

'Yes,' I agree, 'there might be lights and people if we go a bit further.'

'Isn't it dangerous to be wandering about in the middle of the night?' Anna asks plaintively.

'Well, I'm not going anywhere,' Pepper says. 'I'm freezing cold and I ache all over from steering that stupid boat.'

She sets off towards the house.

'She's right,' Josh concedes. 'Let's rest here till dawn and see what we can see in the morning.'

We follow Pepper to the house. As we get nearer, it becomes

obvious that it was once quite grand and far bigger than I first thought, stretching back into a low-walled garden. Though every window is boarded up and the front door so rotten that it collapses with just a few quick pushes, the remnants of lights and carpets and patterned wallpaper are dimly visible in every room.

We find a room upstairs at the back of the house and huddle together for warmth. Outside, just visible through the cracks in the boards at the window, the sky lightens to grey, and pink swirls gather at its edges.

'I can't wait to get a proper meal,' Kit muses sleepily.

'Yeah and a shower,' Pepper adds.

'I want my guitar back,' Josh says with a grunt.

'Did you know a human head remains conscious for about twenty seconds after decapitation?' Samuel asks.

'Er, thanks for that, Samuel,' Josh says.

'I really need to see my mum.' That is Anna. She looks at me anxiously. 'I guess you'll be wanting to go to the police, Evie?'

'I'm going to call my dad first,' I say.

Kit squeezes my hand. 'I can't wait to meet him,' he says.

An uncomfortable knot tightens in my stomach. I nod, feeling helpless. I sense Josh's eyes are on me, but I can't bring myself to meet his gaze. Josh, like everyone else, thinks I'm happy with Kit. He accepts that; he hasn't even asked me out himself.

And I am happy with Kit.

At least I think I am.

I fall asleep, wedged between Pepper and Kit, waking to

find Josh shaking our shoulders and hissing in our ears: 'Someone's here, on the stairs, listen.'

We're all awake suddenly, alert, leaning towards the door.

The creak of a floorboard sounds outside. A light flashes through the crack in the door. Beyond, on the landing, comes the low muttering of voices.

Beside me, Pepper gasps. Anna clutches Josh's arm. I hold my breath, still half-asleep, as two long seconds pass.

And then the door is flung open and a torch glares in our eyes.

'Evie?' a familiar voice calls.

I jump to my feet as the torchlight dips and I come face to face with the last person I expected to see.

Thirty-five

Uncle Gavin stands in the doorway, his forehead knitted in an anxious frown.

'Evie?' he says again.

'Oh!' I let out a strangled sob of shock, delight and relief as I hurl myself across the room and into his arms.

'What are you doing here?' I gasp. 'How did you—?' I stop, suddenly aware that my uncle is standing stiffly, his arms by his sides, not hugging me back.

Behind him, another figure moves. I back away as the torchlight reveals Miss Bunnock, her hair swept off her face in a tight ponytail. Her gun glints in her hand. I turn to my uncle.

'What? I don't . . . what's going on?' I stammer.

'Come with me.' Gavin drags me into the next room and slams the door shut. It's smaller than the one everyone else is still huddling in, though just as empty, with boards over the window and a threadbare carpet on the floor. Behind us, I can hear the others shrieking my name and then Miss Bunnock threatening them.

'Evie, listen, I need the password—' Gavin starts.

'How did you find me?' I ask. It's not the question I really want to ask. That seems too big, too terrifying.

267

'We tracked the *Aurora*,' he says. 'Using the tracker Francine planted on the boat when she hid it in the cave.'

'Francine?'

'Francine Bunnock, my girlfriend,' Gavin says matter-of-factly.

'Oh,' I say, flatly. I suddenly remember how he told me back in Scotland that he was single. It's only a small lie on top of all the other ways in which Gavin has clearly deceived me, but it still hurts.

'Francine loves me very much,' Gavin says with a nasty smile. 'She'd do anything for me.'

I gulp, edging my way nearer to the question that's now filling my mind. '*You* got her to do . . . all the stuff on the island? The ghost and everything? It was *you*?'

'Yes.' In the flickering light of Gavin's torch, I can see the impatience on his face. No concern, just frustration. 'Come on, darling, what's the password to Irina's safety-deposit box?'

'You want to kill me?' The question shoots from my lips at last.

Gavin brushes it away with a wave of his hand. 'The password, Evie,' he repeats. 'It must have been among the papers that lawyer gave you?'

'Password?' I echo blankly as the horrific, sickening reality settles inside me: my uncle wants me dead and is prepared to go to any lengths, including murdering my friends, to make it happen. 'I don't know about any password.'

Gavin studies my face. 'Come on, darling. This isn't anything personal. I just want the information so I can get some of the money straightaway.'

'Money? I've never heard of a safety-deposit box. Or a password. And I'm not your darling.' I take in a quick, trembling breath. 'What are you doing this for? Is . . . is it about my inheritance from Irina?'

Gavin paces across the room, then turns to face me again, his hands clasped behind his back.

'Irina . . . your mother . . . wasn't what you think,' he says slowly. 'She didn't set that trust fund up for you . . . She barely knew what she was doing when she signed the papers.'

I stare at him. 'What do you mean?'

'I mean that our parents organised it. *They* were the ones trying to make Irina get a grip on her life. I think they hoped if she was on top of her finances, she might get on top of her life and start taking responsibility. It wasn't about leaving money to *you*. They hoped that it would turn things around for her.'

'Turn what things around?' I ask, bewildered. 'I don't understand what you're saying. Irina was successful. OK, so she didn't plan on getting pregnant, but she was a brilliant dancer. She was getting back to ballet after having me and—'

'She was mentally ill,' Gavin interrupts. 'I don't think there was a definite diagnosis, Irina refused to accept she had a problem, but she was very unstable. She took a lot of drugs – a few of them prescribed for her, most of them not, which made the situation worse – and—'

'No.' I was on my feet, my fists clenched. 'No, she was just

269

a bit different from other people. She was special, not ill, not some drug user who—'

'She couldn't cope,' Gavin says flatly. 'Especially after you were born. I'm not saying she didn't love you, but she sure as hell wasn't able to look after you. Your dad did all that. My parents helped when they were still alive, but Irina's suicide pretty much destroy—'

'Her *what*?' My blood runs cold. 'Irina didn't kill herself. It was a traffic accident, a hit-and-run.'

Gavin shakes his head. 'That's just how we all agreed to present it – my parents and your dad . . . but none of us were in any doubt that Irina walked out in front of that lorry deliberately. She'd threatened to kill herself that way enough times.' He pauses. 'It wasn't her first attempt.'

My mouth feels dry. What Gavin is saying *can't* be true.

'She made my childhood a nightmare,' Gavin goes on. 'She got all the attention, all the energy. And of course she was a beautiful dancer too, so she got most of the praise and the plaudits as well. I was just the stupid younger brother,' he says, a bitter note to his voice. 'I was a sideshow. And then she died, and our parents lost the will to live, and *they* died within a year or two and I've been living on *their* money ever since, but it's gone now and I need yours. I'm next in line if anything happens to you and I'm owed it, for all the chances Irina took away from me.'

My hand flies to my mouth. 'And you think that justifies killing me?'

Gavin says nothing.

I try to process what he has said. 'Does what you're saying mean my dad *didn't* keep me away from my grandparents, like you told me before?'

Gavin makes a face. 'I guess not,' he says. 'Truth is that after Irina died they pretty much gave up on their own lives.'

'Oh my God.' I can't believe it. So Dad didn't stop me from having a relationship with my family after all.

Another thought hits me. 'What about the car that nearly ran me over in Edinburgh? Were you behind that?'

Gavin gives a swift nod. 'But then straight afterwards your dad whisked you off and I realised I was going to have to be a bit cleverer about it so I looked into Lightsea, where I remembered Irina being sent for a few weeks in her late teens.'

I gasp. 'That's how there was a photo of her at Lightsea? She was a patient here before I was born? Before she met my dad?'

He nods. 'I saw there was a job going, at the institute so I got Francine to apply for it, then once she was in I gave her the photo to plant where you'd find it.'

My mind rushes back to the night Josh, Pepper and I broke into Mr Lomax's office. 'So David Lomax doesn't know anything about it?'

Gavin snorts. 'He knows Irina was once a patient at his father's mental-health institute. But your dad was adamant none of us should tell you about Irina being ill. Lomax was going along with that.'

'So Irina didn't die on Lightsea,' I say.

'No. I just wanted you to believe Lomax pushed her off Easter Rock to encourage you to think Irina was trying to tell you he was her killer.'

'So I'd follow her to Easter Rock where that Bunnock woman could push *me* off.'

'And everyone would think it was suicide after you becoming obsessed with your mother's ghost. Your own fixation on Irina gave me the idea.'

I bite down hard on my lip, misery consuming me. I had thought my uncle loved and cared for me, when all along he was just plotting how to take my money.

'Hey.' Miss Bunnock pokes her head around the door frame and gives Gavin an adoring look. 'Did you get what you need?'

'Evie doesn't know,' Gavin says. 'No matter, we'll get the info soon enough ourselves.'

'You'll inherit everything if I don't?' I ask, though the answer is obvious.

'Yes, but only if you die *before* inheriting yourself at the end of August.'

'Gavin, babe?' Miss Bunnock says, her tone far softer than I've ever heard it before. She hands Gavin a small silver lighter. 'I've filled this like you said.'

'Coming.' Gavin takes the lighter and turns it over in his hand. As he flicks the lighter on, then off again, I recognise it as Samuel's.

'What are you doing with that?' I demand.

But Gavin just slips the lighter back in his pocket and walks

272

out of the room. A split second later, Bunnock ushers Kit, Josh and the others in. Her gun is tightly gripped in her hand.

'You can't do this, you bitch,' Pepper snarls.

I stare numbly as the five of them file inside and the door is closed and locked. Josh rushes over to the window and pulls at the boards, but they're nailed firmly against the frame.

Kit thumps on the door. 'Let us out.'

Anna stands, trembling, in the middle of the room.

I turn to her. 'Did you know my uncle was behind all this?'

Anna shakes her head. 'I only ever talked to Miss Bunnock. I swear I didn't even know the plan was to hurt *you*. I told you, I thought it was just some weird psychological experiment.'

'It's true, Evie,' Kit says quietly. 'Anna talked to me those first few nights. No details. I didn't know it was about you, but . . . but she was asking about whether it was ever ethical to deceive people for scientific reasons. She wanted my opinion.'

'I just thought Kit seemed smart and . . . and more serious than everyone else,' Anna admits. 'I wanted his advice about what I'd been asked to do without explaining in detail.'

I nod slowly. So that was what Anna's interest in Kit was really about.

'Evie?' Josh's voice is low and intent. 'We need to focus on how we get out of here.'

'Right.'

'What will they do?' Samuel asks, his voice small.

'They're going to get rid of us,' Kit says tersely.

'Yeah, Bunnock wasn't messing with that gun,' Josh adds.

'That was real.'

'It wasn't an AK-47 though,' Samuel says. 'And AK-47s are the most popular guns in the world.'

'Thanks for that, Samuel,' Pepper says, her voice hollow. 'But a gun doesn't need to be popular to shoot straight.'

Josh crosses the room to join Kit at the door. 'D'you think we can break it down?'

Kit nods. 'We can give it a go.'

'What's that sound?' Pepper asks.

I listen hard as a crackling noise drifts towards us. A whiff of pungent smoke fills the air.

'What is it?' Anna asks, sounding desperate.

'Fire.' I turn to her. 'They've set the house on fire.'

Thirty-six

There's a moment of total silence as the sound of the flames outside builds. Then Pepper points to the first wisps of smoke curling under the door and Anna lets out a high-pitched scream and panic fills the room.

Samuel shrinks back against the wall. Kit hammers on the door.

'Let us out! Let us out!'

Josh turns to me and Pepper. 'We have to break the door down.'

I nod, the smell of the smoke filling my nostrils. Pepper calls to Anna.

'Stop shrieking and get over here.'

Anna does as she's told. I run over to Samuel, grab his arm and drag him to the door. Kit squares up to it. He points to the area level with the handle.

'That's where it's weakest. Kick there.'

We line up. The smoke coming under the door is thicker now, dark grey in the dawn light. My head reels. Uncle Gavin has left me and the others here to die. It's unthinkable. Horrific.

'Bunnock gave him Samuel's lighter,' I say numbly. 'He'll

leave it downstairs. Everyone will think we took it and filled it with fuel and set the fire by accident.'

'Or they'll think Josh did it on purpose,' Kit says. 'Weren't you excluded from one of your schools for lighting a fire?'

'Let's just break this door down,' Josh says with a frown. 'One, two, three, go!'

I put all my force into the kick. So does everyone else. A series of hammer blows rain against the wood. The door shakes, but stays locked.

'Again,' Kit urges. 'Together this time. One, two, three . . .'

This time we all kick together. Even Samuel is in synch. The door cracks.

'Once more,' Pepper cries. 'Hit it!'

I lunge out, imagining it's my uncle I'm aiming at. The door splinters. Flies open. A gust of acrid smoke whooshes into the room. Kit plunges past it, Pepper at his heels. I take Samuel's hand.

'Come on.'

Ahead of us, Josh propels Anna onto the landing. The smoke is so thick here I can barely see them. I'm coughing, choking. I let go of Samuel's hand to cover my mouth.

Someone grasps my arm and pulls me sideways. It's Josh.

'This way,' he yells, directing me towards the stairs.

Flames writhe up from the hall. The bottom of the staircase is hidden in dense smoke. We rush down to the ground floor. A wall of fire blocks our way to the front door.

'Over here,' Pepper shouts.

My eyes sting with the smoke, my lungs burn as we follow

her into what was clearly once a living room. The base of a lamp on a wooden sideboard and a couple of tatty old sofas are the only pieces of furniture remaining. Across the room, Kit is pulling a long rotten board from across the two small windows. We race over as it hits the floor.

The glass in both windows is broken, with jagged pieces sticking out. Kit and Pepper smash the shards sticking out in the first window. I snatch up the lamp base and swing it at the second. A large piece of glass crashes down outside. Josh shoves at the remaining slivers that stick out from the frame, knocking them away.

'Gavin!' It's Miss Bunnock.

'Francine! Where are you?' Gavin cries.

They sound close. Are they in the house?

"Hurry!" I urge as Josh helps Samuel over the sill. Next to us Pepper is hauling Anna outside. Smoke swirls around them as they pelt across the garden.

"Come on, Evie!" Kit follows Pepper through the window.

'*Evie!*' It's Gavin, he sounds closer than before. I glance over my shoulder. The door and the far walls are hidden by smoke. Is he inside the room?

'You next.' Josh reaches for my hand. He helps me scramble out of the window, my pumps crunching on the glass as I land next to Kit. Smoke is pouring out of the house, swirling into the sky. Pepper, Anna and Samuel are at the other end of the garden, almost at the low wall. There's a field on the other side and a road beyond that. Its rough tarmac glistens in the dim dawn light.

'Run, Evie!' Kit yells, haring across the grass. I set off after him, As he leaps over the low wall into the field, I'm suddenly aware Josh isn't with us. I turn round and face the house. The windows we just climbed out of are shrouded in smoke. Where is Josh? Is he still stuck inside? Panic swirls inside me. I race back to the house.

'Stop!' Gavin's voice rings out across the garden.

I spin round. Gavin emerges across the grass through a haze of smoke. He has Josh in a tight grip, a gun at his throat.

Josh's eyes glitter with fury. And fear.

Gavin cocks the gun.

'Don't.' My voice cracks. 'Please.'

'Get back inside the house, Evie,' Gavin orders. 'Or I shoot him.'

Thirty-seven

'You wouldn't,' I gasp.

'Don't test me, Evie,' Gavin snaps. 'I make my living taking things from people. You've got no idea who I am.'

I stare at him. 'You're a gangster, just like my dad said.'

Gavin meets my gaze, his eyes cold and narrow. 'Inside, darling,' he snarls.

He's ordering me into a blazing house. To die. Fear seizes me like a fist.

'It's going to be OK,' Josh says softly.

'Shut your mouth.' Gavin prods the barrel of his gun against Josh's throat.

I gulp. 'How about if I agree to give you all the money I'm going to get from Irina?' I plead. 'I'll sign anything you want if you just let us go.'

Gavin shakes his head. 'What? So you're free to go straight to the police? I don't think so.'

I keep my gaze on Josh. His eyes flicker sideways, to the gun at his neck. He's going to try and wrench it away. My stomach lurches. No, he mustn't, it's too dangerous.

'Just . . . just please put the gun down,' I plead.

279

'Get inside.' Gavin indicates the door behind him. Smoke pours out of it, flames licking around the edges.

I walk over, my legs shaking. Josh stiffens, readying himself. I keep my eyes on the gun. I'm trembling all over. I don't have what it takes to get a gun off a fully-grown man. That needs strength and timing and guts. I look around. Smoke is billowing all over the garden. I can't see further than a few metres in front of me in any direction. I have no idea where the others are. Far away I hope.

'You can do it.' Josh's whisper is soft and steady. 'Just tell me when.'

I glance up.

'Stop mumbling.' Gavin pokes the gun against Josh's neck. 'What are you saying?'

Josh wants me to help him wrestle the gun away from Gavin, but I can't. I shake my head. Josh stares at me. *You can*, he mouths.

I grit my teeth, hope unfurling inside me. If Josh has faith in me, maybe I should have some in myself.

'Tell me—' Gavin starts.

'Now,' I whisper.

In a single move, Josh rams his head back and up, knocking against Gavin's chin. Gavin staggers back, his fingers loosening their grip on the gun. I grab his wrist, racing round to his side, forcing the weapon away from Josh.

With a roar, Josh breaks free. He turns and throws a punch into Gavin's ribs.

Gavin chokes. I twist his wrist. The gun falls to the ground.

280

I snatch it up and back away. Josh shoves Gavin to the grass, just as Kit and Pepper race over.

Before Gavin can yell out, Kit hurls himself down, his arm at Gavin's throat. Josh drops to his knees and pins one of Gavin's legs, then the other. Pepper grapples with his arms. I fling the gun into the bushes and race over to help.

'Get the wire.' Pepper indicates the length of electrical cord trailing from the lamp base I threw through the window earlier.

I grab the wire, yank it from the base and wind the ends around Gavin's wrists.

'Get off me!' he splutters.

Kit presses harder against his throat as a ray of sunlight breaks through the dawn sky. It glints off the buttons on Gavin's jacket, then his belt buckle.

'Use that,' I urge.

Josh tugs the belt out and together we bind Gavin's ankles, while Pepper fastens the thick wire more tightly around his wrists, pulling his arms so he can't move.

'Stop! Stop!' Gavin yells.

'Oh, make him shut up for goodness' sake,' Pepper snarls.

Kit tugs off his T-shirt, rips it into strips and binds it tightly around Gavin's mouth.

Panting, the four of us step back. Gavin writhes on the damp grass, his shouts muffled by the T-shirt.

'That's better,' Pepper says, dusting her hands.

'Where are Anna and Samuel?' I ask.

'In the field beyond the garden,' Kit says.

'What about Bunnock?' I ask.

281

'As far as we can see, the evil bitch didn't make it out of the fire,' Pepper snarls.

'Oh.' I look at the stone house, engulfed in flames. The sky beyond is pale grey with pink swirls – too beautiful for the ugliness that has gone on beneath. Whatever Miss Bunnock has done, and been prepared to do, I wouldn't wish such a death on anyone.

'She's gone,' Kit says flatly.

I glance at Josh. His face is pale and drawn; he's bent over Gavin, searching his pockets. 'Are you OK?' I ask.

He gives me a curt nod, then draws Gavin's mobile out of his jacket pocket.

'We should call the police,' he says.

'And I need to call my dad,' I say.

There's a pause, then Pepper raises an eyebrow.

'Oh good,' she says sardonically. 'Because another one of your relatives, Evie, is just what we need right now.'

I grin. 'Don't worry, my dad's solid.' I imagine his kindly face. 'Actually, my dad's the best dad in the world.'

Thirty-eight

Three hours pass and the sun rises high in the sky, burning away all the remaining clouds. We have left the cottage – now cordoned off and swarming with police officers – and been taken to the nearest hospital. After being examined by doctors and given a change of clothes, the six of us are interviewed individually by police officers, a social worker sitting beside us. The two women who listen to me are lovely, sympathetic as I cry, describing everything that happened yesterday and today. At last, the commotion dies down and Pepper, Kit, Josh and I sit in a small, private room, waiting for our families to come and pick us up. I've spoken briefly to Dad. He was devastated when I told him how we nearly died – and deeply shocked about Gavin. He and Mum are on their way here now.

Mr Lomax arrived at the hospital earlier this morning, ashen-faced with horror at the danger we've all been in – and at Miss Bunnock's betrayal. He told us he returned to Lightsea in the middle of last night and, before he even found out we were missing, Bunnock had tricked her way onto the boat that brought him and persuaded its captain to take her back to the mainland.

'She said something about a personal emergency so I let her

283

go, though it seemed strange. Once I got up to the house and found out not only that you were missing but that she hadn't said anything . . . that's when I became really suspicious, but by then she was well away.'

Mr Lomax asks each of us in turn to give an account of the past twenty-four hours. Shame-faced, he confirms what Gavin told me about Irina being a mental patient at Lightsea about eighteen years ago, when his father was in charge. However, he refuses to explain more, insisting I talk to Dad.

'I apologise for lying to you about your birth mother, but your father was adamant about that and it's for him to tell you why.'

Mr Lomax leaves in the late morning to accompany a weeping Anna to the police station where she's going to be reunited with her mother and formally interviewed. Samuel goes too – collected by his mother, a harassed-looking woman who doesn't speak to anyone else. I hug him goodbye. Well, I try to hug him, but he feels so stiff and awkward that in the end I let him go.

'Thanks for trying to help me,' I say. Samuel opens his mouth as if he's about to tell me another weird fact. Then he just shuts it, nods and leaves.

Parting from Anna is completely different. She's in floods of tears, still apologizing for her part in nearly getting us killed. The others each tell her that they forgive her, that they understand she was tricked and manipulated.

Everyone is kind and generous. Even Pepper. Everyone except me.

It's just too hard. I still feel furious when I think of how Anna lied about her mum being dead, then dressed up in that coat and hat to trick me into thinking I was haunted by *my* mother's ghost.

Still, as Josh points out, at least Anna tried to help me. There's no such excuse for Uncle Gavin and Miss Bunnock. I can't bring myself to think about them. All I know is that the police officers who interviewed us are certain Gavin will go to prison for a long time. They confirm that Miss Bunnock's body was found in the ruins of the house, that she must have got trapped in the fire, unable to follow Gavin out.

'Wow, so everything that happened was about your inheritance?' says Pepper, sitting forward in her chair. 'Does that mean that you're, like, totally rich now?'

'I guess I will be at the end of the month,' I say, though right now the prospect of inheriting millions in a few weeks doesn't feel real.

'Cool!' Pepper grins. 'Just don't let it turn you into a total arse like it did my dad.'

I grin back. 'I promise I won't be any more of an arse than you are.'

Another hour goes by. Kit, Pepper and I swap phone numbers. Pepper gives hers to Josh and he says he will call her. He doesn't bother to ask for Kit's. Or mine. And I'm too self-conscious to ask for his.

Kit sits next to me, holding my hand and occasionally suggesting we go for a walk along the corridor to get some privacy. I point out that there's a police officer stationed on the other side of the door.

'He'll follow us if we go too far,' I whisper so that Josh and Pepper can't hear. 'We wouldn't have any privacy.'

'Then I want to come home with you when your dad picks you up,' Kit whispers back.

I can't see Dad agreeing to that. Which makes me feel relieved. Which makes me feel mean. I keep looking over at Josh, but since our escape from Gavin he's been strangely quiet and is now, in the absence of his MP3player and guitar, hunched over a music magazine he's picked from the selection on the hospital waiting-room table.

Perhaps he's gone off me. I could hardly blame him after what my uncle has put him through. Or perhaps he never really liked me in the way I imagined. After all, he's never actually *talked* about how he felt. When I think about it, nothing more than that single brush of the lips has ever passed between us.

Maybe he doesn't like me that much after all.

As I hunker down in my chair, the door is flung open and a tall, elegant woman rushes inside.

'Peps,' she breathes. 'Oh, Peps, are you all right?'

Pepper jumps to her feet, her cheeks flushing. 'I'm fine, er, Mum, I—'

'Oh, come here, darling.' The woman extends her arms. She is very slim and dressed in a dark green coat that fits like it's been specially made for her. Which, I reflect, it quite possibly has. Diamonds glitter on her fingers.

Pepper submits to the hug as a big black man strides into

the room. His suit looks as expensive as the woman's coat. He has to be Pepper's dad.

'Is she OK?' he barks.

'She says she's fine,' Pepper's mum says with a sniff, drawing her daughter into another hug.

'Well, don't suffocate her,' the man snaps, an edge to his voice that reminds me very much of Pepper's own.

Pepper herself steps back, rolling her eyes. 'Hi, Dada,' she says.

'Home,' the man says. He looks cross. I wonder if he's angry because of Pepper's behaviour before coming to Lightsea, or because of her mum acting all emotional, or just because he's a cross person.

I suddenly miss my own dad very much.

Pepper sweeps over. She gives each of the boys a swift hug, then pulls me into a bigger clinch.

'Keep in touch,' she breathes in my ear. Then she lowers her voice further. 'Go with your heart; listen to what it tells you. Go with your heart.' She draws back, gives me a huge wink, then sweeps out. She's followed by her parents, neither of whom have given us a second glance.

Once Pepper leaves, the room feels emptier. The atmosphere grows tense as we all sit in silence, wondering who will be picked up next. I really want it to be Kit. That will give me a chance to talk to Josh in private, maybe get a sense of how he feels.

But the next time the door opens, an hour later, it's my own parents who hurry in. After the elegant and expensive whirl of

Pepper's mum and dad, they seem very ordinary, their clothes creased from their journey and their hair rumpled and messy. Dad's face is pale with worry and exhaustion.

As he holds me, some of the tension of the past few days slides away. For the first time since our ordeal, I start to feel that everything will eventually be OK. I look up. Mum is hovering across the room, looking anxious.

I hold out my hand and she hurries over, then the three of us stand and hug. Dad doesn't want to let me go, but at last I disentangle myself, aware that the two boys must be watching us.

'This is Kit and this is Josh,' I say. 'They helped me . . . all of us . . . get away from Gavin.'

Dad shakes both their hands, his thanks pouring out of him.

'Come on, Evie,' he says. 'I'm sure you want to get home as fast as possible. If we go straight to the airport, we can get a flight back in time to pick up the twins from—'

'Wait, Dad,' I say. 'There's something I need to talk to you about before we go. It can't wait.'

'Er, OK.' Dad frowns.

I clear my throat. I've been planning this question for hours, but now the time has come it's hard to speak, especially with the boys here.

Josh seems to sense my awkwardness. He stands up. 'Kit and I can wait outside.'

'Sure,' Kit says. He and Josh leave the room. Mum and Dad sit in their seats.

'What is it, Evie?' Dad asks, leaning forward with a frown.

I take a deep breath. 'Uncle Gavin said a whole lot of stuff about Irina and Mr Lomax told me she was a patient at Lightsea years ago too . . . that she was mentally ill, that she . . . did all sorts of bad things . . .'

Dad's face pales. 'Oh, Evie.'

'Is any of it true?' I ask.

He nods.

I take a deep breath. 'Gavin also said that . . . that Irina killed herself.'

There's a long pause.

'Dad?' I ask, my voice very small.

'Irina loved you very much,' Dad says.

Beside him, Mum puts a hand on his knee. 'It's time.' She looks at me sorrowfully. 'I told Dad you were old enough to hear the truth, but it was hard for him.'

Dad bows his head. I wait, but he still doesn't speak.

'Dad,' I say, my voice stronger. 'I know you want to protect me, but I think there have been too many secrets already, don't you?'

Dad looks up at last, his eyes full of misery. 'It's true. It was a suicide, but not because of you. Irina did love you in her way. It was life that she couldn't handle, the dark stuff that went on in her head . . . She was always either very up or very down.'

'Was *that* why you didn't want to tell me anything about her?' I ask, leaning forward, intent on his face. 'Because she killed herself and . . . and you didn't want me to know I wasn't enough for her to live for?'

Dad nods again.

'I see,' I say, feeling hollow.

'I don't think you really *do* see, Evie,' Mum says gently. 'You can't possibly see fully right now. It takes time to understand properly, to come to terms with something like that. But your dad and I will do our best to help you and there are people out there, professionals, who can try and help too.'

I look up. 'Like Mr Lomax tried?'

Dad rolls his eyes. 'Mr Lomax said I should tell you the truth about Irina from the start.'

I think back to Mr Lomax's awkward reaction when I said I needed to know about Irina's death. No wonder he looked like he was hiding something. He was hiding the truth, just as Dad had told him to.

'I'm sorry, Evie,' Dad says, squeezing my hand. 'There are lots of things I should have explained; I see that now.'

'Gavin said there's a safety-deposit box?'

'Yes, there is. It's part of your inheritance; the papers arrived from Mr Treeves while you were away, along with a letter offering to help find us a specialist financial advisor, like lottery winners have, to help you handle the money. If . . . if you think that's a good idea?'

I nod.

'I *should* have told you everything, but it just never felt like the right time.' Dad looks up, tears in his eyes. 'I'm so sorry, sweetheart.'

I gaze into his unhappy face and squeeze his hand back. 'I'm just glad I have you,' I say with a smile. Then I reach out and take Mum's hand. 'I'm glad I have you both.'

Kit and Josh are waiting outside as we leave the room. Kit hurries over as soon as we appear. He draws me to one side, then leans his handsome face close to mine.

'I'll call you later, maybe we can meet up at the weekend.'

I nod, feeling awkward. It will be good to see Kit. I like him. And he is gorgeous. Everyone at school will envy me if we go out together. And yet that cartwheeling feeling I had the first few times I saw him is long gone. I no longer look at him and fancy him, in spite of his good looks. I no longer think about him when we aren't together. I no longer want him to kiss me.

As he hugs me, I look over his shoulder at where Josh is skulking by the window. Why isn't he looking at me?

I raise my hand. 'Bye, Josh.'

Josh throws me a swift glance, his arm raised in a brief wave. 'See ya.'

He hasn't even bothered to ask for my number or where he'll find me online or how far away from him I live.

Tears prick at my eyes. I pull away from Kit.

'Don't cry,' he says, misunderstanding my tears. 'We'll see each other soon.'

Nodding, I turn and hurry away. My heart feels like lead in my chest as I follow Mum and Dad down the staircase. We reach the lobby on the ground floor.

'I'll bring the hire car round,' Dad says.

Mum and I stand against the wall, waiting. My mind races over everything that has happened, snapshots of the past week speeding through my head: seeing Irina's 'ghost' through the trees that first evening, the stones in the cave spelling out her initials, dancing with Josh as the storm raged, Anna's face when she turned around on Easter Rock, Gavin's gun pressed against Josh's neck, the thought – clear and terrible – that Josh might die, and finally the whisper of Pepper's voice in my ear:

Go with your heart.

My breath hitches in my throat. What did I just say to Dad? That there had already been too many secrets.

Go with your heart; listen to what it tells you. Go with your heart.

'I forgot to do something,' I say to Mum. 'I won't be a minute.'

And then I turn and race back up the stairs.

Thirty-nine

I reach the top of the first flight of stairs. The waiting room is another two floors up. Head down, I charge to the next staircase.

And run smack into Josh on his way down.

'Ow,' he says, rubbing his arm. 'That thing I said back in the cave about you not being clumsy? Maybe I was wrong.'

'Sorry,' I say. My throat is dry. 'What are you doing?'

Josh says nothing. A group of nurses hurry past us, chattering excitedly. They disappear down the stairs. Josh and I are alone again.

'Josh?' My mouth is dry. 'Where are you going?'

'I was coming to find you,' he says, meeting my gaze.

My heart flips over. 'Find me?'

'OK, here goes.' He takes a deep breath. 'I really like you, Evie. That is, I think you can be stubborn and crazy and really impatient when you're not getting your own way, but you're also beautiful inside and out and the most amazing, brave person I've ever met, and I'm not leaving here without letting you know how I feel, which you can throw back in my face if you want because I can see you're with Kit, and we all know he's like this perfect guy, but he's *not* perfect for you, Evie,

293

because *I* am. Just as you're perfect for me. Not perfect. Just perfect for me.'

We stare at each other. Josh's expression is part defiant, part terrified. I smile as something inside me settles into place.

'Wait here,' I say.

I turn and race up to the waiting room. Kit is standing by the door, deep in conversation with a middle-aged man who must be his dad.

'Evie.' His expression brightens as he sees me.

'Listen.' I draw him away from his father.

'What is it?' Kit asks.

'It's us,' I whisper, keeping my eyes fixed on his. 'It's wrong. That is, not right. That is, I like you, but I don't want to go out with you any more. I'm truly sorry I got it wrong . . . but everything was so crazy before and now I know that anything more than being friends wouldn't be right.'

'No.' Kit stares at me. 'We belong together.'

'We don't,' I say. 'I'm sorry, but we don't.'

'I don't want to let you go,' Kit whispers.

I chew on my lip, feeling awful. Why does everything have to be so complicated?

'You have to let me go,' I say. 'Because what you're letting go of isn't even real.'

'Kit? I've got your mother on the phone.' Kit's father strides over, holding out his mobile.

Kit hesitates, his eyes still on me.

'Please.' I smile. 'Friends?'

Kit frowns. 'Of course, but—' He tails off, shaking his head.

294

'Thank you.' I turn and fly back down the stairs.

Josh is waiting where I left him. I slow as I reach him. He raises an eyebrow. I smile.

'Wanna hear my new song?' he asks, leaning back against the wall.

'Is it about me?'

'Hell, yeah,' Josh says. 'Although after *that* being your immediate reaction I'm definitely adding "big-headed" to the list of your personality traits we ran through the other day.'

'Add what you like,' I say with a grin, drawing closer.

'How about adding this?' Josh says.

And he takes my face in his hands and we kiss.

Perfect for me.

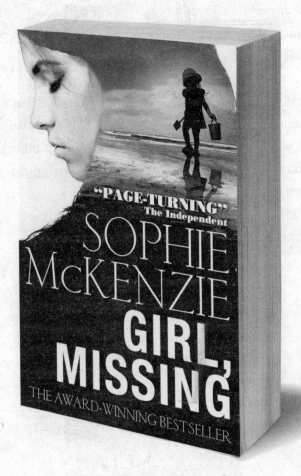

SOPHIE McKENZIE

Life can change in the blink of an eye
– whether you're ready or not.

#HASHTAGREADS

books worth talking about

Want to hear more from
your favourite **YA authors**?

Keen to **review** their latest titles
before anyone else?

Eager to read **exclusive extracts** and
enter **fantastic competitions**?

Join us at **HashtagReads**, home to
Simon & Schuster's best-loved
YA authors

Follow us on Twitter
@HashtagReads

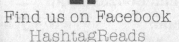
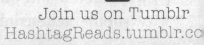